JIM DANDY

JIM DANDY

Irvin Faust

Carroll & Graf Publishers, Inc.
New York

Carroll & Graf Publishers, Inc.
260 Fifth Avenue
New York, NY 10001

Library of Congress Cataloging-in-Publication Data

Faust, Irvin.
  Jim Dandy / Irvin Faust.—1st Carroll & Graf ed.
    p.   cm.
  ISBN 0-7867-0062-9 : $21.00 ($28.50 Can.)
  1. Afro-American men—New York (N.Y.)—Fiction. 2. Italo
-Ethiopian War, 1935–1936—Fiction. 3. American—Travel—
Ethiopia—Fiction. 4. Depressions—United States—Fiction.
I. Title.
PS3556.A97J6   1994
813'.54—dc20   94-4660
                                                  CIP

Manufactured in the United States of America

June 1994

For Jean

Part One

PROLOGUE

ON AN AUTUMN AFTERNOON IN 1915 IN A SMALL, BLEACHED TOWN
in South Carolina, not too far from Charleston, in a tent on a
lot near the town square, a group of men called Tiny Cleveland's
Minstrels sat in a solemn, unblinking row and faced their audience. Some of the minstrels were dressed most shabbily—these
were the no 'count Jim Crows; the others, including the man in
the center, were ruffled and pressed and sleek: Jim Dandies. On
each black face, Crow or Dandy, lay a patina of burnt-cork black;
lips were a circle of thick, bright red. But of all the black and
red faces one stood out: Tiny Cleveland's. And not only because
he was the center man, although that helped. His face stood out
because his picture was all over town, and the picture was something, for right dab square in it, even as now, sat the "World's
Biggest Mouth," and that alone was worth the (somewhat high)
price of admission: an open, amazingly huge thing, a black cavern
surrounded by a loop of red and some more black, a red tongue
filling the cavern like oozing, kneaded blood. To make it even
more amazing, more scarifying, beside Tiny sat a little fellow as
perfect as Tiny was monstrous—neat and buttony and shining,
with a small, red mouth: a miniature, cute cameo Jim Dandy.

The line of minstrels sat and looked out, and the audience, in
shirtsleeves and suspenders, fanning itself with newspapers and
flyswatters, looked right back. After a good minute of looking,
the amazing Tiny nodded, and the sweating white block in the
creaking chairs ceased moving. At that silent instant, the black

3

line rose and opened its thick red mouth and poured out
"There'll Be a Hot Time in the Old Town Tonight." Into the
singing, around and above it, the miniature Jim Dandy, opening
wide his neat, red, button mouth, wove the words and tune—
better, purer than all the rest. The white block smiled. Perceiving
the familiar, and even more, it settled back and seemed to sigh.
Chairs creaked altogether, heads nodded and then smiles turned
to laughter, loud and belly full, for now long arms and legs (save
for little-fellow's; he was a neat dancer) were flailing up and
down and sideways, ignoring the music or the tempo, or ignorant
of it, crazy limbs shooting out in all directions including absolutely by gosh I tell you impossible ones. Yet by some miracle,
the flying tentacles stayed attached to both awkward and dandi-
fied bodies!

Suddenly the song ended, its echo hanging for a shrieking
second. The waving and shooting and flying stopped. A hush
filled the tent. Tiny Cleveland opened the world's biggest mouth
and in a deep voice said, "Gentlemen, be seated." Each silent,
still figure sat, jarring the wooden platform; a sweating face in
the audience-block snickered and said smoothly, "Yeah, gennel-
men." Only Tiny stood, ignoring the voice. He held himself together, then he opened the champion cavern and said in his
quiet, but somehow loud, deep voice, "And now the youngest
member of our company will favor you with a special rendition
of a popular favorite." Then he sat down and looked calm-eyed
into the distance as the little ruffled, shiny figure beside him
stood, took one firm step forward, flung out two supplicating
arms, opened the neat little mouth and filled the tent with "Old
Dog Tray." The voice was high and strong and pure. The white-
gloved little hands moved with the words, but always just a beat
behind, as if they were not tightly connected to the controlling,
shaping redness. He finished with a long, thin vibrato, gloves
reaching for the audience and the redness curved in a V as out
there hands clapped politely together and flyswatters hit a few
heavy thighs. Stepping smartly back, he sat down hard and stared
solemnly out, even as Tiny. When it was doubly quiet, Tiny
turned his head fast, like a New York actor, and said deeply,
"Now, Mr. Tambo, wasn't that touching?"

The man at the end of the line on his right, no 'count, shiftless, old Jim Crow, said to him, "Sho were. De man nex ta me teched me."

"Now, now," said Tiny, shaking his head as a gust of laughter rose up to him, "Mr. Bones, were you touched?"

"Tambo, he touched me for five dollars last night," said the man on the extreme left, all pressed and ruffled and dandied. Another gust rippled to the stage.

"Dear me," said Tiny, and he placed a white hand over his heart. "I mean to say touched *here*."

"Well, Tambo is sure touched *here*," said Bones-Dandy, pointing to his ear. Chairs creaked beneath rocking, hard laughter. Tiny wagged his head and turned the huge red cavern down. "Were you not *moved*?" he asked.

"Ah *moved* las month," said Tambo. "Don'chou member, Mr. Locutor? I teched you fer ten dollars an ah moved." Tiny shrugged and sighed into the waves of laughter. "Shore enough," said Bones, rolling huge pools of white, "we went to a meetin and Tambo moved over so's I could sit down."

"Wal," needled Tambo, "you done *moved* de question."

"Shore did. But you then *touched* on some werry important matters."

The helpless, the frustrated, the imploring Tiny: "Come, come, gentlemen. I beg of you, cease and desist . . ." He covered his offended ears. Tambo stood up and cleared the gravelly throat. "Ahm ceasin de sistuation in order ta say a few tings." He cleared again, expertly, as the guffaws shrank. "Ya might say ahm *moved* to say dese tings." The tent went agonizingly still, no laughter, no smiles, no creaking. Tambo timed his experienced moment and said into the hush, "Mistuh Wilson he done moved inta de White House an he ain't gwine let no Europeen War *tech* us ovuh heah." Into the practiced pause sailed a wave of applause and he smiled with supreme modesty. "Yep, he kep us outa war, but do dat mean we is afeerd a war, *do* it?"

"NO," came the roar.

"Keerect. We is not afeerd. Why, Mistuh Wilson he done send Black Jack Pershing down to Mexico when dat bandage Pancho Villya started movin around an stickin his Mex tongue out at

Uncle Sam"—the audience had fastened on him hungrily—"an ol Black Jack he moved down to Texas an he didn worry bout no border, no suh, not when a bandage is *techin* Merican intrests. Cose Black Jack he fought wid Teddy an Teddy he showed em how ta walk soft an carry a great big stick, so iffn dem furriners tinks we is keepin outa dere war cose we is afeerd dey is *teched,* cose George Washington he done tol it straight ta Mistuh Wilson, he done say don'chou get in no furrin tangles an dat is what dis country tinks, but, says Genral Washington, lettum start sumpn funny an my good pal Black Jack is gwine move a big stick right onta dere numbskulls an ahm tellin de whole wide world Mistuh Wilson he come from de souf an he is foist in war, foist in peace an foist las an always in de hearts of his countrymen!"

Screeching, whistling applause, rebel whoops, stomping feet ran wildly through the crowd and leaped up to him on the platform and he bowed before the anointment. Then he sat down, waited for the storm to subside, only to rise again; he got up, bowed and sat down again. The noise rippled up and back across each row, then cracked back up to the stage, once again flowed back and then reluctantly petered out. Only then did Tiny raise his hand. An emaciated Jim Crow unfolded from his chair and, bending backward from the thin, bony waist, head high, hoisted a lovely tenor into "Tenting Tonight," building the applause and whistling back up even before he had finished, and when all was as it should be, each Crow and Dandy was on his feet, jigging in place to beat all, swinging and stomping and shuffling on that skinny platform. Over it all a voice whooped out, "GO IT, COON!" and the yells answered and each and every face was Monroe-Doctrine jubilant while hammy fists punched European air.

Tiny's head. It moved ever so slightly. The prancing feet stopped, almost in the middle of the air, returned to the stage. A dozen banjos materialized and white-gloved hands sped through a medley of old and appreciated favorites, hands moving so fast that they were huge white hummingbirds. And then silence. On stage, in the audience. And then into the silence the little shiny Dandy, standing straight and proud was singing "My

Country Tis of Thee." High and founding-father pure. He finished up on one knee, fighting to hold his defying balance, but
hold it he did, through the whoops and yells and clapping, until
Tiny touched him lightly on the head. He rose obediently and
sat down and, in spite of itself, the quieting audience went ahh.

At last then, at *last*. Tiny. He rose and turned his stiff, broad
back. All was Appomattox-quiet. Slowly he rotated and yes, cal-
lused palms cracked together. FOR HE WAS DOING IT. The
great rubber redness was stretched a country mile, stretched
around an apple, a whole darn *apple*! And even while that apple
rested impossibly in its socket, the thick red lips stretched even
further, and clear and sharp and true emerged, "Columbia, the
Gem of the Ocean."

GREAT GAWD AMIGHTY!

So then what does he do? Well, with the apple in his trap, he
bows forward into all that applause and straightens up and starts
down the line, head thrown back like a happy stallion, arms
kicking and sure enough if he ain't doing the best damn cakewalk
you ever saw! And the little fellow, he's right behind the prancing
Tiny, kicking and reaching so cute you could die, and so too is
that entire lineup, pulling air and kicking sky so good and exciting that if Tiny Cleveland the Genuwine Coon don't have the
best damn show in the whole cockeyed world, you can just call
me a know-nothing, do-nothing, see-nothing goddam liar!

The head-darting, quiet men were standing outside the tent
and one was holding up a sign.

NIGGER, READ AND RUN.
ZIP COONS AIN'T FUNNY.
THEY ARE SMART
ALEX. ††††

Tiny, lightly touching the little Dandy's shoulder, without moving the smiling mouth, said easily, "Do like I said." The words
were soft as rainwater and just as clear. The little fellow straightened his skinny shoulders. He peeked upward. The famous
mouth was open wide and pouring out was a joyous, "Oh, I wish
I was in the land of cotton," and suddenly all about him every
man in the company had joined the interlocutor. Tiny bobbed

his head even as he sang and the men split into three-part harmony and Tiny bobbed still again and stepped off. Behind him, the little fellow took a giant step, and then all the rest; and, singing to beat anybody's band, they all marched, straight and high, down the middle of paved Main Street. High-kneeing, each foot, without hay or straw, stamping together onto Main Street, they marched past the watching, eye-wheeling men with their sign, past other men who did nothing but smile, past women and children who pointed and clapped and squealed. Tiny's hand swept air and the little man took three great steps and wound up alongside him, and a sweet soprano climbed above all the voices, and a woman who had been clapping bent over her child and said, "Ain't he sweet, Louisa?" "Oh, yes, Mama," cried the little girl, and the ruffled Dandy stretched up higher, stretched out farther. Smiling inside his head, way up in there where no one could see, as his mouth chanted sensibly, he sang, "Ohaway down south where the land is rotten, ol times dere is soon forgotten; go away, go away, go away, Dixie Laaaaand." Oh, he was a Smart Alex all right and he sang that inside his head all the way to the Pullman cars without once changing his eager face or the way his mouth wrapped around the hand-clapping words. For he was doing just like Tiny said.

And in the Pullman car, all nice and comfortable, Tiny said something else. He said to him, "Sonny, you sit right there, for I'm going to tell you a story, and I want you to listen." He nodded and sat very quietly; this was Tiny's serious face. And this was the story Tiny told for the umpteenth time:

"The Ituri forest sits all alone in the heart of Central Africa. It's a thick, damp, solid forest where the trees blot out the sun. It seems to be a fearful place, but it's not, not to those who know it. The animal sounds are pleasing and friendly: elephants, leopards, beautiful black and white monkeys chattering away. There's even the chameleon's cry leading people to the honey. Yes, the Ituri forest is a fine place for the people who live there.

"And who lives there? I'll tell you. Pygmies. Yes, grown people smaller even than you, and they won't grow, as you will. You can imagine how small the children are, although for a few years they do grow. Now, why are the Ituri and the Pygmies important? All right, because they were important to a little boy who was not a pygmy but who lived close to them, on a river in a place that came to be called the Kongo (I like to spell that with a K).

"Now this boy, and I don't even know his name, was about your age when the story begins. He was born, as far as I know, around 1793—that's over a hundred years ago—near the Ituri, and almost as soon as he could run, he sneaked away into the forest to play and have fun with the Pygmies, who taught him to love the forest and not to fear it. Sometimes, like you, he overdid things, and his parents scolded him, as I do sometimes and your mother does at home, but it was always in his best interest, as I'm sure you know.

"Well, one day while he was playing with his Pygmy friends, he heard noises like drumbeats, only they weren't drumbeats. And his Pygmy uncle, that is, a very good grown-up friend just like an uncle, said, 'Don't go home tonight.'

" 'Why not?' he asked.

" 'A bad man is in your village.'

" 'Who is he?'

" 'A terrible man. A friend of your chief.'

" 'Then how can he be terrible?'

" 'Because he is. Stay here tonight.'

" 'I can't. My mother and father would be very angry.' And with the long, low Pygmy loping style, he ran all the way home.

"Well, almost all the way. For close to home he heard the drum sounds again and smelled smoke, so he hid behind a tree and peeked out. He saw fingers of fire coming out of the houses. And he saw strange people rushing all around. They had shaved heads and dark faces that kept darting this way and that. They seemed to be in charge; they were controlling the fires and making the drum sounds and sure enough, one of them was talking in a friendly way with the chief of the village. And then he saw that all the women, except the very old ones, were pressed together in a group, including his mother, which was a great relief. In another group were the men, including his father. When he saw his father all still and helpless, he darted out and ran toward the village. But suddenly a shaved head with a darting face appeared and scooped him up and, before he knew it, he was set down in a pressed-in group that included all the children.

"Yes, the fire ate up the village and they all slept on the ground; and the next morning as the sun rose above the Ituri, the terrible man and the chief lined everybody up, except for the old and the sick, and told them to start walking. The shaved heads had sticks that made the drumbeat sounds; the sticks were tipped with balls of fire and one of them knocked down a good friend of his father who had rushed at the terrible man, so they darn well walked. The boy was tied to his mother, who had a pole across her shoulders, and they walked hard and fast toward the climbing sun. And the shaved heads with their thunder-fire sticks kept that *Coffle* going fast and hard. For that's what it was called. A *Coffle*. Remember the word. It was a thing the Pygmy boys had whispered about, and here he was in one. And at the head of the *Coffle* walked a shaved head holding the flag of the Sultan of Zanzibar, a man like a king or president. Zanzibar was a tough, bad, money-making place where people were bought and sold like shoes and stockings. That was their destination.

"Day after day the *Coffle* walked, the boy behind his mother, his father somewhere up ahead. Down valleys, up steep hills, away from the softness of the forest onto the hard, burning-hot plain. Some of the women and children, and even some of the men, began to weave crazily about under the sun and seemed to go to sleep right on the ground. The shaved heads slashed away their ropes and left them there; the *Coffle* had to keep going.

"They walked past a great lake, which looked like a river but wasn't. He found out that things grew larger as you came close to them; he grew dizzy and funny, as you do when you spin around, but he was darned if he would lie down and go to sleep.

"They passed through villages and they passed other *Coffles*, but they didn't stop except to sleep and drink some water and eat a plant called manioc. They kept on going until they reached a water greater than a river or a lake—the ocean, just like the ocean in Coney Island. And out on that ocean was a long blue shadow."

Tiny looked out the window.

"Zanzibar," he said.

"Well, they crossed over in a dhow, an Arab ship—meaning it belonged to the shaved heads—and the next morning they rode at anchor in Zanzibar town. Off they go and once more start walking. Through animals and beggars and fruit stands until they came to a square. And there they stopped. The boy looked around. In the square young girls were being inspected and ex- amined by the shaved heads, and these persons were looking into their most private and personal parts as if they were doctors, only they weren't. Then they had the girls run up and back. Then the shaved heads exchanged money, and some walked off with the girls, as if they were shoes or stockings.

"The next thing he knew, he was told to run up and back, and he did, for he was a very fast runner and proud of it. Then he was looked at and poked all over, and suddenly he was in another lineup and once again was walking. Luckily, his mother and father were in the same line. Together they walked through Zanzibar town and through the forest surrounding the town, and they came to a beach and out beyond the beach he saw that a large ship was standing and rocking. The small *Coffle* was rowed out to that ship and he was surrounded by new men, not so dark, but with sharp, watching faces.

"His father and the other men of the *Coffle* were placed below. The women, including his mother, and the children stayed up on deck. Other *Coffles* were rowed out and joined them. Soon Zanzibar began to grow small. They were out on the tremendous ocean and the Ituri forest was far away and so were his Pygmy friends; and when he looked back and listened, he thought he could hear the sound of the whistling chameleon."

Tiny looked at the boy. He was asleep. He shook him roughly and the boy's eyes sprang open. Tiny never let him sleep during *The Story*.

"That ship," said Tiny, "was called *The Black Joker* and its captain was a big man known as a tight packer. Meaning he could fit the people of the *Coffles* into every part of that ship without wasting an inch. That trip was called the Middle Passage, and I want you to remember that also. And on that Middle

Passage the boy came out all right, and so did his mother; but his father died down below, all tight-packed in. They unpacked him and threw him overboard. The boy felt awful, of course; but his mother said, don't worry, as a Kongo man he was just flying to his home beside the Ituri forest; and that made the boy feel much better. . . . Stay awake now!

"Well, after many days they came to South Carolina." He pointed out the window. "Right out there, to the city of Charleston. And as they lay in the harbor there was a terrific commotion and new men came aboard and ran all about and began the Scramble. Remember that, the Scramble. For the people of the *Coffles*. And in the Scramble, the boy was carried off by one pair of men, and his mother, kicking and screaming, by six other strong, husky men—that's how many it took. They never saw each other again."

Tiny looked out the speeding window.

"They named him Cicero in South Carolina. They never knew his right name; he never told them. He lived and worked and grew up in a place called Pleasant Pines, not far from here. He grew to be very old. He had many children. Everybody liked him, for he was a good worker, had a nice personality and had a beautiful, natural singing voice.

"But late in the night, like now, he would talk softly about the Ituri forest. He would talk about the chameleons and the leopards and the elephants, but most of all he would talk about his friends, the Pygmies . . ." Tiny looked down and nodded. "All right, you can go to sleep, now."

THE SCARLET CREEPER

WAS A CHARACTER IN A NOVEL. NOT JUST ANY CHARACTER, NOT just any novel. In many ways, the most important character in a (then) most important novel, one written by a Carl Van Vechten, published beautifully in 1926 by Mr. A. Knopf. Called *Nigger Heaven*. And it sold 100,000 copies, mostly, of course, to white folks. And why not? For it was the absolutely inside story of atavistic, hot-stuff Harlem, told—as was well known—by the one white man in America equipped by character, training, experience, inclination, empathy and boldness to do the job.

Terrific Excitement.

For *Nigger Heaven*, to squeals of delight and barks of resentment, showed not only Harlem to the outside world, but Harlem's relationship to that world—world here meaning downtown Manhattan. Or, to use the author's metaphor, the white orchestra to the segregated balcony, well understood by our Southern brethren to be above the celestial place. With Van Vechten as patron, angel, midwife, rushing up and down, recording it all on lovely vellum enclosed in a (what else?) tan slipcase.

And who was the thrillingest, excitingest, biggest carrier-on? Who up in Nigger Heaven lived most deeply and pullulatingly in his blood?

Why, the Scarlet Creeper.

Anatole Longfellow, to be precise.

Splendid moniker.

Why such a smash? He really did not do very much: opened and closed the book and appeared once in between, so why?

13

Because everywhere and over all, his menacing presence brooded; and, at the end, to the immense gratification of all the orchestra-readers, he sealed everything with the bang of his piece, his gat, his internal and inevitably exploding self.

Sweet man (or pimp), male hustler, pusher, the fanciest of Dans, he was any or all, depending on the yearning chemistry of the neck-craning orchestra-sitter; in his skintight suitings, his sueded feet, his pomaded hair, his diamond-pierced cravat he made even the most magnificent prostitutes ecstatic; and who amongst the yearners could accomplish *that*? So they hopped the A train, the yearning, envying downtowners, and debarked at 125th Street or 145th, and climbed onto the Creeper's thrilling world. There to have a shot of gin that tasted more wicked, there to study high-kicking brown thighs that promised the impossible, there to wonder and marvel, and from there to return through the underground to safety, to tell of that place of wild and forbidden fruit.

By actual count, through 1928, there were nineteen Scarlet Creepers in Harlem. With the crash, the number shrank to three and by 1934, only one, by white and general consensus, remained—the vestigial survivor of the Harlem Renaissance, and also the primitive triumphant on the islands of exotica that were surrounded by garbage, sneaky Pete and breadlines. His name was Hollis Cleveland. He had met Van Vechten, briefly, in the Sugar Cane on 135th Street in 1927, a year after the book appeared, and he apparently, albeit anachronistically, parlayed that encounter into identifiable, tight-fitting, suedely clad operations up to '29 and then, as the Depression deepened, just as the shrewd bears did, he stayed in shape and found more profit and a greater market for what he had, and had to sell. (It should be recorded that in an interview with the *Graphic* in 1928, he stated: "I have never claimed to be the notorious person I am strongly rumored to be.") He was in particularly shrill demand at downtown parties, debuts and opening nights. In 1935, one of his admirers, a Sherrill Varaday, originally from Zanesville, Ohio, went so far as to write a play that everyone knew was about him, called *Cotton Candy*, which ran for ninety-three performances at the Shubert. Indeed, after three weeks, Varaday even wrote him into the contract at forty-five dollars a week, for which price he had to appear in the balcony three times a week, arm draped loosely but lustfully over a bare, tawny shoulder. Business immediately picked up, for which Cleveland was grateful, although he confided to Harmon Farmer, the poet, that he thought the play was pretty terrible. This was at one of Sherry's after-theater parties on East 57th Street and Harmon had nodded and said, so was *The Green Pastures*, but that hadn't stopped Dick Harrison from taking money as De Lawd, or prevented him from hiring a white coach to teach him proper Lawd dialect. Cleveland said, Of course, you're right, I merely made the observation. To which, surrounded by Sherry's bronze Masai dancers and lacquered-wood Guinea heads, they hoisted the Mumm's and drank. Holding his glass high, he then moved to the buffet table, at which point, out of the crush, a Negro middleweight named Tiger Jackson leaned toward him and whispered out of a creased voice box that he was wanted down the hall, second door on the right. He smiled at the caviar and, without moving his lips or the smile, said "Who?" The solemn croak told him to "just get his ass down there an don't ask no questions, sweet man." Cleveland smiled and said the fisticuff situation certainly was precarious, Canvasback, and patiently finished his morsel on a toast triangle. With six white men and five white women intently tracking him around their chitchat, he tight-stepped across the room, paused, then walked down the hall.

Five minutes on his Elgin watch passed, during which time he absorbed a bronze dancer by Richmond Barthé and a terracotta head by Sargent Johnson, two artists adored by Sherry for their ability to capture the placid hyperkinesia of the Negro's gift. Then, the door opened. Cleveland rotated slowly and smoothly until he had located the man at the door, who was smiling with what seemed shy apology. The man's name was Sol Winograd and he met Cleveland's eyes with his apologizing but firm ones and, nodding at the Barthé, walked pigeon-toed across the room and sank with a sigh into a red, flatulent chair. Without speaking, he produced a Royal Jamaican from an inside breast pocket, daintily bit off the end and just as daintily expelled it, produced a kitchen match and crrrracked it against a turned-up sole, lit up with total dedication and emitted perfect white circles which rose in layers to Sherry's beamed ceiling. With another sigh, still examining his cigar, Winograd said, in a pleasantly musical voice, "So how you been behavin?"

"Been fine; how you been, Solly?" said Cleveland.

Winograd p-p-p-puffed. "I call you Holly?"

"Nah, you allus calls me Hollis or Kiddo."

"Then," said the puffer agreeably, "if it's all right with you, suppose you call me Sol."

"Sure ting. No problem dere. You is Sol."

Sitting far back and crossing thick blue and white clocked ankles, Winograd said, "And cut out the shuffle-along shit. Talk like a man."

"Okay, Sol." Cleveland smiled. He walked to Sherry's ebony table inlaid with white chess squares and sat on it. "What's on that thing your ass-kissers call a mind?"

The panatela speared a perfect, white ring. "That's better. That I like." Three fast circles escaped from snapping lips. "I asked how you been behavin?"

"Taking care of things."

"Well," said Winograd, studying his ankles, "I just guess you have. Yesirree, I guess you have."

"I do my best, Sol."

"Oh, you do; yes, you do. You mind if I ask a personal question?"

"I don't mind."

He looked up and pushed his eyes against Hollis's. "Have I ever fucked you?"

"Not overtly, Sol."

"Does that mean like out in the gutter?"

"Close enough."

"Well then, have I?"

"No, I can't honestly say you have."

Again the sigh. "Then, tell me something. Why are you fucking me?"

"How ahm . . . in what way have you been fornicated?"

Stubby, English-flanneled arms spread wide. "Hollissss. We're on good terms. We understand one another. I'll ask you a question. Do you want to work for a living? Is that what you really want? If it is, just say so. A liquor store? You want a liquor store? I'll talk downtown and place you in a liquor store. Name your location."

"No, thanks, Sol; I don't want a liquor store. I like what I do."

"Why?"

"Well, I provide a community service surpassing even a liquor store."

"Anything else?"

"It gives me personal gratification."

"Anything else?"

"I like the *gelt.*"

"Now we are getting down to brass tacks. We've established something. Let me ask you a personal question. If you're makin a good dollar; if you like what you're doin; then, why do you want to spoil it? You ever hear of division of labor?"

"That's two questions."

"Oh, a lawyer from Philly. All right, you know about division of labor, don't you, a smart kid like you?"

"Yes."

"All right. There's me, what I do. There's you, what you do. Why do you want to fuck that up?"

"Is that what I'm doing?"

A sigh, almost a moan. "Ah, Hollis, I don't like it when you do that. You ain't talkin to these shitheels in Beekman Place; it's me, Sol; we under*stand* one another."

"Okay, Sol, get it off your chest."

"It hurts me to say it like this, Kiddo; you know how I hate to spell things out . . ."

"Spell, Sol, spell."

He looked down at his Paris garters; he wondered for a moment how it would feel if metal *did* touch that leg; then, he looked up. Cleveland was sitting with his arms folded, gazing into space. Lousy kids, they all let you down in the end. "From now on," he said gently, "you will please turn all receipts over to me personal. You will come on up to the Bronx and be a person and do that."

"*All* receipts?"

"All," he sighed. "'And I want you to do something else. I want you to go back one month, thirty days, and do likewise—"

"Ah Sol—"

A hand under treatment for psoriasis was up. "No pleading, I won't listen. One calendar month. Retroactive. Past that, you can keep all you stole because we go back quite a ways together."

"If you say so, Sol."

"Yes, I say so. I don't want to say so, but what else am I gonna do? I'm painted into a goddam corner. When we get this goin proper, I will personally take out your cut and give it to you and you know my books are perfect. So, unlike some people in this rotten world, you don't have to worry about taking a fucking. How's your aunt, Hollis?"

"Fine."

"I like Aunt Clara, she's a good person." A white bridge of smoke reached Cleveland, then collapsed. "She's a lot like my mother," Winograd said to his socks. "They both had to put up with two wild kids, but they'd go to Sing Sing for them. I'm gonna ask you a question. What else is there in this *shvartz* world except loyalty? You don't have to say anything, just think everything over; after all, you got a head on your shoulders. All right now, Hollis, you can go back inside and give them shitheels a run for their goddam money."

Halos. P-p-p-popping to the ceiling.

On the way out he located Tiger Jackson near the food and drinks, and as a cluster of canapé-chewers looked on with large-eyed disinterest, he feinted with a left, hooked with a grunting right and left Tiger kneeling and vomiting on the lovely Persian carpet.

2

Hollis Cleveland, over and above a variety of skills and abilities, possessed a specific talent. Sherry, if apprised, would close his eyes and call it a blood-gift. It was both simple and complex and it was this: he knew what people were thinking about him. He knew with a complete and swift certainty, and he knew regardless of the other's century, epoch or environment. Just one example: at collection time he knew that Harriet Beecher Stowe thought: "Is *he* what I labored so long and hard for?" Of course, he smiled when she thought this (a polite smile, for Harriet meant well), but it was definitively her thought. Paying off a numbers winner, he knew what Cecil Rhodes was thinking: "He is living proof that with proper training they *can* find a place in society; but *this*?" Booker T. was not enchanted either, for the lad could do so much for agriculture. And George Washington Carver, wagging his smart old head: "That boy is lower than the peanut; if he keeps this up he will ruin my scientific deal." That is how his blood-gift worked, and once the others got started they just wouldn't stop:

Marcus Mosiah Garvey: Now why don't you let me save you from this corruption?

Don't wanna be saved.

Why don't—

DON'T WANNA.

Oom Paul Kruger: And God will descend on you and your immorality.

Uh huh, truck on down.

Jim Dandy: That's the spirit, boy. Remember, I beat Gallant Fox, the heavy favorite.

Ahhhh.

And so it was that with his blood-gift bounding down the hall, he located Sol Winograd's percolating centrality: *The little sonofabeehive, don't he know a Jew is just a nigger turned inside out? Cut us both, we bleed. Don't he know? He knows. So why did he do what he done? Why? I was a father to the little bastard. Better. A real father would kick his ass all the way down the street; I gave in to him. I put what the hell to eat in his mouth, clothes on his back. The boy was moody, I understood, I'm moody. The boy was clever, so what, I'm clever. I made my own breaks, but I went out and gave him a break; is this my thanks? A royal fucking?*

I understand what you are thinking, Sol, I really do. How

can I tell you? Very well, I'll try. No, Jim Dandy will try. Tell him, Jimbo.

Certainly, Mr. Interlocutor.

It seems that there once was a scorpion who came to a river and wished to cross it. But he could not swim. Not for little green apples. So he casts about and locates a frog and he says to brother frog, "Here is all my money; carry me across the river on your back." The frog, aghast at the prospect, replies, "And have you sting me? No, sir." But the scorpion shakes a sad head and says, "But if I sting you, I, too, will drown. I am dangerous, but not stupid. Here, take my money." Frog says, "Of course, stupid you ain't." So he tucks the money away and kneels down. Scorpion climbs aboard and off they paddle across the river. Halfway to the other side, the scorpion reaches down and stings the frog. As he is about to sink beneath the muddy water, along with the scorpion, the frog looks up and entreats, "But why? *Why?*"

"Ah," says the scorpion, going down, "it's my character."

In the beautifully leathered, damasked room, Cleveland stepped about and ate and drank, and then finally excused himself and said he had to run and Sherry murmured but of course and as Cleveland left, gazed carefully at the Cotton Club's Harriet Clive.

Cleveland took the elevator down as the elevator man studied him in the security mirror and walked outside onto the cleared sidewalk of East 57th Street and asked the doorman to please whistle for a cab. The doorman did, tipping his cap for the dollar; Cleveland sat back as the doorman closed the taxi door; he said, "a hundred eleventh and Lenox, please," and ignored the cut of the eyes in the rearview mirror. In fine, squealing loops the cab ran up through the park and halted in a breathless rock before his building. He got out and, after a peeled-off dollar tip, turned slowly, walked slowly upstairs as behind him the cab fled screaming. Then, when his door was closed and bolted, he moved. He jerked a soft genuine leather two-suiter out of the closet that contained twelve suits and opened all his bureau drawers. He pulled out silk and pongee shirts, silk foulard and regimental repp ties, silk athletic shirts, silk, monogrammed shorts, silk and cashmere socks and folded all neatly into the suitcase. He chose two suits, a powder blue cheviot and a deep brown pin-striped flannel, packed them with careful attention to the shoulders. A pair of brown suede shoes, well-treed. He slapped locks and buckles, jerked straps. He walked into the bedroom, flipped back the coverlet, blankets and sheets and dug into the zippered slit in the mattress under his pillow. He pulled out two Mark Cross briefers fat with bills, removed the bills and restored the briefers and zipped. He packed the bills smoothly and evenly into the two money belts that added no more than an inch to the twenty-six waist. Tightly tucked in the white-on-white shirt. Walked out of the bedroom, hefted the bag, and, leaving the reading lamp on, unbolted, unlocked the door, stepped outside, relocked and walked downstairs with calm detachment. On Lenox he whistled up another cab and said clearly, "Penn Station, Long Island side, I'm in rather a hurry." Then he sat back and lit up a Murad.

Ah Sol, it is my character . . .

A SCIENTIFIC INTERLUDE

"LADIES AND GENTLEMEN, PERMIT ME TO INTRODUCE YOU TO SIGMUND the Genu-wine Coon who will unerringly—that means without no errors—interpret your dreamiest dreams. Yes, ma'am, don't be bashful, step right up.

"Well, the other night I dreamt I was down home and I seen mama so clear, jes like you standin there, and I was in bed with the croup and outside my window the birds was singin and the breeze was blowin and I could smell the grass and my little brother was playin so nice and mama she came in and sat down beside me and put a ice cold rag on my head and she smiled down at me, I seen it so clear . . .

"Yes, I see, a cold rag, yes, plus two sore eyes, plus your mother, plus your brother. That comes out one hundred twenty-two, therefore and ergo, that is your number. No ma'am, please don't kiss my fingers. Next.

"I seen the top floor of the Hotel Theresa and up there I seen a great big apartment painted all blue and yellow and jes like that I'm walkin around in that apartment and then I hears a voice and I steps to the winda and I sees three aeroplanes and these planes they flew in my winda and flew all around the room and dumped ten-dollar bills all over the floor and then the planes jes fly out the winda and I wakes up.

"Simple. Six-room apartment, two-months concession, three airplanes. That comes out to six hundred twenty-three; that's quite all right, sir; I do not accept gratuities; thank you, sir. Who is next, please? You there.

23

"*Last night on the Day Line. I'm sailin along nice and easy when this fight breaks out. All of a sudden I sees I'm captain of the boat and I starts givin orders left and right. Oney nobody follows my orders, so I takes the wheel myself and I drives the boat, Sweet Sue is her name, and I drives her onta land and crosstown and onta Lexington Avenue and I keeps her straight on course all the ways down to Wellman, Georgia; and when I hits Wellman, everybody comes outa their house, white and colored, and I salutes them with three big toots on the whistle and they all holler out loud and I toots again and turn Sweet Sue around, oney now all of a sudden she ain't no boat, but a great big Nash, and I drives all the ways back to New York; I seen every single thing like it was five minutes ago ...*

"*Hmmm. Two hundred fifty-seven. That's the number, sir, two hundred fifty-seven. No, sir, I do not accept fish; I do this out of a sense of noblesse oblige and I would appreciate your not mentioning me in your prayers. Well, if you must ...*

"*LADIES AND GENTLEMEN, THERE IT IS AND THERE HE IS, YOU HAVE HEARD HIM WITH YOUR OWN EARS, WITNESSED HIM WITH YOUR OWN EYES, THE EIGHTH WONDER OF THE WORLD. YOU HAVE SEEN CLOSE UP HIS KNOW-HOW, HIS INNER SANCTUM—THAT MEANS HUNCH—SIGMUND, THE ZIP COON, THE MAN OF A THOUSAND PROBING EYES, BUT WILL HE DESERT YOU, LET YOU DOWN? NO, SIR. AS ALWAYS, HE WILL SEE YOU TOMORROW, SAME TIME, ANOTHER STATION, HEH HEH, WHICH WILL BE SUBSEQUENTLY ANNOUNCED— THAT MEANS WE'LL TELL YOU—SO YOU JUST COME AROUND AND FOR A TINY, TINY INVESTMENT YOU WILL FIND OUT HOW YOUR FLUFFY NIGHTTIME ADVEN- TURES CAN BE CONVERTED INTO FRESH, RIPE GREENSTUFF, AND I DON'T MEAN CUCUMBERS, HEH HEH, SO STEP RIGHT UP, SLEEP TIGHT, DON'T LET THE BEDBUGS BITE.*"

BOONDOCK

HE CAUGHT THE NINE-THIRTY OUT OF PENN, WHICH PROMISED NO change at Jamaica. Opening a rather large (though far from the world's biggest) mouth as they swooped beneath the East River, he worked his jaws and swallowed hard, clearing his ears; and he pressed tightly up against the tons of water that couldn't possibly crack through the snouted-out tunnel, and that crackling, gurgling groan was just one of those things (and there were worse ways to go). He insisted that his eyes stay open, which of course they did, though rather unseeing, and then, just as they filmed over, the train sprang into the soft Queens night, and at the Woodside station he lit up. Blowing circles, he let Long Island fly past and, at Jamaica, he moved closer to the window partially but politely for an eyes-front, I. J. Foxed matron returning from an evening in the wickedly thrilling city. As she sat stiffly within herself, he flipped his paper open and carefully scanned Frank Graham and the Old Scout in the *Sun*, where if you read it, Virginia, you better hot damn believe it. He was peripherally aware of Sunrise Highway racing the train, of Lynbrook, Rockville Centre, and Baldwin entering and leaving. And then South Bay.

He swung his suitcase down, expertly close to the matron, who blinked despite the facelift, and he walked through the car and out onto the platform and downstairs to the waiting taxis. He planted himself in front of the open window of a horizon-studying driver, he carefully pronounced the address, and before the

25

deaf-mute could gaze and point to his ears, he had slid in and slammed the door. With a sigh, they lurched away, swooping and clashing south of Sunrise, heading for the bay. When he smelled the water and saw the canals, he sat forward and directed and the cabbie said I only been livin here thirty years. He smiled into the musky dark, paid and tipped generously as he always did, got out, slammed the door as he always did, and walked up the flagstones to the Baltimore-white steps, past the seriously striding black lawn jockey and rang. He heard the chimes and footsteps, one heavy, one light. The door opened and she examined him seriously, carefully, her rimless glasses shining in the lamplight held by the little jockey.

"It's me, Ahnt Clara," he said.

He had a warmed-up baked fish dinner (fresh off the canal that very afternoon) and, in the middle of the mashed potatoes, she said, "Well, are you going back to school?"

Swallowing first, as she'd always insisted, he said, "That's the last thing you said to me four years ago."

"Well, are you?"

"Four years ago."

"This today," she said.

He continued to eat and swallow. "Same answer," he said.

She waited for some more quiet, neat eating, then said, "The country need college men."

"I'm a college man."

"College men with a *diploma.*"

He drank the guest coffee while she sipped her chamomile tea, for it was late and she had to get her good night's sleep; she had to get up at five, she had to dress nice, had to catch that train to Jamaica, she had to change for the Hempstead line, she had to chew the fat and read the *News* with her "girl friends," she had to decamp at Elmont, New Hyde Park, Stewart Manor, she had to be picked up by her missus, she had to clean, cook, nanny. It was very late and he was keeping her up; he drank some more coffee.

"A credential," he said with care, "is a piece of paper."

"You just had six months to go."

"That's right."

"You a expert in foreign languages. Five."

"Four."

"What about English?"

"Yes, I forgot. And English."

"That makes five."

"All right, Ahnt Clara, five."

She sipped her tea and nibbled on an oatmeal cake—she always nibbled on oatmeal cakes. She swallowed and said, "You could pick up Ethiopian no time atall. You could be a real help to Haile Selassie."

"They speak a language called Amharic. At least, *he* does. Along with English and French."

"See?"

"He didn't ask me," he said gently.

"Don't get smart; I never like it when you smart. You know what President Garvey say? He say we should *all* help. It is a *great* opportunity."

"It is?"

"I done tol you bout bein smart. Yes, it is. He say it right in the *Blackman*." She closed her eyes and leaned back and she was in the slanty gray church, her voice a metallic singsong: "Mussolini's Fascist madness and brutality has paved the way toward the hastening of a new national life which otherwise might have been stifled for another century." Slowly she opened her eyes and sighed and returned to her tea.

"Yes indeed," he said, "it sure is a break, a real break, Italy declaring war. Tell that to Mr. Selassie."

"I'm tellin it to you, Mr. Smartman. I'm tellin you what President Garvey say."

"Maybe," he said, and he felt he was back on the rushing train and the brakes were failing, "I could become an Ethiopian Delineator. Like Tiny."

She looked at him over the glasses. "Tiny were the *greatest* Ethiopian Delineator who ever lived, and don't you never forget it."

"I know, Ahnt Clara, I know; yes, I know." He drank his

coffee, and the train slowed down; but then it took off: "It's not at all certain Haile Selassie is Negro," he said.

"I'm certain. He from Africa."

"President Garvey," he said, wrestling with the brakes, "is not exactly sitting pretty."

The metallic brightness again: "The Universal Negro Improvement Association, it rise above any one man and will always continue to live."

He thought very calmly, *Up you mighty race! You can accomplish what you will!* Out loud he said very calmly, "Garvey wants us scooting back to Africa, and you want me to be an All-American boy. Which way do I go?"

"Which is that there's somebody smartern you. He killin two birds with one stone. So just get wise to yourself." She closed her eyes and there it was: the pitch, the Black Star Line, the five dollars a share. "Ethiopia," she chanted, "is in the vanguard, fightin democracy's battle, holdin on while we girds ourself around." She opened her eyes and smiled peacefully.

He thought he might say, you got rotten ships for your blood money, he got his ass kicked out, let his wife do *your* cleaning; but this time he fought and twisted the brake wheel, drew sparks, and screeched to a halt. He drank his G. Washington coffee while Tiny and his adoring sister whistled and clapped for President Garvey and the fancy boys in feathers and uniforms and the stone-serious faces stepping smartly down Lenox Avenue.

The phone rang.

"Scuse me," she said, dabbing with a lace napkin. "It's the phone." She got up and, with her dipping limp, walked toward the inlaid mahogany end table. Oh, that limp, that congenitally short left leg, that jutting hip, and the operation she had been about to get for fifty years . . . "I know it's another absence, but my ahnt had to go to the hospital for an operation on her pelvis . . ." They bought it, and bought it, and bought it, and now it carried her, that sad, handy hip, to the end table where she rested, breathing heavily; she picked up the phone and, softly putting on airs, purred, "Webster residence." She listened with complete attention, nodded several times and said thank *you* and laid the phone delicately back in its French cradle. She hop-dipped back to the table, sat with a deep sigh, and then said, "It was for you."

"Why didn't you put me on?"

"Didn want to talk to you."

"No?"

"No."

He sat back. "All right, what did he tell you to tell me?"

"I'll tell you. He said," and she was slow and careful, "to quote Mike Jacobs: 'Chappie, we were robbed.'" She lifted her cup, her educated pinky neatly curled, took a sip, and delicately lowered the cup; it trembled ever so slightly. "Are you in trouble again?"

"Nothing serious, Ahnt Clara."

"Then, who that? He sounded polite, not that that mean too much nowadays."

"Yes, polite. But very badly informed. Yet presumptuous enough to tell you what to tell me. Well, I will tell you something, something important. The gentleman he blithely quoted was Joe, not Mike, Jacobs. The expression is not *were* but 'wuz robbed,' spelled w-u-z. The context is wrong; he is extremely imprecise. Also, Jacobs would neither use nor understand the term Chappie. Jack Blackburn, a boxing trainer, both uses and understands it. He calls Joe Louis Chappie. On occasion, Mister Louis refers to Blackburn as Chappie; it signifies a relationship your caller could not possibly comprehend." He swilled his coffee. "Ahnt Clara," he said gently, "that caller is a moron. He has never considered the word, diploma, but he's in the driver's seat. Is that what you want for me?"

"Yes, that's right, yes. Don't make no difference he a moron." Eyes closed, head back, rocking: "The ends you serve that are selfish will take you no further than yourself; but the ends you serve that are for all, in common, will take you even into eternity."

When she was finally in bed, and her breathing filled the house, that's when he picked up the French phone and dialed.

"Hello, Ben, it's Hollis; sorry I woke you up ... Yes, Hollis ... I need a favor, yes ... All right, I need a passport; yes, a passport, but not in my name ... Here's the name: Dandy, James Dandy ... That's what I said ... Yes, I also had money on Gallant Fox; Ben, something else: I want to be on the first thing that leaves this country ... Yes, the *first* thing ... I don't care where ... No, next week is too late, understand? ... Work on it, Ben; call me back, I'll be waiting ... Ahnt Clara's ... *Work* on it, Ben."

He hung up, crossed his arms and, facing her spotless venetian blinds and the spotless Long Island night, he dozed the way Bomba the Jungle Boy had taught him, remaining alertly awake even as he slept. The phone rang; he plucked it up, cutting the first ring.

"Mr. Dandy?"

"This is Mr. Dandy; who am I talking to?"

"Ben."

"Go ahead, Ben."

"The first conveyance I can lay my hands on that is leaving the country is not an ocean liner."

"I see. What is it?"

"It is a freighter. Completely seaworthy and fully registered and inspected to meet all international regulations."

"I see."

"It's the *Singapore*. As you might suspect, it's a British boat. It will carry a variety of copper products."

"Will you please get me on?"

"I have already anticipated that request, Mr. Dandy. I've booked passage and you will be expected."

"When, please?"

"At six-thirty tomorrow evening. Pier thirty-eight on Fifteenth Street. It will take ten days to Southampton."

"Fine. Passport?"

"Taken care of, Mr. Dandy."

"I'll need a car."

"Again anticipated. Used but highly serviceable Packard, plus driver. Emerald green. License plate ZYL 492. It will pick you up at two o'clock sharp."

"I appreciate, Benjamin. There'll be a check in the mail."

"No hurry whatsoever; I know you won't forget. Incidentally, you will be the only passenger, but that will present no problem, will it?"

"None at all. Keep an eye on Ahnt Clara, Ben."

He clicked off and gently placed the French phone back in its cradle. He sat back and looked out through the blinds while Ahnt Clara filled the house. A pine pillow, smelling sweet, inscribed with the Latin of the University of Pennsylvania, a rummage sale prize, would be supporting the sad hip. Oh, the hip. He got up and, stepping swiftly to the window, split two blinds. Long Island hunched out there, beneath a Milky-wayed, overarching sky. Beyond the row of houses that stared back, the canal and bay were still and dark. Boats were sleek and quiet. A perching seagull . . . The only thing in motion was the earnestly striding little jockey on the lawn.

He jerked the cord up and lifted the shiny blinds and confronted the flaming cross.

"Cleveland!"

"Please don't go out, Pa."

"Always face the music, sonny."

"Not now, Pa."

"Got to, sonny."

"Cleveland!"

Tiny opened the door and stepped out. A short fat man in white walked up to him and Tiny looked down. The man reached something up to Tiny, something . . . yes . . . a cue ball. A white cue ball. The snowy arm pointed and slowly and with great neatness Tiny stuck the cue ball in his mouth. No trouble atall; cheeks puffed out like a slight case of the mumps. The man reached up and fed him another ball, a black one. "All right, Pa; you can come in now." Tiny shoved it in and smiled. The lined-up snowmen clapped their hands slowly as if their arms were melting. Then the short fat man grabbed Tiny from the back and looped a cord around his hands. Tiny didn't move. Another man walked up and shoved a third ball, the nine ball, into Tiny's mouth and they all hollered, "Sing, nigger!" Tiny's head wagged from side to side, even while he was smiling and his mouth was stretched so far it had to tear, but it didn't. Then they did it. The short man kneeled down behind Tiny and the one in front gave him a push. Tiny went over backwards, arms flailing. His head hit the ground and then it did a very funny thing. His head began to dance, like it was a tap dancer. Up and down it danced, and back and forth, and even crossways it danced. The men were pointing and then, without any command, they were running, running away from Tiny and his dancing head. And the cross, it was burning; and Ahnt Clara, she was bending over Tiny, and the little jockey was solemn and striding . . .

He opened the door and stepped outside. Very carefully, he removed his jacket, folded it inside out and placed it carefully on the scrubbed white steps. He walked over Clara's lawn to the earnest little jockey who gazed forever toward the city. He reached down and cupped the little fellow's chin and, pulling steadily, lifted him out of the hard ground. He cradled the little fellow against his chest and began to step about the grassless lawn. Faster and faster, higher and higher they kicked, little jockey and Cleveland, bending far back, cakewalking into the klanned Long Island night.

FREIGHT

CAPTAIN HUGH ARTHUR BANKS HUNCHED DOWN TO MEET HIS broth, worked his spoon. He remained absorbed and silent until he had finished the broth, cleared his throat, then remained absorbed and silent through the neat, brown squares of mutton. He studiously drank some Scotch and soda after every two bites. Cleveland ate in silence, too, drank his Scotch a bit more slowly. Finally, with a sigh, the captain looked up. "Some more Scotch, Mr. Dandy?"

"No, thank you."

"Gin? Rum?"

"No, thank you."

"Clear away, Bruce."

The cabin boy darted, stacked plates on a tray, scurried off. He hurried back with coffee, poured, then stood at attention in his corner. Both men sipped slowly, and when the rhythm of the sipping had been established, the captain straightened up and drew a pack of cigarettes from his breast pocket.

"Players, Mr. Dandy?"

"No, thank you."

"I have some Camels back in my cabin."

"Some other time, perhaps."

"A cigar?"

"No, thank you, I find them a bit cloying."

"Ah yes, the expensive ones. My first officer has some guinea stinkers."

"Thank you. Another time."

"As you wish."

The captain flamed his Players with a lighter as thick and solid as his hand. He inhaled and swallowed and poured a thin pair of tracks out of his nose. He sighed and sat back, examined his cigarette. Looking up, he smiled and said, "You know, Mr. Dandy, I'm quite certain I've seen you ashore."

"Oh?"

"Yes. In New York."

"It's possible."

"Oh I don't mean on the street. I get around a bit in the big town. I'm referring to the stage. You wouldn't take me for a theater person now, would you?"

"Why not?"

"Precisely. Why not? Well, there it is, it's rather a passion of mine." He leaned forward. "There is one work in your theater that is an absolute smasher. *The Green Pastures.* I never visit your country without seeing it."

"Really?"

"On my honor. It is, in my opinion, more than a stage presentation. It is a moving experience. Of, course, I am only an amateur in dramatic criticism, as it were."

"But clearly, you know what you like."

"Precisely, sir, on the mark. I have seen it thirteen times, so there is a bit of evidence that I admire this work, eh?"

"Absolutely."

"I shall see, and experience, that piece of work, that dark marvel so long as Thee Lawd, as it were, sends me to your shores."

"Which, I hope, will continue for many years."

"Well, at least as long as *The Green Pastures* continues, eh?"

"Oh yes."

The captain inhaled, exhaled. "Which brings me to my point. I tend to take the circle route."

"No hurry."

"Precisely. No hurry. Mr. Dandy, were you not at one time Noah?"

"In *Green Pastures?*"

"The same."

"Oh no. Never."

"Are you quite sure?"

"Quite sure."

"I see." The captain looked at his cigarette and shook his head. "You have an absolutely uncanny resemblance to Noah, you really do, sir."

"Not guilty, Captain."

"Pity. I do hope I haven't spoken out of turn. I was terribly moved when Noah spoke to Thee Lawd and Thee Lawd responded. So when Noah came on board, sans wig and beard, it was, you see, a jolly big jolt. I don't mind telling you, Mr. Dandy, I have had millionaires on this vessel, dealers in precious gems, merchants of death, even South American presidents—deposed of course. I quite fancied having Noah with us. Seemed apt, you know?"

"I have never been Noah."

"Please forgive my clumsiness, Mr. Dandy."

"It's quite all right, Captain."

"One gets so damnably biographical at sea."

"It's all right. As a matter of fact, Captain, I'm a runner. A *top* runner. In a larger sense, a racketeer."

"Sir?"

"A racketeer. A swindler, if you will. Actually a double-dealing swindler. I'm absconding with my partner's money; no, to be precise, my boss's money."

The captain swallowed a ball of smoke.

"Of course, Mr. Dandy," he said solemnly. "Of course. I tend to talk a bit at sea. Of course. I do apologize for stepping over the line." He drank deeply and set his mug down with a plunk. "Really. A racketeer. Little Caesar. Oh, I say."

On the fifth night out, there was a light rap at his door. He looked up from a London *Times* and called, "Come in, it's open." The door swung gently in, and Bruce, the little cabin boy in spotless whites, stepped over the barrier. He was holding high a small, round tray. Cleveland waited.

"Capn's compliments, sir," said Bruce. "Says seein as ow it's a bit rough, you'd like sumpn of a nightcap."

"Thank you, I would." He swung out of his bunk, tossed the

paper onto a chair and sat down at the tiny, bolted-to-the-floor table. Bruce set the tray with its jigger, tall glass half-filled with ice and the bottle of Scotch on the table. From a deep pocket he produced a pint of soda.

"Aig Scotch, sir."

"The captain's favorite."

"Right, sir. Don't drink nothin but Aig."

"He led the troops in the war, didn't he?"

"Oh no, sir, the cap'n weren't even in France. Worked in Glasgow in the yards."

"I mean Haig."

The small head drooped to one side. The boy said, "Why, they does ave the same name. Fancy. Field Marshal an Aig Scotch. Fancy."

"I believe it's the same family."

"Is it now?"

"Yes, I believe so. Would you like a taste of the Field Marshal's Scotch?"

The boy's cheek was translucent; even his acne glowed. "Hit's werry kinda you, sir, but Hi never drinks on duty."

"I respect that."

The boy seemed to glow again and his whites creaked as he stood even straighter. Cleveland carefully fixed his drink and sipped. He smiled at the glowing boy as he leaned back from the waist. Cleveland nodded encouragingly.

The boy somehow managed to examine his gleaming black shoes. "Beggin yer pardon, sir . . ."

"Yes?"

He looked past Cleveland. "The boys as been talkin, sir . . ."

"And?"

"They been talkin about *you*."

"And?"

"Oo you are an like that . . ."

"And?"

"Well, sir." The boy's eyes cut to him, then away. "The boys figger you be workin fer Mrs. Ruservelt . . ."

"Mrs. Roosevelt?"

"Yessir."

"In what way do I work for her?"

"Well sir, the boys they think you be her personal repre-sen'tive, in a manner of speakin . . ."

"And what do you think?"

"Hi allus goes along with the boys."

"I see."

The whites creaked under heavy breathing.

"What *in particular*," Cleveland said, "do I do?"

A deep, whistling breath. "The boys they figger you be lookin inta labor conditions all over the world. So's the workin bloke kin get a fair shake. They figger you be doin that fer Mrs. Ruser-velt." He sighed.

"You think so, too?"

"Hi goes along with the boys, sir."

Cleveland stroked his N.R.A. chin.

"The boys, sir, they wants you ta know somethin."

"Yes?"

"Conditions on board the *Singapore,* sir. Conditions is pos-itiffly turrible."

"Really?"

"Oh yes, sir. In perticular down the ingine room. Down there, sir, a person he can't see a *think*." He nodded violently.

"I thought this was a pretty well-run boat."

"Beggin yer pardon, sir, this here be a ship. A boat is a fing what's aboard a ship."

"My apology."

"Oh everybody makes that mistake, don't fink nothin of it." He continued in a low, excited voice. "Hit's well run, all right. Hit's well run ta the irons. Fair brutal hit's run. Mrs. Ruservelt she be positiffly *amazed* at what we puts up with. *An* if she tol the President, why he would say, 'That be *outrachous.*'"

"You really think so?"

"Hi *knows* it. Would you tell her, sir?"

"Bruce, I don't know Mrs. Roosevelt."

The boy rocked gently once, twice. He smiled very briefly, a brown-toothed smile. "A course, sir. Hi gets it."

"Bruce, I mean what I say."

"A course you do, sir."

"Bruce, I'm on the run."

"A course, sir. Hain't we all? Cept for the cap'n."

"I am on the lam."

"Hi see, sir. Now sir, if Mrs. Ruservelt kin go down the mines, she could tyke yer word fer what goes on in a ship. A ship what puts inta New York in America?"

"I am running for my life."

"A course, sir. You know my all-time fav'rite price fighter? Kid Chocolate. You kin ask the boys."

"I like Joe Louis."

"Oh yes, a great one, oh yes. Fact is you kin put em tagether and you get boxin ability with a killer punch. Oh yes, Hi agrees with that. Will ya talk to Mrs. Ruservelt, sir?"

"I have never laid eyes on the lady. Except in the newsreels."

Bruce set the pint of soda on the table. He picked up the tray with the tumbler and jigger and bottle of Scotch. He frowned, placed the Scotch beside the soda. Holding the tray high, he walked stiffly to the door. There, without turning, he said, "Food is slops, boys they works triple overtime, Jimmy got flunk against a berler las week, he can't hardly walk, nobody knows, nobody knows." He touched a finger to the acned forehead. "When ya talks ta her, please don't use my name, sir." The Dickens child stepped over and out to the corridor, reached a careful hand behind and gently closed the door.

Cleveland sat and stared at the door. Then he lifted the bottle of soda and drained it. Very quickly, he undressed, washed, brushed his teeth, entered his silk pajamas. He reached up and twisted off the bare overhead bulb, blew on his fingers. The darkness was pierced by a sliver of portholed light. He climbed into his bunk against the wall, slid beneath the brown navy blanket, kicked it loose about his feet. The boat—the ship—shuddered through the mattress and the cabin creaked as if it were built of Bruce's whites, and through the open porthole leaked the perspiration of the sea: salt and night and oil.

Part Two

SHOPKEEPERS

AFTER THREE WHISPERED CONFERENCES HE WAS ADMITTED TO the Hotel Piccadilly which was filled with rather primitive paintings of a ruffed Queen Elizabeth. He tipped the bellhop three shillings and carefully explained that piccadill meant ruff and pointed to Elizabeth over his bed. The boy said, Thank you, sir, and backed out of the room.

He washed and changed and walked out past all the Elizabeths into London. It was a beautifully clear day so he walked along the route of Victoria's Diamond Jubilee, thence to Park Lane. He crossed and continued on to the corner of Hyde Park where he listened with arms folded to calm denunciations of Trotsky, Kerensky, colonialism, democracy, Krupp, Gladstone, Wall Street, Leon Blum, Baldwin, syndicalism, socialism and the graduated income tax. That killed the afternoon, after which he drifted off and had ham and eggs and tea near Marble Arch, in the shadow of the Iron Duke. He visited the Royal Geographic Society and explored the explorers of the Nile. Drifted off again, this time to Fortnum & Mason, then back to the hotel of the ruff. And so to a lumpy English bed.

The next morning, after Wheatabix and tea in the hotel, he returned to Hyde Park. He parked near a rat-faced fellow who was poking holes in the air along with the Hoare-Laval agreement:

"And so we have the spectacle of Sir Sam Hoare and Monsieur

P. Laval, that famous trained-seal-and-dummy-act, trained in the clubrooms and *bourses* in chicanery; we have this pair combining to prevent a presumed mad-dog act on the part of Signor Mussolini, who though he indulges in a bit of frothing at the balcony is nothing if not a shrewd and manipulating fox. To accomplish this imaginary end, that of stopping Mr. Mussolini, Monsieur Laval dons his virgin-white necktie and Sir Samuel repairs to Switzerland where he instantly dives to the ice and breaks his busybody nose. These are our diplomatic leaders. Meanwhile, the idiot we have imported from an Institute of the Feebleminded to head our government drones on about sanctions and oil and other paper-tissue threats of which he knows nothing and cares less. Mr. Mussolini merely shrugs his foxy shoulders and drives deeper into Ethiopia. Nothing has moved; nothing has changed; except that Hoare and Laval, representing the world's two greatest democracies, have put their empty skulls together and agreed to hand over Ethiopia if Mr. Musso will cease and desist. In other words, to sell a nation they have sworn to protect down the bloody river. Mr. Musso has it both ways. He knows that the only things that will stop him are closing the canal and throwing a royal battleship at him, neither of which we have the nerve to do."

He held up a modest hand.

"Please save your approval until I have concluded my remarks; it interrupts my flow of concentration. Thank you. Now then, let me put to you a question: Suppose Mr. Roosevelt and Mr. Stalin had got together and decided to hand the midlands over to Mr. Hitler without so much as a by your leave, how would you take it? Think on that. Now think on this: What would our staunch ally across the channel do if those two gentlemen handed over to Mr. Hitler the heart of France?

"Nothing, indicates my friend down here, shaking his head sadly. Why do nothing, sir? Oh, it would prevent war? And that is all that matters, eh? Ah, sir, perhaps you are right. But, if you are, then we ain't what we used to be, are we? For then, sir, we are lost.

" 'Spit in their eye' says my dark friend with the folded arms. Now, *there's* an answer! I'd dearly love to believe we could and would. For though we have fallen low, we are not so low that we have forgotten how to be *men*. Thank you, my dark friend.

"Hold on to the clapping, please . . ."

A pleasant nod, a bit of a smile, and the rat-faced chap was off again.

"Take diplomacy. I mean, *you* take it, not me. For isn't it a pretty name for the business of liars and confidence men. Why, Mr. Stavisky would make a *great* foreign minister . . . Hold the clapping, please . . . Then again he's probably too far above such work. Jack the Ripper would blush purple to be caught in such company. I can only trust that Mr. Hitler is watching and taking copious notes, for Hoare and Laval are surely his masters. Yes indeed. Much here for Adolf to learn. Sir Samuel, whose surname insults a noble profession when put up against his own, could teach Mr. Hitler how best to steal from the poor and give to the rich. And Mr. Laval—he of the pure white tie—Mr. Laval, to aid and abet a bully and a thief, would scuttle both Ethiopia *and* the League. Now, *there's diplomacy* for you. Mr. Hitler, note, observe; you are the soul of *purity* beside this pair . . . Please, my friends . . .

"Well, then, what next? Perhaps Signor Musso covets the tomb of Napoleon, perhaps this very Hyde Park. Hand them over, Hoare-Laval, why not? For it would make Musso happy and perhaps he wouldn't ask for the Abbey or the Tower. In a pig's eye, he wouldn't.

"Because you know what's the problem, my friends? I'll tell you what's the problem. Very simple. The old school tie runs the bloody show. You and I and poor Ras Tafari, we ain't out of Eton and Harrow and Oxbridge and so we don't know peas from porridge. Those thin-blooded ones, those trained seals, they're the ones what count. They make secret agreements we can only read about and if it was up to them we wouldn't be able to read . . . Hold on to your cheers, my good friends . . .

"Do not take my word for it. I'm biased, prejudiced, I admit it. I failed their eleven plus exam, as did many of you, so I'm a wee bitter. No, here's what. Go on over to Parliament, to the House of Lords. Behold them snoozing their lives away, not to mention ours, a gouty foot upon a plush chair. And if that don't make you sick, try Commons. They'd have you think *our* people sit down there. Rubbish. Listen one time and your poor old Aunt Sally wouldn't stoop to talk so stupid. Because that bunch is out of the same cloth. Different bolt, same cloth. I tell you, my friends, I've had it to the bloody gills with the Sam Hoares of this country. A true whore sells what's hers; a Sam Hoare gives away what ain't even *his* . . ."

Cleveland's palms were snapping like pistol shots when the voice behind him and to the right said, "Now, my good man, you just take 'er nice an easy and keep on clappin till I say stop, for the thing you're feelin is a real true gun, a deadly weepin, so do what I say. All right, stop. That's a good boy . . . Now, start walkin in the direction it indicates, away from Park Lane, that's a good fellow . . . Slow an steady wins the race, that's the ticket; don't make me show you how this bit of business works . . ."

The car looped back on its trail several times. This he knew from having gone through it with the Sugar Hill Boys, who had grabbed him in '32, and toured and retoured the Bronx. Then, it was a black eyeshade, the kind you sleep with; now, it was a black silk handkerchief, but it still took an hour to go two or three miles. Sighing, he worked on the major rivers of the world and their tributaries; he was spelling them backwards when the clutch rasped and they came to a screeching stop. They were at the edge of smoothly flowing traffic, but the air was clear. A park; no, a garden. Doors slammed. He was hustled roughly out and across a sidewalk past the openness of the garden, up a flight of stairs. Through one, two doors, into a lift that clanged behind him. They rose one, two, three floors. He was hustled out and down a long, dust-filled, thinly carpeted hall, across a threshold. A pressure on his shoulders and he was sitting in a firm, high, winged chair. He crossed his legs and laced his fingers. A cleared throat and a quiet, civilized voice: "You may take it off now, Lemuel, and make sure to wash it thoroughly and put it away with some lavender." The handkerchief came off and he blinked away the spots. He looked about at the high, beamed ceiling, the clutter of massive furniture, finally at the gentleman before him. This gentleman was sitting tall and slivery and elegant in another winged chair. He had red cheeks which on further inspection were composed of finely broken veins. Pure white sideboards. Beyond all that, however, almost obliterating his physicality, was the uniform. Khaki officer's uniform, beautifully pressed, held together by a tight, gleaming Sam Browne. And a swagger stick. Touching same to wide, marbled forehead, the officer and gentleman said very pleasantly, "Welcome to Gawain House. Please forgive the dramatics. Lemuel is a fine fellow but too strongly influenced by the kinema. I should like to introduce myself. Henry Armitage, sometimes known as *Sir* Henry Armitage, for the family title, which is neither here nor there, has resided with us for some three hundred years. I do not doze, in fact have a touch of insomnia; nor do I have the gout." He smiled quickly below his upper lip. "So much for me, at the moment. Now, as for you. I know, sir, who you are." He lifted the swagger stick. "And who you are not." The swagger stick returned to his other palm and lay there quietly. "You are not James Dandy." His lip rose again; a flash of teeth. "You are, of course, Gallifa, the son of Ras Gugsa of Gondar and, though illegitimate, you are therefore also a Solomonic Prince. Your father, the husband of Empress Judith, was the mortal enemy of Selassie and was slain by him five years ago at Ankim near Addis. You have been a wanderer and you have wandered all the way to me. All this I know. You naturally hate Selassie and thirst for revenge. As a student of the mind's psychology, this, too, I know. I can assist you with your very natural impulse, even if your father did not acknowledge you in his lifetime. Blood is thicker than sherry, is it not? I say, would you care for a bit of sherry?"

Over the second drink Cleveland said, "It's true that, legally, I'm not James Dandy." Armitage raised a lip. "How do you know I'm the son of Prince Gugsa? Illegitimate."

"Gobineau, of course. But that needn't concern you."

"I'll be the judge of what concerns me," Cleveland said, folding his arms regally. The swagger stick saluted. "I don't suppose," Cleveland continued, "there's much point in denying that I *am* Prince ... Gallifa?"

"Nonatall."

"Then, there we are." He unfolded his arms regally. Armitage uncurled from his chair and stood slightly curved beside the mantel.

"Yes," he said in a bit of a mumble, "here we are." "Do you know where that *is*?"

"Galahad House. You told me."

"Aha, you are clever." The lip flashed. "You know quite well that I said Gawain House; you know it quite well. You have chosen another reply. Yet, this calculated reply is by no means a poor one. May I remind you I know psychology. You might have said Lancelot and you didn't. You might have said Guinivere and you did not. Instinctively, you surmised that I detest the philanderer and adulteress above all else. We are adrift, as well you know, in a moral cesspool, exemplified by these two cases. It is ab-so-lute-ly essential that we return to the basic and pure rhythms of the sun. Gawain, Galahad, Gugsa, Gallifa, good. Well, it appears that I've made a bit of a speech. Do you know the G, Prince?"

"Sir?"

"Come now. You have an instinct; and you are a G."

"Sir?"

"Tut. All right, we will play a gifted game. The G. It girdles the globe. Even in Ethiopia they know of it."

"Perhaps in Gondar."

"There. Definitely in Gondar." The swagger stick whipped lightly against a bloused trouser leg. "The all-powerful, all-knowing G." Armitage stepped away from the mantel. "Have no fear, Gallifa, you are safe here, quite safe. You are a guest of the Golden Grace."

"Do I genuflect?"

"Good try, dear Prince, but lacking. Genuflect is a soft G and just will not do." Good, gravy, gamble, game, girl, go, groin, gallop, glory, glow, gift, granite, Greek, Goth, give, godsend, Gulliver, Gordon, Garibaldi." Cleveland stared at (soft G) Armitage, who continued with intent calm: "From the land of the midnight sun to the Mediterranean shore, we will transform the world-cesspool, restore it to its natural state."

"Africa included."

"Practically *beginning* with Africa. Africa needs us."

"Especially Ethiopia."

"Ah, most especially Ethiopia. Despite Tafari-Selassie's moral-istic pleas, you and I both know your country practices slavery. Not"—he flicked—"that slavery per se is evil. It cannot, however, be a birthright like primogeniture, which as you know was the downfall of the middle ages and the reason the Crusades failed. Soft G, primogeniture. No, slavery, or mastership, go-to-the-top-ness, as we call it, must be earned in each successive era. Other-wise you will have a condition of mamelukism wherein the slave becomes the master, the downfall of Egypt, soft G. Your country has never learned this basic lesson. Then, too, it is run by corrupt priests supported by Tafari and this we cannot permit. Yours, dear Prince, is an evil land, despite the proclamations of the Book of Glories, a cleverly borrowed G. Actually a blasphemy. Bit more sherry?"

Cleveland shook his head and settled back against the winged chair. He smelled the dust of Inkerman, Ypres, Mafeking. He looked around the room, nodded very slowly, and said, "Are you connected with Mosley?"

Armitage whacked his trouser leg three times, then flashed brilliantly. "You cannot provoke me. I have complete control of my inner glory." He rapped lightly against the mantel. "Silly old Oswald. Flaccid, Prince, flaccid. An overextender, a poor thing. His BUF? A bluff. Hah, a bluff. In many ways more primitive than, you will forgive my discourtesy, your people."

"You are temporarily forgiven. To return to Mosley, however, you see we have heard of him even in the jungle, whereas you and your . . . group . . ."

"Quite all right, Gallifa, quite. You may say it. I do not take offense, one of Oswald's failings. What you say is absolutely cor-rect. It is our way. Glimmers, glances, goads; we are hardly in the advert business, you know, eh? However"—the stiff, solemn (shy) smile—"we are deeply concerned and involved with the transformation of your—Selassie's—land." He sat down sud-denly, now stiff and straight. "You see, Prince, *Garibaldi* is di-recting operations in Ethiopia."

"... and his commanding vessel is ... Graziani ..."

"How did you know that?" Armitage said quietly.

"It's appropriate."

"It is indeed."

Cleveland leaned away from the dust and said, "Although in a certain position at twilight I'm a bit golden, I fear I don't qualify for grace. So what do you want from me?"

"The point precise. Glorious. Very well. We work with whom we can, when we can. Where we can. An ends-means thing, you know. We make arrangements, a soft word, but softness can be manipulated, used. Quite simply put, Garibaldi needs you. Rome, as you perceived in Hyde Park, is neither universally acclaimed nor understood. Your father was murdered by the tyrant. You are his son, though illegitimate. Your father's cesspoolian behaviour is, however, no fault of yours. You are a son. That is a glorious thing to be, a son. You want revenge. You have every reason to come over to our cause ..."

"And to proclaim it publicly?"

"There *is* a glimmer of the gold in you, Prince, your disclaimer to the contrary notwithstanding. Precisely."

Once again he settled back against the dust. He could take the fruitcake out easily, but there was Lemuel and company. "May we have some lunch?" he said.

"But of course. How uncivil of me. Please forgive me." Armitage rose swiftly. "We will lunch in the Golgotha Greengarden."

That night he lay on a camp bed in the Glowering Godiva room. He was positive someone sat outside his door and beneath each window. He shrugged and briefly examined the reproductions of Goya, Gainsborough and (El) Greco. Beside him on the night table were three slim, elegantly bound books: *The Sun Is All, The Glory That Is Goth* and *Do Not Hate PiGment*, all by Joseph Gobineau, and two pamphlets: *Why We Are Superior* and *RiGor and DisGust: Partners in ProGress*, also by Gobineau.

He picked up *PiGment* and it fell open. At the top of the right-hand page a note was pinned, written in a swooping, Palmerian hand, that said, "Guided reading, my dear Gallifa, will save time, which will not even wait for a Prince. H. A." Each line on the page was underlined in green, beginning with:

DRAPETOMANIA, OR THE DISEASE
CAUSING NEGROES TO RUN AWAY

(A disease of the American slave as diaGnosed by the eminent American physician, Dr. Samuel CartwriGht of the University of Louisiana, appearing in *Du Bow's Review*, Vol. 11, September, 1851, pp. 331–334.)

DRAPETOMANIA is from (a Greek word meaning) a runaway slave, and (another Greek word meaning) mad or crazy. It is unknown to our medical authorities, although its diaGnostic symptom, the absconding from service, is well known to our planters and overseers ... The cause in most of the cases, that induces the NeGro to run away from service, is as much a disease of the mind as any other species of mental alienation, and much more curable as a general rule. With the advantages of proper medical advice, strictly followed, this troublesome practice that many NeGroes have of running away, can be almost entirely prevented, although the slaves be located on the borders of a free state, within a stone's throw of the abolitionists ...

Before NeGroes run away, unless they are frightened or panic-stricken, they become sulky and dissatisfied. The cause of this sulkiness and dissatisfaction should be inquired into and removed, or they are apt to run away or fall into NeGro consumption. When sulky and dissatisfied with cause, the experience of those (overseers and owners) on the line and elsewhere, was decidedly in favor of whipping them out of it, as a preventive measure aGainst absconding, or other bad conduct. It was called whipping the devil out of them ...

In the margin was written in the swooping hand: "However, there is hope. He is a hard G."

He hummed a few bars of "Satin Doll," turned over and went to sleep.

"Good morning, Prince. I trust you slept well?"
"Very well."

"Ah then, let us break our fast."

Scones, marmalade, shirred eggs, three meats, kippers, Indian Ocean tea. He ate slowly. Armitage waited patiently until he looked up and smiled. Armitage said, "Well then, Gallifa, what is your view of things this morning?"

Cleveland dabbed at his mouth with a starched napkin. "I was rather surprised to see the books and pamphlets by Gobineau."

"You are familiar with Gobineau?"

"French Count. Nineteenth century. I've read some of his things. Do you read French?"

"No . . ."

"Really the only way to get at the meat of things. Go to the source."

"You have a point, although I have excellent translations."

"Not the same."

"Let us not quibble, Prince."

"All right."

"I will vouch on my honor that these translations are accurate and convey his every nuance."

"All right."

The flash-smile. "You are a natural diplomatist. The foreign office could use you."

"I have little use for the foreign office."

"Splendid. Gobineau would approve of you."

"I don't know that I approve of him."

"Bravo."

"And he would detest me."

"Then, you *do* know his views . . ."

"I think I do. I believe I have a firm grasp on them. But I am unfamiliar with those particular titles."

"Naturally, although they are of a piece with his other material. I give you my categorical assurance. They are very current."

"One of your French friends is leading you on, Sir Henry. He's been dead for seventy years."

"Oh, that is true. In the corporeal sense. *I* wrote these; Gobineau dictated them."

Cleveland folded his napkin and slipped it through the gold ring. "You are in touch with him?"

Armitage flicked the smile. "Oh, dear no. No spirit nonsense. I am—what was your good word—his vessel. Yes, his intellectual vessel. It is really amazingly simple. When he is ready, I write. He's chosen Armitage, the lucky lad me."

"The lucky count *he*. I mean, to have found you."

"You are kind, Gallifa."

"Only accurate, sir. I trust it was Gobineau who located me and told you who I was."

"Quite so. We Gs are about, we're about. At a critical moment we reach out to each other. Well then, you read a bit last night, did you?"

"A bit. Drapetomania, Dysaethesia Aethiopica . . ."

"Yes, yes, Dr. Cartwright. Excellent credentials."

"Tell me, Sir Henry, according to the eminent doctor, were these maladies present in Africa, that is, when the American slave was in his natural condition?"

"Interesting question, Gallifa. He doesn't say, actually. My own view of the matter is to think not. The admixture of African pigment and the American climate produced the illness, as I see it. Quite a chemical thing, a type of spontaneous combustion, as it were. The American climate is terribly faulty."

"You've been there?"

"Oh my heavens, no. My research has confirmed this. There's no question but that America has quite destroyed its whack at the G."

"Your research?"

"The reading of history, my dear Gallifa. You can always rely on history. America, you see, once had a chance. Two chances, actually. It had two presidents who were of the Grace. Garfield and Grant. But America, or the United States—a contradiction in terms if ever there was one—shot one and besmirched the other. Oh, there is a nationwide will behind such acts, believe me. The G simply cannot survive in such a faulty climate— environment, as it were. I'm afraid it is a Graceless country."

"Great Britain is not, I take it?"

"I am not totally sanguine, but there is hope. We have our G-killers. Our prime minister is an ass, as the chap in Hyde Park told you; our king is a philanderer. We are on the edge of the cesspool, dipping our toes, as it were. There is a certain fascination in cesspools for people of all classes. Yet, there is a matrix of hope here: Goldsmith, Gordon, Gray, Gulliver, Sir Garnet—oh, especially Sir Garnet—all have shown that the Grace flourished once and can flower again." Armitage curved tautly in his chair and continued in a soft, confidential voice. "I will let you in on something, for I feel I can trust you . . . The nation of the future is . . ." He curved a bit more . . . "Greenland." He straightened up. "You see, as it grows in glory, it will return to its past. Eric the Red, the Ericson chap and all that. The Grace, Gallifa, is nothing if not a complete girdle, a going forth and regoing. I've informed Baldwin time and again that Greenland is the future and we had damn well conquer or ally, but of course I've had no success save a thank you and cheerio, the silly ass. But then, as your father well knew, the prophet is without honor et cetera, et cetera."

Through it all, Cleveland listened with unblinking courtesy, though with princely aloofness. Then, he said, "In my country we have heard of a certain Marcus Garvey. Do you know of him?"

The heavy eyebrows snorted. "Indeed I bloody well do. Met him once. At Brighton. Very decent swimmer. Overall quite an interesting chap, the question of pigment aside. Good skull despite a sloping forehead. Longish, though. But a shameless fraud. Complete and shameless. Somehow, and this will happen, you know, he got on to the G and has used it for all its worth. Gobineau has checked him out thoroughly. Real name is Parkhurst. Isaac Parkhurst. Hails from Jamaica, as he claims, and the J is even more flaccid than the soft G. A reader of books, such as they are in Jamaica. Somehow hit on this back-to-Africa business—G-swindlers can sometimes become temporarily inspired—and got the slave population of America all stirred up. Has even upset our coloreds. To no practical avail, of course. Faulty thinker, Parkhurst, with all his Sam Smiles self-help. For in the end Africa will be thrashed out amongst ourselves—if we wake up—Greenland, and Rome."

"So now we have returned to Rome."

"Oh my, yes. Your reason for being here, eh? I will put it to you straight out, Ras Gallifa. Play our game and you can have the throne. You have my word on that. Of course, it will be a bit on the Manchukuo style, but what's the difference? I guarantee you thousands in social credit at home and abroad. Move your capital to Gondar, if you wish; that's a distinct possibility. We will talk to Graziani. Rather, Garibaldi."

"Not Mussolini?"

"Heavens, no . . . The future of Rome is Graziani. He will in due time get rid of Mussolini, who is a necessary interim stage. Also Badoglio, his only rival on the African scene. Ruthless man, Graziani, utterly ruthless. Mean, spiteful, petty, vainglorious, above all, vainglorious. He will conquer Ethiopia, with your help, I trust, and invade Rome with your tribesmen behind him; they are still a marvel with the spear, as well you know. I say, that *is* a juicy picture; naked blacks screaming like demented demons and Signor No-Neck running away like the very devil. I say." His teeth glistened. "You see, Graziani is the completion and return-ness of Garibaldi. The groin and gut-grandeur of Golden Grace as we unite sun, soil, social credit, glory, greenery. No puzzle there, my friend, no mystery, no fuzzywuzziness. Gobineau has arranged all." His upper lip remained poised above his teeth.

Cleveland sat under a dull sun in the brownish greengarden watching Lemuel, who was watching the neighborhood girls walk by on the other side of the fence. Three of the Golden Gang stood at different points of the garden doing the same thing, but they all wore bulges under the left shoulder of their jackets and they seemed in reasonably good shape.

Then he saw him. Elmer Quinn. Leaning on his game leg across the street, beside a telephone kiosk. Congratulations, Sol. Elmer the Great could handle everyone in the garden as he had once handled Strangler Lewis, even if Strangler was on the downslope. Good show, Sol, but not for the wronged royalty of Gondar who detested broken backs.

He got up and as the Golden boys glanced his way, walked slowly into the house. He kept on walking up to the third floor. The library door was closed to everyone, and that meant, sir, *every*one, yes, even royalty. He opened the door and walked in.

Armitage was seated at a campaign desk wearing a tin hat and belted trench coat. He sat very stiffly, staring at a photograph on the wall behind the desk that documented a good portion of the slaughter on the western front. Cleveland hesitated, then began to walk across the room. A whistle sounded.

"Any man," the soft voice said, "whose back does not face me, will be shot between the eyes."

Cleveland said, "Does that include colonial troops?"

The whistle blew again. "I do not command colonial troops," the soft voice answered.

Cleveland began to walk again, but an upraised imperial hand stopped him. In a crisp voice, Armitage said to a point above the photograph, "Yes, I understand. Yes. I know that very well. With all respect, you *do* realize that I am surrounded by bloody fools and flaccid second-raters, do you not? Please! I am doing my best under very trying circumstances. You might give one a bit of credit, you know. Oh, very well then." He sighed and leaned forward in a taut curve, and began to write. A hard scratching filled the room. Suddenly he stopped writing, capped his fountain pen, placed it in a drawer, leaned back and half turned his head. The whistle dangled from a gold lanyard about his neck. He said gently, "We are attempting to work out a problem. One of our people in Prussia is acting the bloody fool with kinema actresses. Either he ends this behavior or faces expulsion. We do not care how important—or unimportant— these people are; there is very little Grace in the missionary position. Is there something on your mind, Gallifa?"

"Yes. I'm accepting your proposal."

The lip flashed and the eyes flickered, but that was all. "Ah, I see. Well, I must admit we are a bit ahead of shed-ule . . . I frankly anticipated a bit of trouble with you."

"I make up my mind quickly. I always have. There is one condition, however."

"We are flexible, dear Prince."

"I want to go to Ethiopia. I want you to get me there. Now."

"Isn't that quite dangerous for you?"

"Perhaps, if I go gunning for Tafari. But I want you to get me to the Italians. Pardon, the Romans."

The clear brown eyes closed for a beat and a straying hand toyed with the lanyard. Then, he nodded.

"It will be a great coup for us, you know?"

"I suppose."

"Gobineau rather likes it."

"Good."

"But, if I may ask, why, my dear Prince?"

A glance toward the telephone kiosk. A quick review of Sol's blotless escutcheon where the double cross was concerned.

"I want to be on the winning side."

"Ah, indeed. I can understand that completely." Armitage rubbed his hands together and stood up. He saluted smartly. "We move quickly. You will leave tomorrow morning at the first glow of globelight. Everything will be arranged. Transportation. Wardrobe. Everything. Graziani will be briefed. So will the press." The swagger stick whipped a bloused leg. "All will be Sir Garnet, oh yes, all, *all*. I must bid you good day now, for I have a great deal to do. Oh my, I must tell you, Gobineau is very pleased, *very* pleased . . ."

VICTORS OF VERDUN

THEY AWAKENED HIM AT FOUR-THIRTY. LEMUEL SAID, "IF YOU WILL proceed to the dressing room, sir, when yer ready, yer clothes be all laid out," and he opened an adjoining door and pointed.

Cleveland poured ice cold water out of a fluted pitcher into its white, scalloped basin and noisily splashed face, arms, hands and chest (as Tiny Armitage had surely done at Eton, Harrow or Rugby). Patted himself dry with a square of Irish linen. Then, with Lemuel trailing, he walked into the dressing room. On a straight-backed chair was laid out a white garment.

"That be a *shimma*, sir," Lemuel said.

"Solomon's children would be a bit upset. It's a *shamma*."

"Well," Lemuel said, frowning, "it's yer cuppa tea. And so's the Joffers." He pointed. The jodhpurs stood at gleaming black attention in front of the chair; he let it go at that. He dressed slowly; everything, including the jodhpurs, fit perfectly. With Lemuel trailing, he strode out and downstairs.

In the breakfast nook, Armitage was waiting with a chubby-faced man dressed in boots, khaki trousers, leather jacket, white neckerchief and Lindbergh helmet, with the goggles pushed up to his forehead.

"Splendid," said Armitage, rubbing the swagger stick. "Royalty will always out. You simply must avoid our silly togs, dear Prince." Flash-smile. "Permit me. I introduce you to Jacques de Lesseps. A *nom de guerre*, of course, but rahther necess'ry to our work. Jacques, this is the *personage speciale* I have told your people about."

57

The chubby aviator held out a thick hand and as Cleveland shook it, threw back his head and uttered a shrill, falsetto cry.

Cleveland glanced at Armitage. Armitage was frowning. "You must forgive Jacques," he said. "He fancies himself a Casino humorist. That noise purports to be your famed war cry. As you well know, forgive me for carrying coals, it goes like this." Flinging his head back, he screeched something at the ceiling that resembled a Lily Pons aria. Jacques mustered a Chevalier-lip. Armitage said, "But that will scare the wooly underwear off the Sicilian peasant, eh? Come now, gentlemen, to table."

As they clacked sterling and Sheffield against Spode, Armitage sketched out the drill. The honored guest and Jacques would take wing from a private aerodrome in a de Haviland Comet; twould be appreciated if the whereabouts of the aerodrome would remain in the family, as it were. Jacques would then point them east and let out the throttle for Paris and Le Bourget, which, heh, one trusts he could find for he had once gotten lost over Nancy, eh? Jacques, who had had two confirmed kills in the war, lofted a pair of eyebrows to the skies. Once in Pah-ree, Armitage continued, Jacques' people will see you through. They are rahther poor cousins to the Grace, still fighting agaynst poor old Dreyfus, who has gotten his own back with Blum, eh, old boy? Jacques curled a lip, said nothing. Reflecting that things do indeed spiral out, Armitage clacked his cup down. He stood up and whipped a trouser leg while Jacques sucked on his tea. Armitage sighed and looked over the horizon. "Ah," he murmured, "to be going out. I'd give all, *all*."

Jacques looked up. "Perhaps you could give a gold ring to the cause, eh what?"

"Oh dear," Armitage said, flashing his teeth, "Jacques, the Casino humorist. No, my good fellow, I will leave rings to the Roman *signoras*. Bit of a sign, though, eh? Band of steel for a band of gold. Quite unwittingly, old boy, you do make a point."

Cleveland said quickly, "Might we leave the back way? I really think one of Tafari's mercenaries has found me."

"Really? But I can have Lemuel and his troop take care of that instantly."

"No, Sir Henry. I don't want any fuss."

"But of course. Decent point. Ah well then." He suddenly thrust his head back and closed his eyes. Jacques winked at Cleveland and twirled a finger in the ear. "Egad," intoned Armitage, "to show them our sand. To regain our soul. To track the nobility of valor!" The narrow shoulders lifted and squared. *To play the game of games.*

The head came back and he opened his eyes and looked blankly around the room. Then he whipped his trousers, got up, strode to Cleveland and held out a thin, marbled hand. "Ras Gallifa, Count Gobineau wishes you GracefulGolden-GloriousGodspeed."

2

The father of Jacques de Lesseps was a postal clerk and a Boulangist. Both occupation and preoccupation were to him extremely compatible, for he dearly loved his little job and his country. He loved his duty and he worshiped men who loved theirs, especially where France was concerned. And Boulanger, without the glimmer of a doubt, was that man. The dashing general, indeed, was nothing less than another Bonaparte. To be sure, the father of the father of Jacques, also a postal clerk, had seen nothing less than a Bonaparte in his nephew, Louis Napoleon, but as the sadness of 1870 had shown him, one must choose a hero who has the spirit to restore with the greatest care and examination. The father of the father had thereupon sat back, when not doing his duty, and watched with wary eyes as Boulanger dashed up the greasy pole. Not so, the father of Jacques. For this young clerk, weaned on Austerlitz and Marengo, Boulanger was truth, resurrection and restoration. He was a return to glory. He was, that is, until the critical moment when with the Elysée in the palm of his hand, as well as the inept republic, he chose to go to bed with his mistress. The father of the father sighed and turned away, but the father was so shaken that he did not speak for five years, even to his co-workers. It was not a conscious choice or decision on his part, it was a thing, quite simply, that he did. Rather, did not do. Even when Jacques was born, he only stared. He did his duty well and efficiently, of course; after all, he was a French public servant; but he did not speak. It might have continued indefinitely, this muteness, but the army took the matter into its own hands and shattered the great silence. It was the Dreyfus case that brought this about. Not only did the case make one stand up for one's army, it exposed the republic and the socialists in all their rotten, corrupt and anti-French tendencies, which bordered—one says bordered, for the father of Jacques was not a radical man—on treason. It was, at last, a simple thing in the mind of the father: you were for the army and France or you were not. The Dreyfusards were not. He was.

Thereafter, he never stopped talking.

Guilt or innocence? Socialist irrelevancies, confusions for the clearheaded French brain. Devil's Island? Why is a Jew an officer in the first place and why so close to secret documents? Lying generals? The lion fights for its young; let the jackals beware! Zola, Clemenceau? What do they know of the army? The rest of the world? What world is there outside France?

He never stopped talking.

Nor, in his own way, did Jacques. Until Dreyfus, he had been a quiet child who never quite looked you in the eye. And, of course, he had had no verbal communication with his father. Suddenly, the father took a great, a consuming, interest, in his son; and Jacques in his turn took a great and consuming, albeit youthful, interest, in the monstrous Dreyfus. He educated his schoolmates on all the fine points of the matter; and if some stopped talking to him, so much the better for France and the army; one must choose, my son, one must choose. They talked, they communicated, they *believed* one another, father and son.

When Jacques, the first male child in a long but undistinguished line of male children, gained entrance to the École Polytechnique, it was the topic first class, the premier excitement for the father of Jacques; and, next to the perfidious Dreyfusards, the central subject for monologues in the bistros about rue de

Vaugirard. When he failed out, was the father of Jacques crushed? Is the smart old lion crushed? Bloodied perhaps, but *crushed*? A smile, a wink, a bit of calvados; those bastards are trying to get back at me through the boy. It is all very simple. If you hate the army, ergo France, you kick out the brilliant son of a real Frenchman. With one stroke you get revenge and you continue to weaken the nation. So simple, is it not?

Very well, one sits back, one waits, one watches, one even buys drinks for a decent fellow who confides that Zola had connections with the mistress of Boulanger. Oh, one supports the great war effort, of course; after all, France is France, and the hell with perfidious Albion and upstart America. But, I tell you something. Regard the mutineers. There is much to be learned there; ask Pétain. Do natural French boys mutiny against France? Of course not. It is an unnatural act. They have been made *un*natural, *corrupted* by the socialists, the Dreyfusards. Again so simple. Ask D'Esperet; ask Pétain.

One waits.

And one is rewarded.

In 1933, Jacques—an Ace (two confirmed kills, three unconfirmed; his squadron leader was a Protestant)—this good son enters the house of his father. He is wearing an insignia, this fine boy, and his first real smile since 1918. He informs his father that not only is he a big shot in the Victors of Verdun, he Jacques is the *air arm* of the Victors of Verdun. The father of Jacques folds his postal worker's hands over his patriotic belly and goes to sleep forever with happiness in his heart and the words, "A bas Dreyfus" on his lips.

Now what of Jacques?

To begin with, it is important to understand that he had worked—no, struggled—to achieve 1933. Such things are not simple. In '15, in desperation, they had plucked him out of the post office and set him down in the mud of the trenches, which he did not care for at all. Not that he minded true suffering if it helped France, oh no; it was just that eating mud, tagging dead comrades and tearing lice out of his hair was not helping France. Or the army. But, up above, up there in the clean and noble blue, that was the place to make your contribution, to enable France to become again France. And he argued and pestered and cajoled and even begged—for sometimes you go below the mud to rise above it—until finally a (Protestant) major had said, "All right, by heaven, go, and good riddance!" fully expecting failure or an early end or, worst of all, ridicule.

Instead, the lion cub, the true son of monarchy turned out (naturally) to have magnificent vision and exquisite balance. They shrugged and gave him goggles, leather, scarf and five weeks of training and again—wonder of wonders—the Royal Fly (as he came to be known) succeeded in becoming a loving unity with his little Spad as well as a fine and generous comrade to his squadron mates. A bit impatient with jammed guns, a bit reckless on the prowl, a little too much wine between patrols, but truly in his *métier* at last, a Bonapartist of the clouds. Once Coli flew with him and grinned across the friendly bridge of space; Nungesser shook his hand twice. For Jacques, the sky, the sun, the glory—despite the ineptitude of the republic and its leaders—burrowed deep into him and never thereafter did they ever leave the caverns of his body, the yearning spaces of his head. And 1933 and the Victors had restored, if not Bonaparte (and that was always possible), at least Jacques. (In '35 the Victors joined the Croix de Feu, but always made it very clear they were its fine, pure and special cutting edge.)

So, that is why now, as soon as they were away from Dover, as soon as they had shaken off perfidious Albion, as soon as they were over the Channel, he tapped his Important and Special Passenger on the shoulder, gave him a Coli grin and reached back for 1916 and magnificence. In his targeted bit of cloth and fine French machinery he heeled over and came down out of the sun, flipped over and let the Boche have it with hard, merciless thumbs. Then, in a graceful, swooping fade, he was up and away as the smoking Fokker spun out of control, and he was off to the next big challenge. Grinning with even more Coli-wickedness, Jacques dived, dived, dived and let the faceless troops have it, pulling out, dizzy and half gone but gloriously alive at the last, last, last instant. The grin taped to his face, he climbed a Matterhorn of a cloud while the eyes of Sir Important Passenger lolled blankly and without sight.

Struts groaning, the brave little plane looped, twisted, spiraled and gallantly accepted the challenge of Udet and Goering and showed the perfidious limeys how to fight skill with skill. By the time they had crossed the water and entered the clouds of Le Havre, he had five kills, *confirmed*. At that point, he reached forward, patted the tense but Important Personage on his knotted-up shoulder, nodded encouragement and smoothed out his clumsy but serviceable British machine. Carefully, calmly, he proceeded toward Le Bourget.

3

At a bistro in Montparnasse, Jacques sipped and said, *"Vous parlez français, n'est-ce pas?"*

"Oui, je parle français."

"Bien sur," and he gave him his acrobatic grin. "Well," he said in French, "so you are the Ethiopian big shot."

"That is what Armitage says."

"That one. Rich as the king of England, but . . ." pointing to his ear. "Hey," he said, confidentially, leaning in, "we both know who you are, don't we?"

"Do we?"

"Listen, my friend, I'll tell you something. They sent me to the Ruhr in '22; what do you think of that?"

"France was the boss in those days."

Jacques sipped some more and stopped grinning. "Believe me, we were boss and we showed them in the Ruhr. Hey . . ." He waved at Cleveland, who folded his arms. "Okay, sit with your ass on a pillow, Okay." He sipped again and resumed the grin. "Hey, in the Ruhr, you know who was there? I'll tell you. The Senegalese, that's who. Oh, how the Boche loved that; oh, they loved it. Didn't they?"

"Actually," Cleveland said, "I'm American."

"And I'm Adolf Hitler. Hey, come on. You were famous. You

were a baby and famous. *François le Bébé*. The great baby. The *fraus* got on line for you."

"I'm on the run, Jacques."

"*They* were on the run. The married ones, especially." He drained his wine and waved for more. "The comparison was too much for them, wasn't it? Come on now, did you really have ten *fraus* in one day; tell an old comrade; it's true, isn't it?"

"Whatever you say, Jacques, and think."

"Oh, I think so."

"Fine. Listen, can we see Baker while we're here?"

"What the hell do you want with Baker? I can get you some white meat. There's a redhead at the Casino who faints at the thought of Senegal."

"I'd like to see Baker."

He drank some more and said we'll see ... Baker ... shit. Then, he looked up and said, "Hey, baby, who was the greatest explorer in Africa?"

"There were many."

"The greatest! And no bring them back alive shit. I'll tell you, big baby; it was a Frenchman, Du Chaillu." He sat back. "What do you think of that?"

"A bit sensational."

"Is that what you think? Of course, sensational. He was the greatest of them all, just like you ... Hey, the gorilla, some sensational baby, what do you say?"

Cleveland said nothing.

"You know what? The gorilla forces women to submit to his desire. Du Chaillu says it. A scientist. Some fun those gorillas have ... Hey, big baby, did you see the film of *Trader Horn*?"

"No, I read the book."

"Of course. Hey, the girl in that film, you know who she was? I'll tell you. Her father killed Abraham Lincoln."

"Her uncle."

"I don't give a damn; it was her *family*. You know something else, big baby. They said she got a disease of the blood in Africa and that's what killed her; that's what they *said*." He looked around and leaned in again. "That's shit. Gorillas, they are the missing link, you know? They are in with the American Negro;

they found out who her father was, you know? They got their orders." He leaned further. "When she got to Africa, a gorilla took her." He sat back. "She died from gorilla clap." He grinned. Then shrugged. "It's just as well, you know? She'd never find a man like that gorilla." He folded his arms.

Cleveland said, "The gorilla has sexual intercourse no more than once a year. His penis, at full erection, is approximately an inch long."

A big fist hitting the table. "Shit! He's the King of the Forest! Don't tell me! Du Chaillu says it and I don't have to listen to you."

"No. Can we see Baker?"

"Changing the subject, that's what you're doing . . ."

"Yes, I'm changing the subject. I'll go without you."

Jacques looked up. "You won't go anyplace without me. Ah, shit, we'll see Baker; but, I won't hear any more shit about gorillas, is that clear?"

"Finish your wine, Jacques; it's getting late."

Jacques finished his wine.

He saw Baker in two shows, but decided not to buck the backstage lineup. A gentleman sitting in the back, who bulged above the left ventricle, reinforced the decision, and so they hurried back to the hotel. Very early in the morning, he was eagerly ready when Jacques and another man bustled him out of the room, into a Citroen and on out to Le Bourget. He and Jacques climbed into a waiting Nieuport and Jacques circled once over an awakening Paris, then *sans* acrobatics, turned south. Racing their shadow, he was able to trace orchards and canals and World War rivers and national highways and all the people doing their beloved little jobs. Some waved at the humming plane and he waved back. Then he fell asleep.

When he awoke, they were taxiing into a huge red hangar, beyond which was a cluster of blue and white houses set against a rippling blue sea. Jacques parked carefully; they climbed down and Jacques flipped up his goggles and said, "Grasse."

"Very pretty," Cleveland said.

"Of course," said Jacques, "a rich big shot owns it. Every bit as much money as Armitage. Hey"—he winked—"if I told you his name, you would fall over in a dead faint. Come on."

They walked to the biggest and prettiest house in the cluster and were immediately taken in hand. They bathed and changed clothes, Jacques emerging in soft blue silk and Cleveland in a fresh white *shamma*. Jacques winked and said, "Come on, Senegal, we'll have a bit of lunch."

They ate in a square blue room that overlooked the blue of the Mediterranean. As they were beginning their Chartreuse, the door opened and a small, blocky man in heavily soled shoes clopped in and walked firmly up to them. Jacques stood quickly. The man shook hands with him, then with Cleveland, pumping once, twice.

"I congratulate you," he said in French.

"Why?" said Cleveland.

"For understanding our mission."

"I'm not the man you think I am."

"Never fear, my friend, you will be. We will help you," Jacques, behind the small man, poked a finger into a circle of thumb and forefinger and winked. The small man glanced at him and he snapped to attention. Small man turned back to Cleveland.

"Tell them," he said, "the Cross of Fire is with them." He pumped once more, about-faced and clopped out. Jacques poured more Chartreuse and sipped delicately. "Ahh, these bastards know how to live." He waved an expansive hand toward the Mediterranean. "Personally, I have nothing against the spaghetti-benders," he said, "but I remember Caporetto. You know what I think? I think Selassie might just kick them all the way back to the Fontana di Trevi. Oh, this is good stuff. Mussolini is okay, however. He's got the right idea, just the wrong country. Come on, Senegal, drink. Shit, we need them; we lost too many in the big one. So, what do we have now? I'll tell you: nothing. Ghost children, *that's* what we have; these are hollow years, Senegal. What's the matter, you don't like Chartreuse? Who knows, maybe a French Hitler will show up and take charge . . . But I'll tell you, he better not have that queer mustache, and especially no fat bastards who think they're better than Fonck!"

He fell asleep at the table.

Part Three

THE DARK CONTINENT

AN ITALIAN NAMED EMILIO, VERY NEAT, BELTED AND PRESSED in his Fascisti uniform, and all business, escorted him to a large plane which he announced in impeccable French was a C. A. 133 of the *Disperata* squadron, which—with modest pride—happened to be the squadron of Bruno and Vittorio Mussolini. He informed Cleveland that he would have company—pleasant, he trusted—on the flight to Massawa. The company turned out to be a journalist from Milan who had worked on the *Popolo d'Italia* during the war; indeed, there were those who said he kept it going until Mussolini came back and that Mussolini would grant anything he asked; Ethiopia? Done. There was also a young poet from Turin who looked away from people, and an elderly, ramrod-thin politician from Rome who had hitched his wagon to Mussolini's star when he was still a socialist and whose thoughts and murmured words invariably returned to '96 and the utter need for revenge. Jacques, winking wickedly, shook hands and said, "Good hunting, big baby."

The pilot meticulously greeted each passenger and said he would find as much smooth air as possible, but please remember this is a military aircraft, and in wartime contingencies do arise. He then took off with a roar and a rush.

The poet immediately began to scribble on thin sheets of foolscap; the journalist stared out at the history that was approaching; and the politician sighed and occasionally murmured. Cleveland gazed down at *Il Duce's Mare Nostrum*, dappled and blue and glistening, with the Royal Navy never in sight. Once, as they curved over the Red Sea, he thought he saw a destroyer or cruiser, but could not identify it; in any case, they were soon climbing and away. Now, the outline of a coast appeared and the poet stood before the other passengers and bowed stiffly. Still looking away, his chin jutting, he thrust a sheet of the foolscap at each of them. Cleveland said thank you, and read in Italian as the sunlight streamed past:

> Oh noble dead with clanking propeller spears and
> thoughts of Adowa machine guns British
> Though oil and Suez mix with
>   your blood
>   and Walwal camels
>   scream
> You will find us faithful never minding
>   the taunts of
>   pound poltroons and
>   Bovril

The poet waved a hand and yelled above the motors, "My gift to you, keep it, keep it," sat down and began to write again. The journalist leaned over to Cleveland and behind a cupped palm hollered, "Don't scan it too hard; he's a Futurist," and nodded with his shoulders. He leaned a bit more and hollered, "One of D'Annunzio's babies, you understand," and wrinkled his forehead. Cleveland said yes, thank you; and the journalist smiled and sat back and stared out at the coast of Eritrea, and his own immortality that was rising up to meet them. He already had the title of his book in his head: *Black Monsters, Black Shirts.* All he had to do now was fill the blank, yearning pages. For all he knew, there was a second book down there; suddenly, the flooding sunlight, the mysterious coast, the magic colors were omens for his destiny. He sat back and loved this war.

The politician was nearly overcome with the thought of a 40-year stain at last being wiped out, and not just for Italy, but for all of Europe. Very quietly he began to cry.

✿   ✿   ✿

The C.A. 133 made a creamy three-point landing on a field that was still wet and bruised after being gouged out. Cleveland asked where they were.

"Massawa," said Emilio, the host and guide. "It is the gateway to our new empire." He smiled modestly. "Our neighbors will have some competition."

The vice consul, Signor Brancatti welcomed them. They were bathed, fed, reclothed. Relaxed and comfortable, they sat, that evening, on the veranda of the consulate and looked out at the bay where the ships of the Italian Royal Navy were anchored, trim, gleaming, aloof from the bustle of tankers and freighters that waited their turn to berth, Eritrean workers filed from boat to quay with cases of guns and ammunition and tins of food and parts—parts for planes, for trucks, for bombs. The air grew cool as the flaming sunball plummeted into the Soudan and the mists blurred the outlines of the rising tableland beyond the bay where the sons of steel-banded *signoras* chased the barefooted spear-wielders, and they sipped their anisette, and the cigar-wielding vice consul explained how each day forty ships came in and disgorged and went back and that the biggest problem was the need for more quays.

"An engineering problem of the first rank, Prince," he said, "but we are solving it."

The poet squinted toward the rich plains of Kaffa, the lush forests of Juma, the gold and platinum of Yubdo and Birbir—in short, the treasures of Prester John—and said, "Of course, we are solving it; is there any doubt? Marconi and Fiat have transformed the world and the human spirit, to say nothing of British tranquility."

The journalist, sipping and savoring, confided to the company, "He does not care for the British."

For the first time, the poet looked directly at Cleveland. "You love them, I suppose, after what they have done to the nigger?"

Signor Brancatti said swiftly, "Do you enjoy football, Prince?"

"I do, indeed," said Cleveland. "I played it at school."

Emilio broke in. "There will be time for football after the war. The Prince must go to the front tomorrow, very early."

"Which one?" demanded the poet.

The vice consul looked at Emilio, who nodded. "The southern," he said.

"Graziani?" asked the journalist.

"Yes," said Emilio.

"Why not Badoglio?" asked the journalist.

"That old fart," said the poet.

"It is all arranged," said Emilio with a frown as Cleveland
gazed calmly out over the harbor. "I suggest we retire now.
There is a long day ahead."

"Of course," said the vice consul. "Prince Gallifa, you will
have the ranking guest room." The politician shrugged, the journalist smiled, the poet pouted. "Gentlemen?" said the vice
consul.

They all rose. The journalist, lifting his glass high, said, "I
would like to say something, somewhat in the nature of a bene-
diction." All except Cleveland raised their glasses. The journalist
looked to the tableland and in a throbbing voice said:

> "Hardworking, warrior people who
> Follow your leader, Mussolini,
> We'll open up the way for you,
> You shall have bread for your bambini."

They all drank deeply, except Cleveland, and the politician,
his cheeks burning red, exclaimed, "In '96, this is what we sang:

> 'Baldisare, hey beware
> of these black folk with woolly hair!
> Menelik, you're dead—here comes
> A shower of lead, not sugar plums!' "

His eyes gleamed with memories of youth and the hell with
tomorrow and he flung his empty glass over the verandah railing.
The vice consul shuddered slightly at the sound of crashing glass.
All was silence. Then, Cleveland encompassed them with his
harbor-gaze and said quietly, "Menelik gave you quite a whipping
in '96, didn't he?"

The politician grasped the table. The vice consul sighed. Emilio turned to stone. The journalist smiled thinly. The poet stared at the purple horizon.

That night, lying in the ranking guest room with hyenas shrieking, with the oily waters of the modern harbor lapping hard against the noises of the disgorging ships, he settled back and listened to the argument:

"We will go to the magnificent, decisive, hot, burning southern front," said the poet.

"What of the nigger?" said the journalist.

"The hell with the nigger," said the poet.

"The *Duce*," said the politician, "has sent almost everything to Badoglio."

"That," said the poet, "is merely to balance out the scales. One Graziani is worth a thousand Badoglios."

"Badoglio is very thorough," said the journalist.

"We were not thorough enough in ninety-six," said the politician.

"The hot, red hell with thoroughness," said the poet. "He's an old fart. You must also love ancient Paolino."

"I confess a certain admiration for him," said the journalist. "No doubt you prefer Carnera."

"Carnera is the future," said the poet. "Paolino is the empty stallion of yesterday."

"Ah," said the journalist, "now we have Marinetti."

"Menelik was a shrewd old bastard," said the politician.

"And what is wrong with Marinetti?" said the poet. "He is the motorcycle of tomorrow."

"I thought that was D'Annunzio," said the journalist.

"He was so splendid in Fiume," said the politician.

"D'Annunzio is the airplane *and* the motorcycle of tomorrow," said the poet. "He understands Marinetti completely, even if you don't."

"I admit a bias against Graziani," said the journalist. "How can I follow a man who murders his own family?"

"The *Duce* had absolutely nothing to do with Matteotti," said the politician. "I swear it."

"To save them from the evil Sanussi in Libya," said the poet. "You are supposed to be a writer; complete the statement."

"I do not understand D'Annunzio," said the politician.

"Here is a complete statement," said the journalist. "Badoglio will beat Graziani to Addis."

"When the desert freezes over," said the poet.

"It is quite cold here at night," said the politician.

"Badoglio will do it first," said the journalist, "even if Graziani has all those American vehicles bought from the British."

"British motor turned against British guns," said the poet.

> It is the wily track of the fox.
> When twilight leaps to parchment faces
> vomiting in Downing Wall Street
> We will bomb the wells of Kenya
> as the Suez Canal explodes with oilcan
> beauty.

"Go to the north. Go to Badoglio. Go to hell. I go to Graziani."

"I am still a bit hungry," said the politician.

CHIAROSCURO

THEY FLEW SOUTH THROUGH THE DAWN, FROM ERITREA, AT THE head of Ethiopia, toward Italian Somaliland, at its feet. Cleveland, Emilio, the poet, a lieutenant of engineers and ten truck drivers who were about to make more money than they had ever seen in their lives. They climbed up over the mountain *massif*, above the great inland plateau and soared over towering, snub-nosed *ambas*, the hard, sheer fingers of Ethiopia that everywhere pointed straight at the sky, above beautiful Lake Tana and its Blue Nile that snaked toward Khartoum, above the gouged-out valleys and their surrounding lush meadowlands. They flew over avenged Adowa (a few huts, several wavers), dipped low over Addis Ababa, then climbed and veered southeast above the single railway that ran from Addis to Djibouti on the Gulf of Aden and French Somaliland. Which was beside British Somaliland, Emilio pointed out, adding above the three roaring motors that soon *we* will have the biggest piece. The lieutenant remained dignified and aloof and the truck drivers pointed and chattered about oil and the gold of Ophir and the poet scribbled furiously and not once, as Emilio noted with care, were they challenged by the Ethiopian Air Force.

Over the southern provinces, Graziani's pathway to Addis, they soared and shortly after noon they landed in Dolo on the Italian Somaliland border. The field was patrolled by Dubats—Somalian soldiers—as they piled out and split off, the truck drivers in the charge of the lieutenant hurrying excitedly to the motor pool where GM, Ford and Chrysler trucks stood gleaming and waiting; Emilio, the poet and Cleveland climbing into a Mercedes and being snappily driven to headquarters.

There was a good deal of heel-clicking and saluting as they swept down the corridors and into a huge, comfortably furnished room with a twirling overhead fan. As they entered, and a pair of escorting heels clicked, he turned from a huge wall map and glanced at them. Rodolfo Graziani. He was very tall and broad and clearly well conditioned, like the retired heavyweight who pushed himself off the floor a hundred times each morning. He wore a white burnoose and dark trousers beneath. His face was very dark, as dark as Cleveland's, and it was downturned, as if there were something bitter in the hot, swirling air; and indeed there was: Badoglio, Badoglio, Badoglio, everywhere doddering, festering, preferred Badoglio.

The poet darted forward and dropped to one knee:

> "Oh noble Caesar of mechanized heroes,
> You are the Primo Carnera of Africa who
> will slay evil darkness and Disraeli traps
> which lie across mountain passes to Anglo-Saxon
> Knockout!"

"What the hell was that?" said Graziani.

Emilio stepped quickly forward, hoisted the poet by his shoulders and pushed him firmly back to Cleveland.

"He will put you into a book of poetry, Excellency," said Emilio. "He is of the spontaneous school."

Graziani lifted a shoulder. "Tell him to uncurl his brain," he frowned. "Well, what is it?"

"We have arrived, Excellency."

"So I see." He looked very briefly at Cleveland. "Askari (Eritrean) Spy? Deserter?"

"Excellency, we have come from Sir Henry Armitage."

Graziani sighed and his burnoose quivered. "Oh, yes, that one. As if I didn't have enough on my mind."

"This," said Emilio, "is Ras Gallifa, Excellency."

Cleveland remained very still.

"Yes, yes. Convey my welcome to him."

Emilio turned and said, "The General indicates that you are welcome." Cleveland remained still. Graziani rubbed his smooth face and said, "He can report to the Askaris. Let him have a troop."

Emilio hesitated and Cleveland said in Italian, "I don't wish to be with the Eritreans. I wish to fly."

"He is a pilot?" Graziani said, looking at Emilio.

"Are you a pilot?" asked Emilio.

"No."

"He is not a pilot, Excellency."

"Well then, have him go to the Somalis. Give him a troop of Dubats."

"I wish to fly," Cleveland said.

"He wishes to fly, Excellency."

"In an Italian plane?"

"Do you wish to do this flying in an Italian plane?" Emilio asked.

"Yes."

"What will he do?"

"What will you do?"

"Observe."

"He will observe, Excellency."

"Observe what?"

"What is it that you will observe?"

"That a ruthless and powerful attack from the air has been mounted and cannot be stopped."

"Excellency, the Prince will observe that—"

Graziani lifted an arm. "I have ears. So. No nonsense about humane and civilized warfare?" He swiveled quickly to Emilio. "Put that question to him."

"There will be no nonsense regarding the question of humane and civilized warfare?"

"No. No such nonsense."

"No, Excellency, there will be no—"

"All right," said Graziani. He turned to his map and clasped his hands behind his back and twirled his fingers. He turned back again. "Give him to Cipriotti. He's the roughest son of a bitch we have." He raised a hand in dismissal.

The poet stepped forward and said, "Excellency, I beg of you to let me partake of cold steel hot bombs."

"What's he saying?"

"He wishes to go along with this Cipriotti," said Emilio. "It is his spontaneous way of expressing himself."

"Well, he'd better talk straight to Cipriotti or he'll get a spontaneous kick in the ass. All right, now, get the hell out of here. I have this godforsaken war to win and I have to do it with one hand tied behind my back, the bastards."

They took off after a huge Italian breakfast. One of twenty bombers that would sweep Gorahei to the northeast in half-hour waves. Cipriotti grunted and said we go for the Mad Mullah's fort, we go after Afewek; he's black, but a man; and the poet began to write frantically.

They rose high, Cipriotti leading the formation, and flew over the great river of the south, the Webi Shebeli. Cleveland sat near the bombardier, who was very meticulous and constantly cleaned and adjusted his sights and equipment as if they were a brand new uniform. He could see Cipriotti clearly: calm, self-contained, objective; and, below, he could see desert. Then, Cipriotti was pointing and they were swooping in a long dive. He looked ahead and saw a classic medieval fort with turrets at each corner, then a wall and the town of Gorahei pressed tightly against the wall.

On one of the turrets of the fort was a gun and behind the gun waited a man. Cipriotti motioned to Cleveland and against the dive he made his way to the front of the plane, sat and wedged.

"Afewerk," Cipriotti yelled, jabbing his hand downward. "He's crazy, but we could use one like that." He shook his head and, as he did, heeled over and dived deeply for the fort. The meticulous bombardier laid his eggs and the walls of the fort exploded about the lone gunner, but Afewerk in his *shamma* and jodhpurs remained an island in the geyser of mud and stone and sand and streamed flak at them. The right wing was grazed and Cipriotti shook his head and smiled. He pulled up and banked away, passing the second wave on the way to Gorahei and the single gunner. Cleveland returned to his hard iron seat.

When they landed the poet presented his tribute to Cipriotti:

> Tough guy bird of glory
> you soar with no wax to the solution
> finding black betrayal with no problem.
> Trace bang shoot love your desirable job
> and hand out retribution from Rome
> for all the pathetic world to see
> while a mad slave-owner shrieks and sends
> infamous
> dum dums from obscene walls!

Cipriotti tore it up.
He shared a bottle of wine with Cleveland that night.

"Ask him," said Graziani, "if we are sufficiently ruthless."

"His Excellency wishes to know if the Air Force has been ruthless enough for your taste," said Emilio.

Graziani said, "Merely ask him what I said, if you please."

"His Excellency—"

"Ruthless, inhumane, brutal, unfair," said Cleveland. "Please tell that to the general."

"Ruthless, inhumane—"

"Yes, yes," said Graziani. "Will he tell that to Armitage?"

"His Excellency asks if the Prince will convey those sentiments to Sir Henry."

"Why not?"

"Ras Gallifa responds that there is no reason not to do so."

"You're as bad as the idiot poet," grumbled Graziani. "Nobody gives me what I want, nobody . . . By the way, tell Armitage I need fifteen medium weight General Motors trucks, one and a half tons. He will know. Also a Packard automobile for my personal use. Specify that blue is the only color I will accept."

"Yes, Excellency." Emilio wrote quickly.

"What did the poet do besides shit in his pants?"

"What," said Emilio, "occupied the poet during the bombardment, aside from experiencing personal discomfort?"

Graziani sighed.

"He wrote a poem."

"The poet celebrated the occasion with his art, Excellency."

"Some shitty art. And Cipriotti, what of him?"

"His Excellency asks what Major Cipriotti thought of this art?"

"No, no," said Graziani. "What does that one think of Cipriotti? I don't give a fig what Cipriotti thinks of a shit poem."

"Cipriotti," said Cleveland, "does his job exactly and efficiently."

"The major fulfills his duties—"

A dark, thick stop sign of a hand. "What of Afewerk?" said Graziani.

"His Excellency wishes to know what—"

"Crazy," said Cleveland. "Quite crazy."

The smooth brown head nodded with satisfaction. It gazed broodingly out the window at the Ogaden. "Have him go out with Cipriotti until we get the maniac. He wants to observe, give him something to observe. Tell him that they fight cream cakes in the north; the chief obstacles are down here." A great sigh rumbled out of the burnoose, then Graziani smiled. "All the tough ones, the fanatics, want only to go up against Graziani . . . Well, it is the price one pays. . . ."

They went up after him again the next day, after Afewerk. Cipriotti made three rooftop passes at the man with the gun on the turret. The bombs hit and much of the fort disappeared, but he remained, firing. Cipriotti dived again. Flak streamed into the belly of the plane; Afewerk wheeled and pointed his gun. Cleveland heard an exploding roar; a ball of flame rolled from the center of the cabin back to the tail and the bombardier threw himself on his sights and spread his arms like a mother protecting her child. The navigator stared at his maps even as the fireball struck him. The poet mouthed a prayer to D'Annunzio. The co-pilot jerked at levers and buttons; Cipriotti looked around at Cleveland once and smiled and nodded. The desert rose up to meet them . . .

He was crawling clear, pulling the poet by his limp, twisted legs when the fire ate up the rest of the plane. He could recall Cipriotti nodding and smiling and then, for some reason that he fought against, unsuccessfully, he confused him with Prester John. Then he was gliding into long, soft darkness.

AN HISTORICAL INTERLUDE

"LADIES AND GENTLEMEN, STEP RIGHT UP AND SEE WHAT I GOT FOR YOU. In this corner, wearing a sneer and white trunks, I give you the Saviour of the World, Prester Johnny Cipriotti. Now, in the other corner, wearing black trunks, out of Portugal, I give you the challenger, Rod da Lima Cleveland. I should add that in Rod's corner is his manager and trainer and a darn good priest, Daddy Alvarez. In Prester Johnny's corner is nothing but five hundred years of brain power, lots of myths like a palace roofed over with precious gems and rivers of fire and millions in Christian wealth. Naturally, ladies and gentlemen, Rod, his trainer-manager and the boss of the syndicate, the king of Portugal, cover all this stuff. Now let's proceed to mix it up a little.

"First off, it's the year 1520, a pretty good year for challengers and tough Rod comes into Prester Johnny's territory by way of Massawa, which is the city of challengers. Right off, he turns an Arab mosque into a church, delighting the daylights out of Daddy Alvarez. Then, he continues from Eritrea into Ethiopia. Meanwhile, Prester Johnny, also called the Negus by his fans, is keeping an eye on Rod with hundreds of spies and messengers who slink along beside him on the Delaware Lackawan, but are careful to lay low or Johnny will chop off their tobacco-stained fingers; maybe he ain't De Lawd, but he is some powerful. Prester Johnny, remember, came up the hard way, out of Sicily, and has got lots of boys in his camp who are very skillful in turning out cement overcoats.

83

*"Well, challenger Rod moves on in, all the while taunting Pres-
ter Johnny with such phrases as da Preem is a scream; Johnny
just smiles and covers up. He dangles dreams of his title before
Rod, for Johnny is a very cute guy, much in the mode of Bat
Battalino. He ducks into his blood-red tent, which is in the center
of hundreds of other tents, and he says, by way of interpreters,
what kind of gifts do you bear me from the syndicate?*

" 'I bring silk and velvet, Negus ol boy,' says Rod.

*" 'Whathehell you talkin about? No thundersticks? No bang
bang things? Am I De Fool?'*

*" 'Relax, Johnny boy,' counters Rod. 'These gifts are much
more precious; ask Dickie Burton, ask Jack Speke.'*

*"Johnny says like fun and starts talking with his dukes. Now,
while all this dancing around is going on, Daddy Alvarez is
copying everything down in his notebook, which Prester Johnny
and his outfit are not too happy about, for it smacks of a little
sneaky stuff, and they come out and say so and before long all
parties are arguing about this, that and the other, trying to get
a little bit of an edge. For a good half a dozen years, they waltz
each other around and in the end it is an Ethiopian standoff. In
other words, Carnera cannot touch Kid Chocolate, but the Kid
cannot sting da Preem. So Prester Johnny takes the silk and
velvet, for a winner takes all; but without thundersticks, who
wins? Rod hits the road for Portugal in 1526, leaving Johnny
still champ, still King of Kings, still Lion of Judah, and so on and so
forth, still black but comely, still sleeping the sleep of a thousand
years, still forgetful of the world, still forgot by same. In other
words, it is a draw and John boy is still De Saviour.*

*"Now then, will Prester Johnny hang in there for all time
to come?*

"Will he grab his jock and yell foul?

"Will Yussel Jacobs take him under his wing?

"Will Sol Winograd buy in for a hundred and ten percent?

"Will Islam raise its ugly green head?

*"Will a Falasha like Benny Leonard or Buddy Baer come along
to challenge our boy?*

*"Will Josie Baker and her brown thighs lead the Amazons
against De Duce?*

*"Will said Amazons cut off their right breasts in order to ac-
commodate a Browning automatic?*

*"Will the good people of Harlem start rocking a few nosey
cars?*

"Will Marva Trotter land Prester Johnny or Rod da Cleveland?

"Will Joe Louis Barrow let her?

*"How the hell do I know; am I the Great Thurstone? Besides,
my goddam head is killing me . . ."*

FUTURISM

THE POET GROANED AND SAID, "I WANT DUSE."

"You can't have her," Cleveland said.

"I want her."

"D'Annunzio fucked her and deserted her."

"No . . ."

"Yes. She died in America."

"You nigger, she is buried in Venice. I go there . . ."

"Did you see D'Annunzio?"

"I don't answer you . . ."

"Do you want some water?"

"Give me sand. I order you."

"Go to hell."

"Leave me, nigger."

"I wanted Duse, too."

The poet began to sob.

"The little rat beat me to it."

Between the sobs, the poet screamed, "NO."

"Duse would like what I have."

The poet stopped sobbing, closed his eyes and whispered, "Oh mother lying in moist earth—"

"Idiot."

"Now fly home, come to me—"

"Idiot."

"I will fly to you—"

"Idiot."

"Ignore black bastards you love only me—"

"Idiot."

"White love home bombs fuck pure hell sand—"

"Idiot. Would you like some water?"

"Marry sanctify heaven sun black . . . you have water?"

"Yes."

"Love red bullet tracer hot . . . First clean flask . . . gasoline . . . have gasoline?"

"Yes."

"Filth sorrow tears joy black clean . . ."

"Here, it is now clean."

The poet grasped the canteen and murmured, "Nigger no dream fuck Duse sing heaven." He gazed at the canteen, arching his neck. *"Never love black hot sand guns bomb victory."* Trembling, he lifted the canteen to his lips. Cleveland reached over and slapped it away. It clanked and bounced over the sand. The poet stared at it, at him. Cleveland gently smiled and forced his hand around the hand of the poet. Briefly, the poet struggled, then he began to sob into his death rattle. As the Futurist died, the brown hand was closed tightly about the soft white fist.

THE GUNNER

HE DREAMED THAT GRAZIANI WAS WHIPPING HIM WITH A SWAGGER stick, and he jerked awake. A coffee face with blade-thin nose and lips was staring down at him. For a moment he thought it was Graziani, but then he saw that the face floated into a white *shamma* that, here and there, was caked with blood. There was blood, too, on the smooth, white jodhpurs.

"Dubat?" asked the carved face.

He shook his head slowly.

"Are you from Kenya?" the face said mildly in English.

"No."

"Would you care to divulge your name?"

"Franklin Delano Roosevelt."

"Ah, you do not care to divulge your name." The face and the thin body beneath it bowed very low. "However I will tell you my name. I am Afewerk."

"I know. You shot me down."

"Yes, you were in the Italian plane. Thanks be to God, you are well."

"My head hurts."

"I have examined it. It is not broken anywhere. I will send you to hospital if you wish."

"No, thanks. I wish to suffer."

The face inclined. "Sometimes that is quite enjoyable."

"Are you enjoying it?"

The face seemed thoughtful. "The answer is I do not think so, but perhaps I do."

"The Italians think you're crazy. They're probably right."

"Perhaps. The Italians are insane for invading us. No invader has ever succeeded with the exception of Napier who was polite enough to withdraw. The Italians are not polite."

"But they will beat you."

"Yes. But we must fight them."

"With one gun?"

"Oh yes. An Oerlikon thirty-seven. Would you care to see it?"

"I've seen it."

A modest bow. "I think all but you have been killed."

"I think you're correct. Are you happy?"

"Yes, thanks be to God. If I may ask, why were you with Graziani? I thought Americans loved our cause."

"How do you know I'm American?"

"Everyone knows."

"Then why did you ask where I was from?"

"Oh, that is only polite."

"Shit."

"Perhaps. But Americans love our cause."

"Don't kid yourself. The Sons of Italy don't; they love Musso-lini and his cause. They hate Negroes. A lot of Americans hate Negroes."

"But we are not Negro."

"What are you?"

"Thanks be to God, we are Ethiopian. And Christian."

"Oh, well, that makes a big difference."

"That is true. We are very fortunate."

Cleveland looked at the solemn face. "You and the Italians," he said, "can both go to hell."

Afewerk again bowed. The left side of the *shamma* was now a bright red. Cleveland sighed. "You'd better get to the hospital before you pass out and become useless. Let someone else fire the gun."

"Will you do it?"

"No."

"That is my problem, no one else will do it. And if I go to the hospital, my men will run away."

"Screw them then. They're not worth fighting for."

"Perhaps, but while I am here they will not run, and the Emperor has charged me to remain."

"Let *him* fire the fucking gun."

"He could, thanks be to God, but he must be elsewhere, while this is my post."

"Shit."

"Perhaps, but—"

"Stop talking, my head hurts."

"Oh forgive me, I will stop." Afewerk sat down with a small smile beside Cleveland.

"Do you think you can help him?"

Turning his head slowly, Cleveland saw a slender little man in an immaculate *shamma*. The little man bowed.

"Help who?" Cleveland said. "The Emperor or this nut?"

"If you will help *Gerazmatch* Afewerk, you will help the Emperor."

Before he could answer, he heard Afewerk. "Walda-Ab is the son of the father, but he is like a mother. Pay no attention. Will you please excuse me, I must return to my gun. Would you care to remain here or shall I send you back to the Italians?"

"Shit."

Afewerk bowed.

Walda-Ab had studied English at the college of General Gordon in Khartoum. He was an excellent student and felt that he was redeeming General Gordon by becoming adept at his language, for Walda-Ab, an exemplary Christian, hated the Mahdi and the Khalifa as much as Gordon had, or *should* have, for Gordon seemed to love everyone, Now, far from the Arabs, Walda-Ab said a thankful prayer to the severed head of Gordon, for he could understand almost everything that passed between Afewerk and the American through two days and two nights. The Italian planes would come over in waves every half hour, and Afewerk would excuse himself and, dragging his left leg, climb up to his gun and fire at them and, dragging the leg, climb down. As Walda-Ab listened.

"Gangrene has set in. You'll die without help."

"Yes, but no one else will fire the gun."

"One gun can't change anything."

"It is all I have."

"But it's useless, can't you see it's useless?"

"Oh yes, but it is better than no gun."

The American would rub his face. "Your leg is getting worse. It's beginning to smell."

"I beg your pardon. Please sit elsewhere."

"I'll sit where I please."

"Oh yes. Has Walda-Ab given you enough to eat?"

"Plenty. Don't you know that thousands of your soldiers have gone over to the enemy?"

"Oh yes."

"Not one Italian has gone over to your Emperor."

"But the Italians are going to win, so that would be foolish."

"Jesus Christ."

"Oh yes."

The American stared into the distance. After many hours, Afewerk said, "I beg your pardon, but may I ask you a question?"

"Go ahead . . ."

"Would you join us?"

"You told me that the Italians are going to win, so why should I join you?"

"Because they were incorrect in invading us."

"That and a nickel will get you on a New York subway."

"An interesting thought. Do you know that men have come to us from Sweden?"

"Well then, you'll conquer all of Africa."

"Oh no, Sweden would not care for that, nor would the Emperor."

"You are still up shit creek without a paddle."

"Pardon me but I am here with a gun of very good quality."

"You do not have a goddamn prayer."

"Oh but we have many. Pardon me, please, I must fire my gun."

❁   ❁   ❁

Night. A huge, pale moon. Afewerk: "Pardon me, but aren't you a Christian?"

"No."

"Are you a Jew? Falasha?"

"No. How is your leg?"

"I cannot feel it, thanks be to God. We were once saved by outsiders from Portugal."

"I'm not from Portugal."

"In the sixteenth century. A great man named Christopher da Gama came with but four hundred men and he saved us. He was killed by the Moslems, but he gave us the strength to know ourselves. He was a great son of a great father, Vasco da Gama. Have you heard of him?"

"Yes. I'm a lousy son."

"He fought Gran, the Left-handed One, an infidel. Gran had thousands, Christopher had four hundred and he won. Pardon me, there are the airplanes of Graziani. Could you please help me to the ladder?"

Beneath the desert sun: "Gran tortured Christopher, then slew him."

"Let me take you to the hospital."

"Will you look after my men?"

"No."

"Would you not enjoy fighting Graziani?"

"Drink some water . . ."

"Of course."

While Afewerk fired his gun and the stench from his leg covered them, Cleveland said to Walda-Ab, "He should be dead by now."

He lasted until the following afternoon, falling across the gun that was so hot his flesh was seared, adding to the stench. They carried him down as the planes came in and then circled like vultures. And as they laid him out, the men came running out of the fort and continued to run north, away from the planes. Cleveland muttered that he hoped Afewerk was happy now, which, of course, he was, and then he and Walda-Ab wrapped Afewerk in a white sheet and Walda-Ab beat his fists against the sand

and howled at the sky and tore at his *shamma*. They buried
Afewerk in a shallow grave in a part of the fort that hadn't been
destroyed, and Walda-Ab, quiet now, sat on one side of the grave
while Cleveland sat on the other side. For a long time, Cleveland
looked at the grave and at the gun.

THE RIGHT-HANDED ONE

THEY MOUNTED A PAIR OF MULES THAT HAD AMERICAN SADDLES and rode out of the fort. They rode through the desert, the mules sliding and digging in and sliding, but they made headway as Walda-Ab cajoled and Cleveland jabbed with his heels and cursed. Through the afternoon they rode, beneath an outraged sun, until, wet and sore, they reached the mud-hut town of Hamanlei. That's where they found Afewerk's men, digging into the sand while the sand filled in the holes they had just dug. Cleveland cursed some more and Walda-Ab asked a man who was staring at the disobedient sand, "Please tell me where *Fitauri* Gongol might be?" The man kicked at the place that was supposed to be his haven, looked up and pointed to the end of the line. They rode along the ragged line. Cleveland asked, "Do you know this man?"

"I have heard many speak of him in very good terms."

"Does he speak English?"

"I believe he speaks it a little. Many of our officers speak it a little, though none as well as—"

"Tell him in your Amharic that Afewerk's life cannot be wasted. He and those fucking men cannot make a fool of Afewerk. Can you say those things in your language?"

"Oh yes. Thanks be to God, you will help us."

"I don't give a shit for you. Tell him what I said. I'll wait here."

"Oh yes."

Dipping low over the head of his mule, Walda-Ab rode to the

95

end of the line which curled away from the town. He reached a *shamma*ed man who was peering through German field glasses. Walda-Ab politely waited, for Gongol was studying a great dust cloud that shimmered far off. He nodded at the cloud which he could not understand, then lowered his field glasses and turned to Afewerk's lieutenant. He hoped with a full heart that there would be no ill will in the unblinking eyes because the men had not gone back; he was very glad that they stayed here and tried to dig in, but, of course, would not say that. He bowed.

Walda-Ab, whose eyes were clear, said, "And how have you passed the day?"

"Thanks be to God, as well as can be expected. And you?"

"Thanks be to God," said Walda-Ab, "as well as can be expected with the loss of a great leader. How are your sons?"

"Thanks be to God, one has perished fighting for the Emperor while the other still fights. Was your harvest successful this year?"

"Yes, thanks be to God. Are your cows healthy?"

"Oh yes, thanks be to God, but my bull is sick."

"That is sad," said Walda-Ab. "The man with me is an American. He loved *Gerazmatch* Afewerk almost as much as he loves the Emperor."

"Then he is a good man. He has a most able appearance. Has he come to help us?"

"Oh yes. He understands war. He is of the great da Gama family that saved us from the Left-handed One."

"Oh then he must know war, unless his blood has been watered down."

"Oh no," said Walda-Ab, shaking his head, "his blood is very thick, his name is Christopher, as was the hero's, he is clever, he was with the Italians so he could learn their secrets, and now he will help you."

"Oh I will be proud to fight beside him. I plan to attack the Dubats, for the Italians always send them ahead."

"Oh that is a fine strategy," said Walda-Ab.

"Thank you. I am somewhat concerned about that great cloud of dust that seems to be coming at us and may interfere with my attack. Perhaps your guest would care to observe this thing, which is quite strange." He held out the field glasses. Walda-Ab accepted them with a deep bow, and, excusing himself, trotted his mule back to the American whose fingers were moving impatiently with each other. "Well?" he asked.

"*Fitauri* Gongol loves *Gerazmatch* Afewerk almost as much as he loves the Emperor and he offers you these field glasses so that you may study the dust cloud that approaches."

Cleveland took the glasses and focused. "Holy shit!" he said. Walda-Ab bowed.

"They have to be fucking tanks!"

"And will that be a problem for you and *Fitauri* Gongol?"

"Yes, they will. Tell your friend to get those tin soldiers—to get his men—back to Gorahei."

"Oh that is impossible. He wishes to attack the Dubats. Thanks be to God, he is now putting that plan into operation."

And shrilling their war cry, the men were running toward the cloud of dust, with Gongol leading the way.

"*You goddam fool,*" the American yelled, "*not toward the fucking tanks.*" And much to Walda-Ab's satisfaction and pride, he lifted his dangling legs and pounded them into the sides of his mule, which instantly clattered forward. Walda-Ab violently kicked the flanks of his own mule and was soon dashing after the American. Indeed, everyone was rushing toward the enemy; the disgrace of the fleeing troops would now be removed. Walda-Ab murmured a prayer of thanks as a bullet sang close to his ear.

In the calm nobility of the late afternoon, Gongol led the charge, followed by his men who were followed by Cleveland and Walda-Ab, all of them running into and through a shower of machine-gun fire, for the Dubats of the Italians were obeying their European officers who had told them exactly what to do. And they obeyed well; many of the running men buckled or dropped or dived into the sand. However, none turned and ran away, warming Walda-Ab's heart and surprising the American. They weaved their way through the charging, falling men and they reached Gongol who bowed as he ran.

"Get me a rifle!" yelled the American.

Walda-Ab, riding along beside Gongol, repeated the request.

Gongol nodded and swept a rifle from a screaming soldier, who was instantly killed by a Dubat bullet, and, with a bow, handed it to Walda-Ab who bowed and handed it to the American. The American spurred his mule straight at the cloud of dust that rolled toward them, ahead of, and on the right flank of the Dubat line. Walda-Ab rode after him and he was followed by Gongol who had been a champion runner in his village before the invasion.

The cloud of dust was strange. Within it was the thing that had surely created it, solid, large, black, very ugly, but quite interesting. Gongol, who had caught up, yelled softly into Walda-Ab's ear, "Do you know what that thing is?"

"A tank," Walda-Ab said in English.

"And what is that?"

"I do not know. But Christopher da Gama knows."

Cleveland had dismounted. He waved at Walda-Ab, who also dismounted. Then Cleveland pointed at two black tusks that sprouted out of the tank. Even as he did, the tusks moved and began to shoot at them. Cleveland dropped to the sand and yanked at two sets of legs. Walda-Ab and Gongol reluctantly joined him in the sand. "Stay here!" Cleveland shouted, "I don't want any fucking heroes," and then he raised up and in a crouched posture loped forward to the clanging, lumbering, tusked tank, and, surprisingly, flattened himself against the lower portion. This was clever, for the tusks could not bend toward him, but continued to fire over his head—splendid for him but most unfortunate for the soldiers charging behind. Now the American raised himself up swiftly—he moved with a certain deftness which was unusual for large men—and thrust his rifle against the tank. Walda-Ab and Gongol exclaimed in huge surprise, and Gongol said, "The tank has eyes!" "Indeed, it does have eyes!" agreed Walda-Ab. And as they spoke, and agreed, the American blinded the tank: his rifle shot out the eyes!

Slowly and clearly with great pain, the black tusks began to tilt downward, as if they were melting in the hot sun. They were soon pointing sadly at the ground and bullets did not come out of them. Gongol could not help feeling sorry for the tank, but even as he did, another tank rolled forward wrapped in its own cloud of dust. He jumped to his feet, ran around the dying tank, darted between the tusks of the second tank, stuck his rifle into the eyes and, closing his own eyes, fired. When he opened his eyes, the tusks of the second tank had drooped to the ground in agony and surrender. Oh, but this was exciting!

By the time they had finished creating blindness, the three of them had killed five tanks.

"Please convey my gratitude to Christopher da Gama," Gongol said to Walda-Ab. Walda-Ab bowed and thanked Cleveland, who stood to one side and murmured, "You're welcome, they're pretty fucking brave now, aren't they?" nodding at Gongol's men, who were chasing the Dubats toward Gabridihari.

"Oh yes," said Walda-Ab, "thanks be to God and your knowledge of killing tanks, they are brave."

"Well tell him they better not get too close to the town. The Italians will machine-gun their moxie out of them."

"Oh yes," Walda-Ab said, "but *Fitauri* Gongol knows this for he is a good commander."

"Okay," said Cleveland with a shrug.

And, yes, Gongol was now chasing after his men, shouting, shooting over their heads until they stopped. He shouted some more and they came trotting back. He lined them up and pointed, and they began to clamber all over the dead tanks, calling with excitement to each other, for some of them were hauling forth dead Italians.

"That is very interesting," Walda-Ab said. "They have been planted in the tanks like giant tapeworms."

Cleveland grunted. But it was a soft grunt. Afewerk would not be too displeased.

Gongol said via Walda-Ab, "I would be most satisfied to have you remain with us. Ras Desta will soon join this command with his own command and we will have a splendid offensive."

"No," said Cleveland. "I've done enough."

"Oh yes, you have. Your family will be very proud."

"Sure."

Gongol appreciated the modest shrug. "Where will you go?" he asked, "if you do not mind the question."

"I don't mind. I don't know." He looked at Walda-Ab. "Where should I go?"

Walda-Ab answered swiftly, "*Gerazmatch* Afewerk would be most contented if you would go to Addis."

"What for?"

"Oh in order to help the Emperor."

"How do you know Afewerk wants that?"

"Oh it is very clear," Walda-Ab said, looking politely away. "*Gerazmatch* Afewerk was completely loyal and true to the Emperor and you have been completely loyal and true to *Gerazmatch* Afewerk. Therefore, thanks be to God, you must be loyal and true to the Emperor."

Christopher da Gama lifted and dropped his shoulders as if they were riding on the wind. Then he said something that Walda-Ab could not understand, nor of course, could Gongol, although when informed, he thought it sounded most interesting.

This is what Christopher da Gama said:

"Finessed again."

THE GLORY OF THE KINGS

AFTER SAYING FAREWELL TO GONGOL THEY MOUNTED THEIR ANI-
mals and rode west to skirt the Italians, then when that was
achieved, turned to the north. They rode in silence through the
silence of the desert and continued silently onto the incline of
the dense, lush lowlands and then sharply up onto the wooded
hillsides, climbing constantly toward the central highlands. They
moved slowly, but the mules were sure and had clever feet and
made steady progress as they dipped down into the valley and
continued to pick their way past the beautiful small lakes that
the great Lake Tana had flung south like gleaming beads on a
necklace: Margherita, Awasa, Shala, Langana, Zway.

They rode on through cool days and cold, crystal nights,
through coffee forests, maize, great clumps of acacia and past
the spread of *kosso* plants. It was there that Walda-Ab politely
cleared his throat and asked Cleveland if he cared to have the
silence broken? Cleveland said, Break it.

"*Kosso* is an excellent purgative for tapeworms," Walda-Ab
said.

"I see."

"There are tapeworms in the Ethiopian belly because we eat
the raw meat of the cow. But surely you know that."

"I've heard."

"Many outsiders think we are savages for eating raw meat."

"That's their problem."

"Oh yes. There are reasons for everything and there is a good reason for the raw meat."

"And what is that?"

"I am very glad you asked. The famous James Bruce of Scotland wrote down that we ate raw meat and people laughed."

"Well what is the reason?"

"We do not care that people laugh. As long as God approves."

"What is the reason?"

"The reason is a very sensible one."

"And what is it?"

"They do not understand. People cover the lack of understanding with laughter."

"You said a mouthful. What is the reason?"

"As you know, the Moslems invaded our country three hundred years ago. The Italians are not the first."

"I knew they weren't . . ."

"Many nations have envied us."

"I see."

"The Moslems were at first quite successful, just as the Italians."

"I see."

"We then retreated."

"Yes?"

"Into the caves. Where else could we go?"

"Makes good sense."

"Oh yes. But the caves were a problem, for if we lighted fires in them to cook our meat we would be discovered."

"Ah, so then—"

"Oh yes. we cut the meat off the backs of our cows and ate it raw so as not to be discovered and this was a sensible thing to do, but a sensible thing may lead to unfortunate results . . ."

"Tapeworms."

"Oh yes."

"It adds up."

"We have continued to eat raw meat and continued to have tapeworms and we continue to call on the *kosso* plant for assistance, so you see, it is well taken care of."

"Yes, I see."

"I am glad you understand. It is so simple."

2

They stopped at *tukuls*, mud huts with cone-shaped thatched roofs, where they were welcomed and fed maize and raw meat and given *kosso* pills which, the next morning, worked very well. And after polite farewells, they rode on. Past the towering pylons Walda-Ab called *ambas*, past elephant, leopard, pink-bottomed baboon, gazelle and striped hyenas. In the evening, after a day of silence, near Lake Shala, Walda-Ab said, "*Ambas*, you see, have been very important to us."

"Yes?"

"Oh yes."

They camped beside the lake. After washing and eating the next morning, they mounted their mules and rode past the deep blue lake and up a long, smooth incline. When the sun was high, they stopped to drink and sat against some trees. Walda-Ab said, "Theodore's mother was a seller of *kosso*."

"Oh? The mad Emperor?"

"Perhaps he was and perhaps he was not. His enemies jeered him, behind his back of course. Do you know why they jeered him?"

"No. Why?"

"I told you," Walda-Ab said, shaking his head. "His mother."

"Oh."

"They made jokes. He hated jokes. He never forgot."

"I can understand that."

"Yes."

Hours of silence. At the apogee of the incline, a wide, clear stretch, Walda-Ab said, "Even if he was mad he was a great soldier and a great king. He knew all the psalms of David. He knew them better than the priests."

"Perhaps they were mad."

"Oh some of them were. Some were not."

The mules walked daintily down into the valley.

"His mother was very poor and sold *kosso* to send him to school. He studied hard. He studied the psalms and our history and he hated the Moslems. He became a *shifta*. A robber, a bandit. Do you think less of him for that?"

"He probably had his reasons."

"Oh yes. How else could a learned man and a great fighter get on in that time save by being a bandit?"

Cleveland moved in his saddle. They rode on for several hours more. As he gazed into the distance, Walda-Ab said, "Although he was a *shifta,* he helped others, except the priests. He moved into the house of a rich man, Ras Ali. Ras Ali had a daughter who was a great beauty, Tewabetch. As all who knew him, save the priests and his enemies, she was drawn to him. The people wanted them to marry, so they married."

"What about the father?"

"He was very angry."

"Fuck him."

"Oh yes."

They stopped for the night under a tremendous spray of stars. The next morning, after riding for three hours, Walda-Ab said, "They were very happy, it was the happiest time of Theodore's life, everyone knows it . . ."

Late in the afternoon, he said, "It was only when she died that he grew mad, as they claim . . ."

"Yes," Cleveland said.

"He drank *tedj*. He conquered all of his enemies. Queen Victoria of England sent him a brace of silver pistols because he was such a great soldier."

"That was nice of her."

"Oh yes. He was very important. She sent him a consul . . ."

In the evening, he said, "Theodore sent a letter to Queen Victoria proposing a treaty of friendship."

"One ruler to another."

"Oh yes. It was a very pleasing letter."

The next morning, as the sun climbed out of the Somalilands, he said, "She did not answer Theodore."

That night, he said, "He grew very angry. He drank more *tedj*. He threw the English consul into chains. He threw other Europeans into chains. Oh he was very angry. The queen sent an envoy. A Christian Arab. A great insult. Theodore would not give in. She sent an army. The army was commanded by General Napier. Theodore was somewhat pleased. She had not sent a lesser officer. But Theodore would not surrender. He would not give up his prisoners. He did a great thing. He had his German workers who were his prisoners build the largest cannon in the world. They did so. He went happily up the *amba* at Magdala and waited for the British with his great gun. But he did not fire that cannon. I will tell you why. To do so would have destroyed all the unborn children carried by the women of our country. And so this insured his defeat. This act of a mad Emperor." They rode on and Walda-Ab stared straight ahead for several hours. Then he said, "The men ran away. He watched them. He watched as General Napier advanced. Still he did not fire the greatest gun for the sake of the unborn babies. He did this: He placed a silver pistol that Queen Victoria had given him into his mouth and pulled the trigger. That is how he ended his life. General Napier was a gentleman and did not dishonor him. He took out the prisoners and went home to England. He became famous as the general who had at last defeated Theodore. He received great honors from his queen."

They slept beside Lake Langana. The next morning they washed in the lake and mounted their mules and ate some stale bread and raw meat as they rode. After an hour, Cleveland said, "He was mad; he should have taken a powder."

3

They came to a small, shabby *tukul*, beside which sat an iron-grayed old man soaking in the morning sun. The man stood and

bowed stiffly and Walda-Ab spoke pleasantly to him as he nodded. With a stiff dexterity then, the man dropped to his knees.
He spoke in a flow of jagged Amharic and stared at Cleveland's
shoulder. Cleveland tried to catch and hold his eyes, but he kept
talking and staring to the left of his head and down at his shoulder. Cleveland glanced down, saw nothing but the shoulder of
his *shamma*. Then he clutched Walda-Ab's arm. "You finagler,"
he said, "you've told him I'm Theodore."

"Oh no," said Walda-Ab earnestly. "You could not possibly be
Theodore. All know he is dead many years, killed by his own
hand with a famous pistol. This old man is not a stupid fellow.
He says you are the Emperor Menelik. He apologizes greatly for
having so humble a dwelling."

ROYAL

THEY CAME DOWN FROM THE HILLS TO SEE EMPEROR MENELIK, the wily conqueror. Sitting in a simple chair, he said, "You sonofabitch, you're screwing your own people."

"Oh yes. To them you are Menelik. It would be wrong to say otherwise."

"Balls."

"Oh yes, it is their belief."

"I've done some reading, finagler. Menelik's been dead over twenty years. He's as stiff as Theodore."

"Oh yes. That Theodore is dead, this they know. But they do not know of Menelik. He is ever the Emperor."

"Then tell them, you cruel bastard."

"Oh no, *that* would be cruel. They are happy now. Let us put it so: you are a royal impersonator."

"And you're a royal con artist."

"Oh yes. To be a royal impersonator is a very honorable thing. When Menelik died there was a royal impersonator for a number of years. This was so in Addis. The people do not want an Emperor to leave them. You have a duty to make them happy."

"Give me some more goddam *tedj*."

They crowded around him that night. They bowed down and when they rose they spoke to Walda-Ab, the words rippling between them.

"What are you cooking up now?" Cleveland said from his huge chair.

107

Walda-Ab looked up at him. "They wish to hear of your great victory over the Italians at Adowa."

"That was forty years ago."

"Oh no, it is yesterday."

He looked out at them. "All right."

"Ah, you will do it then?"

"Yes. But in English."

"Oh they do not care about that. The Emperor speaks any way he wishes."

He drank some *tedj*. He looked down at the rapt faces. He gazed into adoring eyes.

"I was born in Alabama. We had a terrible life there, no life at all." Several heads nodded. "Seeing this, experiencing this, my mother brought us north. To Detroit." Many smiles. "But Detroit is a hard, tough, ugly city, don't let anyone tell you otherwise ..." Several old women sighed. "We had to go on relief. Yes, I could have gotten on the line, but I didn't want that." Those in the first row shook their heads. "Mr. Ford could keep his five bucks a day, in fact he could shove it." The same row smiled happily. "So, with nothing on the horizon, I joined a local boys' club. I learned how to *box*." Murmurs ran through the crowd. "I had a punch from the beginning. I was a fast learner. Despite what you've heard, however, I had a few very tough bouts. But I kept moving. All the way up to an A.A.U. championship. I was still just a light-heavy." He smiled down, they nodded and waved. "I turned pro. My first purse was a sensational fifty dollars." A woman called out, she was hushed. "Two real pros named Julian Black and John Roxborough spotted me. They liked what they saw. They said, We'd like to manage you. I said, Sure. They hired a great oldtimer named Jack Blackburn to be my trainer. He called me Chappie. *Chappie*." Solemnly, they leaned toward him. "I had twelve fights my first year as pro, I won them all, ten by knockout. I began to get a rep. The rep climbed up to Mike Jacobs. You know who Mike Jacobs was?" They leaned in. "Only the Garden promoter, a *Yiddishe* Tex Ricard, *every*one knows of *Tex*." Several in the first row, leaning in, scowled. "Mike, or Uncle Mike, as he was known, went out on a limb for me; I was really untested and also the wrong color.

Still Mike took a chance, and also his lumps. But Uncle Mike knew the ins and outs. He lined up some very decent paydays and I kept up my end by belting my opponents into Shanghai, where some of them can still hear Chinese music." Two people applauded and were quickly scolded. "I bought a house for my mother. I paid relief back. I gave them every fucking penny." Ahhhh ran through the crowd. "THEY SAID I NEVER SMILED." The faces looked shocked. "It was true. For I had a purpose, a goal. And so did Uncle Mike. He set up tougher matches. I came through as always. The world, such as it is, began to sit up and blink its eyes." He smiled benignly, drank some *tedj*. Walda-Ab dabbed at his mouth with a white handkerchief. "Now then. There existed a giant in this world. He was almost as large as Theodore's cannon. He was from Italy. His name was Primo Carnera. He stood six feet six and a half inches. His fists were steel hammers, his head was iron, he was uglier than Detroit, thereby terrifying his opponents. That we should meet was inevitable. And so we did. At Madison Square Garden Bowl in Long Island City." Every face was turned up, wide-eyed.

"There was a great white moon that night. The lights of the arena were a cluster of tiny moons beating down on me as I climbed into the ring. Beads of sweat rose on my forehead. The giant stood on the other side of the ring with an expression of anger, loathing, even contempt on the huge, prognathous face." They sighed. "We were introduced. Carnera scowled down at me. I gazed back, as I always did. I walked back, shucked my robe. Jack Blackburn said, Now remember what I taught you, Chappie, and listen to me all the way. I nodded. I always listened to Jack. The bell rang. We walked out." He drank some *tedj*. Walda-Ab ministered to him. The crowd was happy.

"Carnera towered above me. He scowled again. They ate it up. There was a great roar. The moons beat down. For an instant I thought I was in Alabama beneath the noontime sun, but only for an instant. For the giant, in a huge, winging arc, brought his hammer of a fist around. I flicked my head to the side. The fist sailed by my head as if it was a boat on the sea. Another roar. Then." He looked down, spread his hands. They blinked once. "Then I jabbed three times with my left, measured him, clipped the thrusting jaw with a right; his head snapped back." He folded his hands and sat very still. So did they. He stared out over their heads, then returned to them. "From that point on, very scientifically, I went to work, for this was a day at the office. I went to work, chopping down that huge, thick, ugly, soft pine tree. I worked very economically, as well, traveling no more than six inches with each fist, constantly cutting into the great pillar of white . . ."

Slowly, he rose from the chair. Every eye clung to him. He tucked his chin behind a hunched shoulder. He stepped down from the chair and they cleared a space for him. He stepped into the space, and with great economy slid forward, then back, then to each side, and as he did he jabbed the fabled six inches. Then he hooked, again the short, power-packed distance. A terrific roar split the Ethiopian night. He nodded. Beneath a gleaming moon, he advanced and once again measured the giant. With great precision, he worked the enormous softness over. Snorting, clenching his mouthpiece, Cleveland slipped around the giant, always finding the belly, the heart, the chin. Finally then, as if the air was liquid, the giant began to float to one side, floating interminably, until at last he was on the canvas. Cheers of delight. Cleveland stood to one side, patiently waiting. The giant floated to his knees and as if he was treading the liquid air, rose to the surface and stood there waiting, smiling curiously. He moved in carefully, jabbed, hooked. The giant this time did not float. He crash-dived. And so it continued: slide, jab, hook, crash. The cheers grew louder. Time after time the huge tree came smashing down, the puzzled face was shattered into a hundred pieces, yet each time he struggled up. Until at last, the will that drove it gave in, and he lay there, the only movement a quiver of the enormous right leg; it twitched and bounced with a life of its own. And then even that was still. The roaring ceased. A waiting hush. Cleveland turned and raised both hands over his head, clasped them. The Ethiopian war cry pierced the night. Arms hurled imagined spears. He stood in the center of his wildly excited troops, pointed to the north, toward Addis.

"GO AND DEFEAT THEM," he commanded.

They charged away from Madison Square Garden Bowl, hurling the deadly spears, screaming, crowding hard on each other's heels. He turned to his *dejatch*, shrugged and said, "Maybe Tafari can use them."

"I do not wish to offend an Emperor," Walda-Ab said solemnly, "but they will soon come home and sleep away their *tedj*. Alas, they do not know that the Italians have invaded again."

A DEMENTED INTERLUDE

"LADIES AND GENTLEMEN, YOU HAVE SEEN THE EMPERORS IN ACTION. *Now I don't wish to put down the great King Menelik, but to be perfectly honest, which is the onliest way to be, he is not too terrific at the interview game. As you can clearly see, unless you picked up some African eye disease an there's a lot of that goin around, Emperor Theodore got what it takes to fill up your headlines not to mention selling a couple of million papers because as you know if you read the funny papers, normalcy don't make good copy. So you just step right up and meet Emperor Ted here, the Sweet Sultan of Salubrious Insanity. You ask him any thing your little heart desires at this press conference and I guarantee he'll be absolutely peachy and unimpeachable. In other words, we gonna have a fireside chat with no fires on account of them Moslem invaders. You there, no, not you, you."*

"Emperor, Your Topness, what do you think of Queen Victoria?"

"Heck, that's easy. Gimme a tough one, Chappie. Okay. Why I want to marry up with the lady. I want to take off them twenty petticoats an pile them up beside us like a silk mountain and then go to town. We will make a great color combination, pink and burnt sienna. Naturally, I speak of Victoria Paranuccio of East One hundred seventeenth Street, who sat in front of me in royal classes in P. S. Eighteen. Next."

"Emperor, Mr. Sensational, what's your opinion of the invaders?"

113

"*I will never consider myself a true Emperor till I kick the Uhlan shit out of Max Schmeling.*"

"*Emperor, Sir-ness, did your mother ever sell* kosso *for a living?*"

"*I'm glad you asked me that. She did not sell* kosso, *Feen-a-mint, Ex-Lax or Citrate of Magnesia, and she did not take in laundry or clean up any houses except her own. What she did do was keep that house neat as a pin and take beautiful care of her husband, the king, and her son, the prince, known as me.*"

"*Emperor, oh Sultan, what is your opinion of Menelik?*"

"*I assume you refer to Menelik Two as opposed to Menelik One, who was Sol's problem. On the other hand, Sol's problem was somewhat similar to mine in that I took Menny in as a boy, reared him up, taught him how to be a king and what does he do but hit the goddam road first chance he gets. But then again, now that I think about it, ain't that what I did to Sol, which only shows to go you.*"

"*Emperor, Big Boy, give us a psalm.*"

"*Screw unto others before they screw unto you.*"

"*Emperor, Your Royalty, what is your opinion of priests?*"

"*I confess they got me buffaloed. They eye me warily, I eyes them ditto. You might say I don't trust them. Then again, who does I trust? You there, with the upraised fist.*"

"*Emperor, oh King, were you a shifta, like they say?*"

"*Heck, I was shifty. But so was Albie Booth. So is Kid Chocolate. But I tell you one thing; the Brown Bomber, now, he moves straight ahead.*"

"*Emperor Lord-ness, why didn't you set up your throne in the Cotton Club?*"

"*Are you kiddin? Ain't no colored allowed in there.*"

"*But Emperor, Big Boy, it's in Harlem.*"

"*Next question.*"

"*Emperor, Glory Guy, are you mad?*"

"*Sure I am, an sometimes I get sore as hell, but I tell you one thing: they ain't never gonna put me away on Ward's Island.*"

"*Emperor Magnifico, would you give us one last psalm?*"

"*Sure. Let's see. Yeah. I make more money than Hoover because I had a better year. How's that?*"

"*Quotable. Thank you, Emp, oh Tremendous Upper-Cutter.*"

MENELIK'S CITY

WAS ADDIS ABABA, OR ABEBA, MEANING THE "NEW FLOWER," FOR that is what the unifying Emperor desired, a fresh blossom of people intertwined with buildings in the center of his restored land. He wished to create a controlling eye that could gaze out and touch each part of all he had achieved; this eye would send out waves of power and knowledge which would hold his lovely land together, at the same time drawing to itself the loyalty and love of his people. It would be, Addis, both overseeing Oerlikon gun and giant magnet (a magnet as powerful as the one Tafari was supposed to have erected outside the city that was to suck to their destruction the evil Italian bombers). So, in 1889, after all his internecine victories, he began to build his capital, his new flower. Believing them to be the best in Europe, ergo the world, he imported Swiss architects to design his city. Needing more European skill, he sent the Italian survivors of Adowa to Addis in '96 to build his Cathedral of St. George; they built a magnificent Italian church for him, pleasing him so much that he reprieved them to Eritrea without cutting off their hands. Then he looked around and noticed the Australian eucalyptus trees in the garden of the British legation and he ordered the eucalyptus to blanket his city; and it did, budding at his command. He built his palace in Addis and reigned in that palace through royal entertainments, diplomacy, intrigue, invasion, victory, world-wide fame, decline, death and royal impersonation. Addis was his child, his toy, his hobby, his creation, his monument.

115

All this Walda-Ab explained with care and attention to tiny detail so that the American could understand the meaning and the modern significance of Addis as they rode easily toward the celebration of conquest and unity, this oneness that held power and benevolence, this monophysite city. Each day, as they traveled, he grew a bit more calm, a bit more nervous, a bit more polite, informative, apologetic, pleased, proud:

"You must not expect to find London."

"You will see a church as great as any in Europe."

"There is a great deal of mud in the streets."

"The new streets are wide and beautiful."

"There are too many lepers in the streets."

"If you do not look at them, you will not see the lepers."

"The entire world thronged there in 1930 for the coronation."

"The European newspapers spoke of wild hyenas."

"Their newspapers spoke of the Emperor's lions."

"It is not ancient like Axum."

"It has electric lights."

"It was once bare."

"It has a lovely green beauty."

"There are whores everywhere."

"The women of Addis are very chaste."

"There are poor wooden houses."

"The foreign legations are splendid."

They rode on in silence and suddenly, very quietly and with great care, Walda-Ab said, "The lepers will be cured, the whores driven away in shame, the mud covered over." A little further on, he turned and said, "But who can say when?" And they rode on, until he said cheerfully, "The Italians would dearly love to bomb Addis; would you care to view the possible bombing from the hills of Entoppo?"

"Thank you, no," Cleveland said. "We go to Addis. After all, it's *my* city."

"So it is," Walda-Ab said, his face calm and twitching with anticipation.

Across the lone railroad track that ran east to Djibouti they clattered and then climbed sharply. For several days they climbed and Cleveland's heart thumped and his breath came quickly in the thinning air, until finally they reached Entoppo where they briefly stopped and looked down. There it was, the new blossom. Spread out like the maps he drew in grammar school. Running into all its quarters were Menelik's eucalyptus trees, green fingers that wound around the buildings and enveloped the city in camouflaging beauty. In the center of the winding green rose the great octagonal Cathedral of St. George, the Renaissance legacy of the Italian prisoners. It made no sense at all, but then again, why should it? As he examined the relief map, single-storied stucco shops appeared, Ethiopian taxpayers, and then the houses that the Swiss had built as if they surrounded Lac Leman instead of Menelik's palace. Now Tafari's new palace loomed up out of the green: bigger, baroque, ugly. With a controlled face, Walda-Ab pointed to the Moslem quarter, which of course smelled bad and was very dirty. On the other side of the city, running up a eucalyptus mountain, were the villas of the foreign legations, safely apart from the mud, the carts, the bustle and clutter. Cleveland studied the map and its hurrying pygmies and said, "Well, New York, Chicago, London it's not." Walda-Ab flashed his polite smile and replied, "Thank you; shall we go down?"

"Yes."

As the mules picked their way through the people and the mud, Walda-Ab said, "If you do not disagree, we can stay at my cousin's house."

"Thank you, but no, we will stay at a hotel," Cleveland said. "Which is the best hotel?"

"The Imperial. My cousin has gone north to fight with Ras Imru, so we can stay at his house."

"No, the Imperial."

"It is very expensive to stay there. My cousin has told me so."

"We will stay at the Imperial and I will pay."

Walda-Ab dipped his head gracefully. Cleveland said, "I suppose they will take American money?"

"Oh yes. A man from Greece, a Greek, owns it, and he honors any kind of money. My cousin has told me about him. He would be happy to change your money into thalers. In the event," he added quickly, "that you should want thalers."

"We'll see."

"Shall I lead the way?"

"Yes, you lead the way."

He led them politely, firmly, through the mud-filled streets, through beggars who quietly held up their hands, past a gleaming pile of bones which was carefully identified as a leper, past two whores who smiled and waved and were surely Moslem, past motioning Armenian shopkeepers whose prices—frown—had recently gone up, through the piazza of the cathedral as grand as any in Europe (the piazza a square of mud), to the guarding stone wall that enclosed the Hotel Imperial. Through an open door in the thick wall they rode, into a courtyard that had been packed hard by mules, by the guests drawn to the war from around the world and by the solemn, drilling children who couldn't wait to face the invader. The Imperial sprawled before them, a two-story, mud-walled, iron-roofed building.

They dismounted and left their mules in care of a smiling, undernourished boy in khaki shorts who saluted smartly for the sixteenth of a thaler Walda-Ab gave him, accepting with shrugging grace the loss of the dollar that had been swept from his hand and returned to Cleveland. Up the smooth, worn steps they walked and into a long, dark lobby. Behind the desk in the half light loomed a thick slab of a man who was making clicking sounds with his fingers; as they approached, the clicking sounds turned out to be amber beads which jiggled impatiently in a heavy hand. The clicking continued as the man said to Cleveland, "Are you with newspaper?"

"No."

"Journalist people stay here," said the man, clicking away.

"Well, I'm not a journalist. We want two rooms."

"You are not journalist?"

"No."

"You drive ambulance?"

"No."

"You fly aeroplane?"

"No. It's none of your business. We want two rooms."

The clicking hung for an instant and then started again. "Four dollars a day, forty cents for bath, forty cents for game of billiards win or lose, everything in advance."

Cleveland reached into his *shamma* and removed a sheaf of bills, counted out sixty dollars and passed them to an unjiggling hand. "A week for both of us, plus five baths apiece," he said. "If we're satisfied, we'll stay awhile."

The man laid his beads on the table and with a wet thumb counted the money, folded it carefully and tucked it into a thick billfold. "You get breakfast and dinner, same price you eat here or not eat here, is *your* business, no whistling in billiard room, no typewriting after ten P.M."

"I'm not a journalist."

"No typewriting anyway, rule of house. Sign book, please." He pushed a ragged leather-bound book at him and Cleveland signed *J. Dandy*. Walda-Ab signed in Amharic. The man bellowed and a small brown boy dressed in a mixture of uniforms complete to Sam Browne suddenly materialized. "We have no luggage," Cleveland said. "We lost everything in the war in the south."

"Boy show you up with, without luggage," the man said, "is rule of house. If you wish, I tell you where to buy clothes, you only say I sent you. If you don't wish, I don't tell you."

"Thank you, I'll let you know if I wish."

They followed the long-striding boy to the staircase and walked up a creaking flight to a long corridor that crouched darkly beneath cobwebbed chandeliers. No light came from the chandeliers. Walda-Ab whispered loudly, "That was the Greek my cousin told about," and the boy, stopping and standing at attention in front of a door, said softly, "Mendrakos. Tough baby." Cleveland smiled and this time waited for Walda-Ab to hand over the sixteenth of a thaler. The boy saluted and opened two doors with a flourish. Handing over the keys, he saluted again and strode away with long, bandy-legged strides.

"I'm going to bed," Cleveland said. "I'll see you in the morning."

"Oh yes. It has been a long journey, but thanks be to God, we are here."

"Yes, we're here."

"Do you think this is a good hotel?"

"I've seen worse."

He closed the door on a grateful Walda-Ab. He flicked the switch beside the door. An overhead bulb flared. He walked past a drooping bed to the window that had a torn, black shade. He pulled down, the shade bounded up and came down in his hands. He flung it aside and looked out. In the glare of the hotel lights the troop of children was marching up and down on the hard mud of the courtyard. A man in uniform, astride a mule, his legs dangling, rode out through the wall. Another man, in civilian clothes, hurried up the steps, briefcase in hand. He turned back and walked to the bed. His *shamma* on, he lay down. The bed dipped and creaked but stayed up. He folded his hands behind his head and looked up at the bare bulb. A fly buzzed around it. He gazed at the flaked ceiling, inhaled the musty bedding, the dirty, feather-filled pillow. Overhead, the clacking of typewriters. A beleagured and courageous capital was holding out against overwhelming odds. He dozed off. He awoke with a rush. Ten PM., an armistice had descended, the Greek was enforcing it. In the silence then, a rush and a scurry. He rolled over, looked around, then looked down. A platoon of beetles was marching across the floor.

The next day, cool, sparkling, dry, Walda-Ab excused himself and went to visit the family of his cousin. Cleveland questioned the skinny bellboy (for a price), then rode off through the mud, garbage-cleaning hyenas, slave women selling peppers and handkerchiefs, to the clot of Armenian stores on Ras Makonnen Street. He dismounted and tied his mule to a slanting telephone pole and examined the cracked window of R. BALAKAVIAN FINE CLOSE BOTTOM PRIZES.

Balakavian, compact and smiling in the doorway, wriggled his fingers. "Don't be afraid," he called out, "you got no obligation."

"I don't have thalers either," Cleveland said.

"So I don't have leprosy, we can still be friends."

"I don't have thalers."

"I ask you, can you beat American dollar?"

"How do you know I'm American?"

"How do I know the moon ain't green cheese? Whatsa difference long as you are? And you ain't American we still be friends, it don't cost, but I tell you something, I do business with a Yankee before even my own. On the other hand if we don't do business nobody takes out a gun and shoots you at Balakavian, so come in, take a cop and a gander."

He walked inside. A counter was heaped with khaki cotton pants, shirts and shorts, stamped "Boy Scouts of America." Balakavian's fingers writhed in disgust. "Don't waste your time, this here is a waste of time, you follow my lead, no obligation." Steering him lightly by the elbow, he moved him through the khaki, between gauze drapes, through a kitchen where a woman with a mustache glanced at him and returned to her stove, into a large room filled with racks of neatly hanging jackets. "This," said Balakavian, "is the real juice. We give you alterations on the spot. Buy or don't buy, you know you been in a real store."

He walked slowly through English flannel, Paris silk, a gray cheviot by Hart, Schaffner and Marx, an olive gabardine by Palm Beach, ten glen plaids by Hickey-Freeman, a collection of slack suits by Saks 34th Street.

"You're a perfect forty," Balakavian said. "Such an easy fit I could die on the spot, I had them like you business would be a pleasure instead of a headache, I tell you we got the best buncha forties in the whole dark continent."

An hour later a man in a bespoke linen suit from Bond Street that had been made for a legation secretary who dropped dead from sunstroke, a light blue silk shirt and a navy and red repp tie, white silk socks with blue clocks, garters, all from Harrods, thickly soled and heeled white bucks from Paris walked out of Balakavian's. He pulled his mule to him, carefully mounted, and, feet dangling high, rode stiffly back through the mud and hyenas and slave women and lepers to the Hotel Imperial.

2

"Do you mind very much being called the Black Devil?"

He looked up from the forty-cent billiards game. "I beg your pardon."

"I beg *your* pardon." The man had a thin, pointed face that resembled a quizzical sea horse, except for the tiny, goldfish mouth. He wore like a sack a heavy black suit that had a shine at the shoulders and puffy knees, and a black tie that was pulled into a hard, tight knot. His hair was shaggy and flecked with dandruff. He ran a hand through the hair and a sprinkle of white floated onto his shoulders. He said, and the Adam's apple struggled against the pressing knot, "I shouldn't have startled you, but I rather fancy initial reactions, first impulses, as it were. An occupational disease, I fear. I am Warner Brady and I am recording this godforsaken war for the *Toronto Evening Leader*. Might I talk with you?"

Cleveland straightened up and rested the cue on the scuffed flannel of the table. "Did I pass?" he said.

"What? Oh, first reactions. You were absolutely neutral, passed with flying colors. Might we talk?"

"Why?"

"My dear chap, you're good copy."

"Is that what I am?"

"Oho. A philosopher. Well, do not belittle good copy. Practically the entire world is abominable copy. What do you say? I'll make every effort to give you a decent shake."

"But you won't guarantee it."

The little fish mouth tapped air. "In this noble land, dear chap, I guarantee only tapeworms."

Cleveland lined up a shot and made it. He looked up. "Why did you call me that?"

"What, dear chap?"

"The thing you called me."

"The Black Devil? I'll give you a decent shake, but don't come the innocent with me."

"Why did you call me that?"

"Heavens, you don't know?"

"Why?"

"I believe he truly doesn't know. You really *have* been fighting a war. I practically envy you. Why, you are a celebrated figger. Or soon will be."

"Am I?"

"The innocence of nobility. Is it genuine?"

"It looks like we're talking," Cleveland said.

"Ah yes. I've always had that repulsive knack. But I will turn about and exit gracefully if you so desire. I will perforce describe you from afar."

"But you'll describe me."

"Of course I will, old man. We *all* will. I'm first, that's all. Think of it this way: consider our miserable lot; we have an insatiable hunger which is forced on us by the larger hunger as it were; simply put, we need all the color we can find, if you'll pardon my putting it so crudely. Please continue your game if it relaxes you."

"I'm as relaxed as I ever am. Don't you take notes?"

"Oh my, no. When I retire to the inner sanctum, I scribble a few bits, but never in the presence of my client. I always say client since my six months in law school. Filthy habit, notes. They make you concentrate on all the wrong turns. What about the Black Devil business?"

Cleveland set the cue in the rack, turned and leaned against the table. The reporter's heavy black suit exuded Imperial cooking odors and camphorized sweat. "I've been called worse," Cleveland said.

"I dare say you have," said the sea horse with the goldfish mouth. "Did you really knock out eight tanks?"

"No."

"How many?"

"Does it matter?"

The tiny mouth tapped out a smile. "Quite right, how stupid of me. You knocked out a tank. Enough. Please excuse my asking, but the great unwashed are palpitating for this one: what is it about the Ethiopian cause that touches your innermost soul?"

"Emperor Theodore," Cleveland said promptly.

Brady pursed. "The mad king?"

Cleveland grinned and spread his hands. "I'm also known as the Black Joker."

". . . splendid . . . May we try that again?"

"I fought because of Afewerk."

"Of course. The splendid chap with the machine gun. We made a great fuss over him, turned him into Samson, Joshua, et al. Was there then a racial bond twixt you?"

"Nope."

"His men?"

"His men ran."

"Cowards then?"

"No, they just weren't fools."

A sea-horsey smile. "You rallied them and saved the day. Tally ho."

"In a way. But Afewerk had a pretty good man under him. I helped him."

"How, pray tell?"

"I told him what a tank was."

"Oh dear, they really are that ignorant, are they?"

"Yes. They also keep slaves."

"So they do. It's rather a wicked old country, isn't it?"

"I suppose."

"Shall we leave it for the moment? Rumor has it that Graziani offered you fabulous sums to come over. Is that true?"

"No. I was with him originally."

"Oh, delicious. Were you fighting for him?"

"I observed."

"Oh? For the League?"

"For myself."

"Aha. Of course. And is he the compleat scoundrel?"

"Yes."

"Excellent. His people, in case you didn't know, gave you your title. Any comment?"

"Well . . . yes. He's as black as I am. He has a magnificent suntan."

"So much for Rodolfo. Is this a great adventure for you?"

"No."

"A lark?"

"No."

"Are you running passionately away from the States?" The smile with the hole in the middle.

"In a way."

"Oh? As a man of . . . color . . . do you find the States a den of evil, not to mention iniquity?" The pinhole camera of a mouth took a smiling picture. "Rotten question, but necessary."

"Perfectly good question. No more wicked than Canada."

"Been to Canada?"

"Never."

The goldfish smilingly puffed air. "My dear fellow, I have ofttimes bitten the hand that feeds me, but I must now rise to the defense; we do not have a Negro problem."

"Only because you have no Negroes."

The huge head dipped in shaggy salute. "The *Toronto Evening Leader* thanks you; its dashing war correspondent thanks you."

"Is that all?"

"Why yes . . . Did you expect the inquisition? The old third degree?"

"Yes."

"Splendid. I say, old man"—and the shaggy pile dropped again—"would you . . . that is, what do you think . . . well, would you care to share a carefully hoarded bottle of Courvoisier? Been holding it for what your fellows in the battered fedoras call a scoop. Now you've given me one. Brady is nothing if not a grateful sort . . . Of course, if you have better things to do . . ."

"I was going to fuck Greta Garbo. I'll give her a rain check."

The typewriter stood guard on a small table. "My machine gun," Brady had said, patting its head before he broke the seal and poured the Courvoisier into a pair of cloudy tooth glasses. After three half-glassfuls he began to look up and talk, grant an interview; he grinned through the goldfish aperture, it's the only *fair* thing to do. Cleveland, sitting in a kitchen chair, listened silently, sipping slowly; indeed—another pinhole grin—he was the perfect interrogator.

"Born, bred and nurtured in Halifax," Brady said through the cognac. "Beastly provincial little place, but it had a citadel high up in the middle, built to fend off the wicked French in the old days, fancied myself king of the hill up there. Yes ... that is, when I wasn't longing to escape to Buffalo. Quite a corker that. Buffalo. To my feverish little brain, Buffalo *was* the States, therefore everything Canada and I were not. Oh, the perfect little idiot, Brady. Another?" Cleveland nodded. Brady poured. "Buffalo," he mused. "Actually thought the great beasties, *your* great beasties, roamed its streets; my home on your range. Idiot." The thick eyes drooped. "Oh well ..." He touched the typewriter and sat up straight. "Pater now was quite another story. Detested your great nation; disloyal, filthy traitors, uncouth rebels, all of that. Dad was an imperialist, he was, true blue, oh yes, true knight of St. George. Disraeli was his hero and Daddy hated Jews; never owned up that Dizzy was Izzy. Hip hip hoorah. Raised me up on Tom Brown and the compleat works of Samuel Smiles, chap who taught every Victorian child how to build his bloody character and paternalize the world. Dear Sam, dear Guv ... tightened my character *and* my jaw, made me speak bloody British, oh yes ..." He tipped the other kitchen chair precariously against the wall, leaned back and stroked his machine gun. "Volunteered in '15, me Dad, yes he did. Gassed at Wipers. Bloody white cross in a field of bloody white crosses. Flanders Field and poppy, yes indeed ... Mum plastered his khaki picture all over the bloody house. Went west, me Dad." He poured cognac into the tiny opening and somehow it got past the Adam's apple which struggled against the stone-hard knot of the tie. "Sold newspapers, I did, to help me mum and the two little ones. Man of the family. Pater. Till '18, good little newsboy, wuxtry, wuxtry." The Adam's apple struggled again. "Then, Halifax blew up. Did you know Halifax blew up? Exploded all about one; did you know?"

"No."

"Of course not. Not important enough in El Dorado. That's what it did, though. Cross me heart. Blew the bloody hell up. Thought it was the hand of God reaching down to destroy me because I coveted Buffalo. But God overreached and blew up the whole bloody city, plus Mum and the wee ones. Wiped all off the bloody map. Sodom, Pompeii, San Francisco, Halifax. Biggest thing to happen in a century and you didn't know . . . Bloody ship in the harbor carrying dynamite, very un-Godlike. Another?"

"A short one."

"Of course. Always in bloody control." He poured and Cleveland said that's enough; he said, of course, and filled his own glass, held it up and drank. "Always admired the control boys; am I boring you?"

"Not yet."

"Stout fellow. Not . . . Yet. Must remember that. Well then, Not . . . Yet, bummed me way, burns and all, to Toronto, looked up Mum's brother, rich uncle, played the poor waif, reeled him in. Fed me, clothed me, put me through university, started me off at the law. Hated it, hated uncle—stolid burgher, no imagination, Canadian through and through. Took to the rails and headed straight for Buffalo. Me vision of heaven. Resided there for three years before realized how bloody awful. Miserable city. Addis Ababa of El Dorado. Landed me a job on a miserable little paper on the strength of me Canadian background. Bloody fool editor thought I was a Mountie with pen in hand. Lasted three years, saw the real Buffalo, hopped it for Toronto. Bloody fool editor took me for product of great American journalism. Credentials, that's what they want, romantic credentials. Drink up, old man . . ."

"I'll sit tight for a while."

"Not really, sit tight, oh dear. You *are* a watcher, aren't you? Yes, you are. Nothing wrong with that, mind you, it's what you are. Line I'm in, I ought to be a watcher, but I'm a performer. My curse and my gift. But it's what I am. Performer. Laid me low in the Lindbergh case, yes it did. Practically broke it open single-handed, performer that I am. Did you know? Of course not. Rode the wrong horse. Oh, love to have that one back . . ." Fat fingers slid over the keys, depressed them gently; the keys rose, then fell, like tired arms. "Put all me money on Irving Bitz and Salvatore Spitale. Your grand underworld. Entranced by rods, molls, flash and dash. Tommy guns, violin cases, bulging armpits. Marvelous credentials. Adored the grifter, the informer.

Absolutely sure I could break the case and restore golden child to golden parents. Irving and Sal, passports to glory. Wrote like a bloody angel. Had Toronto on its bloody panting ear, excuse the mix. Sensational lead atop sensational lead. To the king of leads. Oh my . . ." Fat fingers through shaggy hair, snowfall on black keys. "Frogs Martin was his name. Moniker. Alias. Tracked him through the bloody Rockies. Up Pikes Peak and down. The Mountie. Cornered him in Cheyenne, extracted ten-page confession, thing of beauty. Golden child tenderly held in Havana. Flew off for grand rescue, golden child turns up in New Jersey grave. Flummoxed. Up to me bloody ears . . . Reeled in . . . Performer that I was . . . am . . . What do you think of that, watchman?"

"You asked for it."

"That's the ticket! True blue to the watchman's code! So right, though. I did and reaped me just desserts. But tell you something, watchman: never be flummoxed again . . . never . . . take this bloody war and shake it by its bloody tail . . . make it say uncle . . . what ho?"

He began to slide limply out of his chair—a long slow glide, smiling. Cleveland caught him under the arms, lifted the dead weight and dropped it on the bed. He opened the window and the door, located some Aqua Velva, doused the bed and the floor. Air whistled thinly through the pinhole mouth. Suddenly the eyes opened and stared up at Cleveland.

"Much thanks, old man," Brady said. "Could never drink. Another curse. You may leave me now."

"Do you want the light on?"

"Look awful, don't I?"

"Yes."

"Watchman says yes. Daddy love you. Black Watch. *No* light. Not at all necessary . . ." The air whistled and the eyes fluttered, then they opened hard. "Old man," he said, "slight correction. Pater never gassed. Never in Big Show. Greengrocer. In Toronto. Died in bed. Peaceful. Mousey chap. Read Thomas Brown, Sam Smiles all on me own. Toronto. Never lived Halifax . . ." He closed his eyes and the pinhole whistled; his eyes still closed, he said, "Blew up, yes; true fact, history, *could* have broken Lindbergh case, yes, Bitz, Spitale, Frogs . . ." A whistling sigh, then the little goldfish smiled; the eyelids struggled but remained closed. "Believe?"

"Do I have to?" Cleveland said.

"Aha, *en garde*! Careful does it. Lindy was careful. Flummoxed me, he did. Spoiled great story. Yes?"

"If you say so."

"Good, good. Wily Black Devil. Keep it up, up. You may go far, then again you may not, then again ah yes. Never to flummox me, old man . . ."

Cleveland walked to the door, listened to the whistling rise and fall, looked at the hillock on the bed, the typewriter standing guard, smelled the cognac and sweating wool and Aqua Velva, turned the light off and walked out.

3

Walda-Ab was unusually quiet when he returned from his cousin's house, although, thanks be to God, all had been well there, and his cousin was fighting heroically on the northern front. He remained quiet for several days. One evening, after the Imperial dinner of rock-hard chicken fried in rancid butter, he said, "May I tell you something?"

"Sure."

"May we walk outside?"

"Sure."

They walked out to the courtyard where the children were drilling. Walda-Ab said, "I trust you have been well since coming here?"

"I'm okay."

"That is good. Are you amusing yourself in the city?"

"Spit it out, please."

"I am familiar with that expression. Bad people spit out on the floor of churches. I shall leave tomorrow to join my cousin in the north."

"Oh shit."

"Oh yes."

"To fight Badoglio?"

"Oh yes. My cousin is with Ras Imru and I must join him."

"You don't have to do a goddam thing."

"Oh yes."

"Is it written in the Book of Kings that you must be killed?"

"I do not know. Perhaps it is not. Perhaps it is."

The children swung noisily past them. "Ras Imru is a fucking idiot. He can't win."

"Then he must lose. For if the invaders win, then he must lose." He bowed. "It has been a true honor fighting by your side and traveling with you and coming to the Hotel Imperial with you."

"Then stick around, you goddam fool."

"Thank you, no, but I thank you."

Walda-Ab bowed and walked back to the steps. The children stomped past.

Three sheets of onion skin, typewritten, double-spaced were lying on the floor when he returned to his room. He picked them up and walked to the window. On the legation hill, lights were brightly shining despite the threat of air attack. Music of the Ray Noble orchestra wafted tinnily through the cool evening air, above the slave women, tarts, lepers, careening Fords and Austins. He looked down at the onion skin.

Colored Crusader Fights Fascism
by Warner E. Brady

He is of medium height, straight and very thin. Our guess is that he is thinner than usual for he has been quite busy fighting the scourge of the desert, Rodolfo Graziani. He wears a spotless white uniform and a sardonic smile. He is, as my American colleagues might say, the real McCoy. For he is the famous (infamous, if you choose) Black Devil. The very name chills the nationalistic fervor of the Alpini (even in the desert). It is said that one must not mention his name in a certain Roman palazzo or the occupant of the mansion will lapse into frothing, stamping rage.

Who and what is he? And why has he become in such a short span of time a sepia Lawrence of Arabia to millions of his racial brethren?

Digging hard and deep for answers to this and a number of other questions, this correspondent was able to elicit much (although hardly all) of the amazing substance behind the dark shadow. For obvious reasons, we cannot overstep the bonds of friendship and propriety, but we did manage to evoke shrugging consent and to obtain some solid information. He fights alone, he trusts few. We are honored.

We shall call him James. To reveal more would delight the Italian intelligence service, which at this very moment is trying frantically to search out and eliminate this *eminence noir* from the African stage.

We can reveal that he is American. He hails from an eastern metropolis and he says, "No, I do not mind being known as the Black Devil." With a sardonic smile, he adds, "If it serves as a rallying point for my people, they can call me Adolf Stalin."

In that exchange, this correspondent believes, lies the key to the Devil's personality. To be precise, it lies in the phrase, "my people"—two words that he utters more than he may believe. Curiously enough, he does not identify the invader as being purely Roman.

"It is infinitely more complex than that," he says in tones that reveal a childhood of flailing desperation mingled with the cadences of a sustaining spirituality. "I see," he continues, "that the invaders are negative charges of force, as it were, striking deeply into positive bodies. Or, to put it succinctly, good versus evil. It is really as simple, and as complicated as that. Complicated, because the world has made it so." He smiles thinly. "The choice was an easy one for me. Not because I am heroic, although (he grows serious) we are all capable of heroic deeds. It was easy because there was no other choice."

"Are you saying," we ask, for we have also heard the

fakirs of the world choose the same sentiments, if not quite the same words, "that there *are no* other choices?"

"Of course there are for others. Not for me. You see, you, that is, I, had to choose at the *outset*. That is my nature. Once that was done, it was a simple matter to come here and go up against evil."

We study the composed features for a sign, a flicker, of false sentiment. We do not find it.

"One thing troubles us greatly," we counter.

He arches an eyebrow. "Yes?"

"How can bare hands and exposed chests and spears fight planes, tanks and mustard gas?"

"But I have just told you," he replies.

Now it is our turn to smile. "By the way, how many tanks *did* you knock out?"

"A few."

We shake our head, for the count, as every street corner in the civilized world has proclaimed, ranges from six to 60. "Of course," we venture, "there is only *one* Black Devil."

"I suppose," he replies carelessly. "But in a test of basic values, the scales have a way of balancing out. I have seen the great Afewerk accomplish this at Gorahei. Morality *can* shoot down a plane. It can and will do a great deal more as the legions of the dark press in. Look at it this way." A film of brooding intensity covers the finely carved features. "Someone has to stand up to the *Duce* and his gangsters. Why not us?"

The Black Devil smiles fleetingly. Suddenly he is gone. We think we can see a shade of white, like the coming of a new dawn, slipping into the grove of eucalyptus trees, but we are far from certain. In any case, the shade is soon gone; we are alone. We turn and stride thoughtfully back to the hotel, the Waldorf, the Ritz, of Addis. As we walk, the planes of the invader scream overhead, and we wonder: Can he possibly be right? Can he, as the French say, have reason? Can this one man possibly know more than the "great leaders" of this crazily lurching world?

We do not know, not at this early juncture. But as we

hunch over the typewriter keys, and the hyena screams back at the planes, we continue to wonder. That wonder permeates the very paper that carries these words to a waiting world. And it may well be that this is the gift the Black Devil sends out to a writhing, infected planet: HE HAS MADE US WONDER.

Slashed across page three at the bottom, in pencil: "Please to forgive. I am no hero and the machine must be fed. I exit to report bombs and yperite. See ya in the funny papers."

LION

A WEEK AFTER WALDA-AB WENT OFF TO FIGHT THE WAR, CLEVE-
land was sleeping late one morning when he heard an insistent
knock at the door. It was like the pattering of rain on leaves.
He cracked his eyelids against the white morning, sat up, swung
warily out of the creaking bed and padded to the door. Mrs.
Mendrakos, plump, breathless, pink faced, in a stained Joan
Crawford suit. "So sorry to bother you, sir. Monsieur Georges
would like to see you very much."

"What for?"

"What for?" she asked, frowning in amazement. "How could
I know?" She turned and walked away, shaking her head.

He washed and dressed slowly and walked downstairs and
slowly drank his chicory and boiled milk and ate his iron roll.
He gazed blankly at a correspondent who sat opposite, pointed
at his ears and mouth, smiled and finished his breakfast. Then
he got up and sauntered to the storeroom where Mendrakos
spent his day when he wasn't at the desk. "Your wife said you
wanted to see me."

"Not me personally."

"Who?"

"A gentleman has been waiting, Mr. Dahndy." He motioned.
A man rose from a chair in the corner and walked toward them.
He was small, well-balanced, had a darkly smooth face with a
pencil mustache. He wore a black serge suit that was cut very
well, a sparkling white-on-white shirt with a hard tube of a collar.

135

Black silk tie, gold tack. The man glanced at Mendrakos, who hesitated, smiled and then walked away.

Cleveland said, "I do not speak to journalists of any color."

"That is not unwise," the man said. "But have no fear. My name is Ato Lorenzo Taezaz and I am the chief political advisor to the Emperor, the King of Kings. I have come to tell you that the Emperor wishes to talk with you."

"Why?"

The padded shoulders of the black suit rose and patiently fell. "Naturally, I know the reason for I am his chief political advisor, but I do not place words in the mouth of the Emperor, as do others. I would like you to come with me, please."

"Do I have to?"

"Yes."

"Now?"

The smooth forehead was lined for an instant. "But of course, now." He walked to the door, turned and gestured gracefully.

They rode in a Rolls-Royce with a rumble seat along Ras Makonnen Street, past the movie house where a Johnny Mack Brown western was playing, past the press office, the Armenian stores, to the end of the street and up to the New Palace. Through the gate, past a guard who stared through them. The chauffeur pulled up beside the palace steps. Taezaz said, "After you, sir, please," and Cleveland got out and waited. Taezaz followed, said, "Please follow me, sir," and walked up the steps. They walked a long way through tall, thickly carpeted corridors until they came into a small room where Taezaz stepped aside and waved him to a leather-covered sofa. Cleveland sat down and Taezaz joined him, carefully adjusting his trousers. They waited beneath the gaze of a stern Woodrow Wilson and a foppish Prince of Wales. Then Taezaz rose, walked to the door and gestured. Once more through a softly cushioned hallway. To a pair of double doors which had been drawn back like folded wings. Taezaz grasped Cleveland firmly by the elbow and lightly pushed. He walked through the folded doors with Taezaz behind. The room within was huge and high ceilinged. Before a pair of wide windows sat a huge, ornately carved desk. Behind the desk, a long, olive-skinned face seemed to float above a black collar and cloak. The face seemed too heavy for the narrow shoulders, but somehow it remained aloft. It was balanced above by a puff of coarse, black hair, below by a circular mustache that circled down to a beard. Beneath the lower lip an inverted triangle pointed its apex at the beard. Moist brown eyes gazed out at Cleveland. A tiny hand fluttered like a small dove on the edge of the desk's glass top. Taezaz said, *"Je reste?"*

"Ce n'est pas necessaire," said the floating face. Taezaz glided out of the room. The face suddenly rose and the tiny Emperor stepped precisely from behind the barricade. The black cloak parted as he walked, revealing splendid white jodhpurs. Cleveland thought briefly of Earle Sande, feather-stepping out of the paddock.

"Je ne parle pas Anglais très bien," said Tafari.

"Je parle Français," Cleveland said.

"Je sais." A dove of a hand fluttered. Cleveland sat in a white, corduroyed chair. Tafari rotated on his slender core and returned precisely to his place behind the great desk. In a gentle voice, in French, he said, "I thank you for fighting for us."

"It was an accident."

The smile was sad and semitic. "Many things take place by accident. The important thing is that you did fight for us."

"Yes, I did."

They watched each other for several minutes. Tafari sighed and said, "Did it take you long to reach my country?"

"No. I proceeded slowly."

"Of course. Was it very hot in the desert?"

"Yes, but hot for both sides."

"Ah, that is a good point, I must remember that point." A dove glided over a pad with a golden pen. Tafari looked up. "I hope you did not suffer."

"I'm here. Afewerk is not."

"Ah yes. I loved him like a son."

"He behaved well."

"Thank you."

They watched again. A dove rose, fluttered wearily to the glass top. "I trust the scenes at his burial were not undignified."

"There was a little dignity."

The long face floated a nod at Cleveland. "That is pleasing. Do you find it not pleasing being called the Black Devil?"

"People keep asking me that."

"It is the Emperor who asks," the face said gently.

"I don't particularly enjoy it."

"Would you prefer that I ask you something else?"

"You are the Emperor."

The sad, long face agreed. "Then," it said, with eyes as wet and shiny as a eucalyptus leaf after the rain, "the Emperor will ask you this. Would you like to become an officer in my army and command my men?"

"No."

"Are you so sure?" and he sighed quietly. "Would you not want to think about it?"

"I'm very sure," Cleveland said.

"I see. You are very sure."

The tiny doves fluttered and folded together on the cool glass top. They twitched for a long time. Tafari stared down at them and his face was stern but fatherly. The doves grew very still. There was a long, calm pause. Within it, Cleveland could hear the muted sounds of palace life: carpeted voices, carpeted footfalls, carpeted commands. Then, into the soft parenthesis Tafari said, "Do you not wish to fight for the people of your race? It is also your struggle." A feathery finger struggled up, then dropped back.

Cleveland said, "You are not the people of my race. Or, are you?"

"Of course not." (Very clearly, exactly, Cleveland could see the jockey stepping neatly to the podium at Geneva.) "However," Tafari said with sudden firmness, "the world does not understand these things. It cannot deal with such distinctions. To the world, we are the same, and we must not disappoint the world. The world detests disappointments. I really think you should enlist with us."

"But there is a large problem with that. Here is the problem: We are not the same."

"Agreed. But, that is a small matter now."

"Not at all. It is a large matter. You and your people are far above me."

This time a dove rose impatiently and was hauled down. "Of course," Tafari said. "But then, we are also far above the rest of the world. So you are not alone in this inferior condition." He sighed with the simplicity of the whole business. "My dear sir, we are in a desperate struggle to retain our greatness and you can be of immense value in this struggle."

"The Italians said that."

"But you are not Italian."

"I am not Ethiopian."

"Alas, no. Not all can have that good fortune. But consider what you do have. You have a talent for bravery and ferocity. You have a great value. I will see you are well rewarded for that value."

"May I go now?" said Cleveland. "I would like to go now." He got up. With a rushing, fluttery sweep, Tafari waved him back to the chair. They sat silently for fifteen minutes, watching each other. Then, Tafari sighed and said, "You may go now. I am not a dictator."

Three days later, Lorenzo Taezaz in his tightly cut business suit came for him and conducted him in the Rolls-Royce down Ras Makonnen Street to the New Palace.

"Is it that you love the Italians?"

"No."

"You admire Signor Mussolini?"

"He made the trains run on time."

"My train to Djibouti runs perfectly. Why will you not fight for me?"

"Again?"

"I must be persistent. God has always told me to be persistent."

"You have slaves here."

"Now we have them. The Italians say that to the world. They are always saying that."

"Isn't it true?"

"Ah, you see how you think? Of course, it is true. But the

Italians knew that when they supported us for the League. When
they came to my coronation. They are so two-faced. I never lied
about slaves."

"Congratulations."

"See, you are honorable and appreciate honesty. In any case,
I am changing our ways. It is very slow, like rowing a boat with
hands for a paddle."

"If you are so superior, why do you keep slaves?"

"I have tried to explain. That was the old way. I am changing
that old way. Do you think we are *perfect*? A superior nation is
not necessarily perfect. Also, I must be honest and say that slaves
were once necessary."

"They are treated well. They are happy."

"Why, of course. You see, you *do* understand when you let go
of that stubborn attitude. But, happy or not, I will make them
free, for I have told that to the world and I never go back on
my word. But it takes time. Will you fight for me?"

"No."

"Very well, I will not ask you again."

"I have sent for you to tell you I am going north to Dessie to
fight the Italians."

"I wish you good luck."

"And success?"

"You will not have success."

"There could be a way. Would you like to come with me?"

"No."

"I will have with me my Imperial Elephant Shooter and my
Imperial Aeroplane Shooter Downer. I will create for you the
title of Imperial Tank Destroyer. With all that power beside me,
I would win."

"I don't want to go."

"Do you only do what you want?"

"Most of the time, yes."

"Suppose what you want is ignoble?"

"I can't bother my head with nobility."

"Ah, that is why I am an Emperor. I have so bothered myself

since the age of three. Will you come? I will point out the wonderful ancient sites."

"No."

"I could put you in chains and make you come."

"Like Theodore?"

"Oh, so you know Theodore? Those whom he put in chains grew to love him."

"I don't hate you."

"Well, that is progress. The world is growing to love me."

"That is for the world to decide."

"And it is deciding wisely. Will you come?"

"No."

"Even my daughter will come part of the way. Naturally, I would not permit her to come the full way because it is so dangerous. But she *wishes* to come the full way."

"She is a good daughter."

"Indeed she is. She loves me. Not only does she not hate me, she *loves* me. She insists that I do not keep the red umbrella over my head as the ancient Emperors did. She says the umbrella would guide the aeroplanes to me. What do you think?"

"She is right."

"I will have my Imperial Aeroplane Shooter Downer beside me. I have no fear in raising the red umbrella."

"I'm sure you don't."

"I would gladly sacrifice myself, although it would be a tragedy for my people and the world."

"Probably."

"Probably? I think I prefer your no. I will also have a huge iron box in which to hide when the bombs begin to fall. I told my daughter I would hide in the box because she loves me so, but of course I will not. It would be too undignified."

"I can understand that."

"Well, a bit more progress. Then you will come?"

"No."

"You fought for Afewerk."

"Only after he was killed."

"Oh, then you will fight for me when I am dead?"

"Probably not, but I will decide then."

"But I have explained to you why I must not be killed. The people must have their Emperor."

"There are those who think Menelik is still the Emperor."

"There, you see? The Emperor never dies."

"Theodore died."

"Theodore, my dear history-student-sir, ate a pistol ball sent by the queen of England. I could never do such a thing, especially when sent by a queen; it is too undignified. If the queen of the Netherlands sent me a pistol ball, I would carefully wrap it up and send it back to her. Will you come?"

"No."

"Perhaps I will hold up the red umbrella."

"I still won't come."

"I will not hide in the iron box."

"I still won't come."

"Well then, if I hold up the umbrella and do not hide and the Italian bombs find me, will you be dignified at my burial?"

"No."

"What will you do?"

"I will weep and beat my breast because it will be for nothing."

"Ah."

Emperor Haile Selassie I, King of Kings, Lion of Judah, dressed himself in khaki and motored north toward Dessai with the princess. After 30 miles he kissed the princess good-bye and promised, when the time came, to hide in the iron box. The Italian planes flew overhead and he drove forward to meet them. Stepping out of his Rolls-Royce, he waited until his machine gun was properly in place, then he curled the doves that were his fingers around the handle and as it danced, he clutched at it and spattered defiance at the diving planes. He was untouched, and for miles around the people spoke of his daring and strength and immortality.

The Black Devil walked to the movie house on Ras Makonnen Street and for three days sat through the Johnny Mack Brown western. The film broke many times. Each time it broke, the audience cheered.

*   *   *

The Emperor motored back to the palace. The princess welcomed him, as did the people who came with their complaints. The foreign legations congratulated him for being a leader who did not hide in cellars. The Italian consul said he was a very brave man.

"Listen," said Mendrakos, "don't be so sure you spoke with Selassie."

"What does that mean?"

"They love their royal impersonators over here. I have heard Selassie is safe and sound in the palace cellar."

"Isn't *any*body who they say they are?"

"Of course. *I* am Mendrakos."

PASTA AND BUTTER

ONE AFTERNOON AFTER THE BATTLE AT DESSIE, HE WAS LOOKING out of his window, as lately he often did, at the foreign legations, when he heard thin, piping shouts that seemed to have something to do, he could almost swear, with boll *weevils*. He turned from the legations and looked down into the courtyard. There was the troop of little boys who had always been busily, solemnly marching, now drawn up at attention in three ragged lines, craning their reedy necks up and waving scrawny arms as they shouted, their mouths working like hungry little birds. He opened the window and the soft Addis air wafted in, along with the shouting which leaped now to a falsetto screech as bony bare feet stomped the packed-down mud in accompaniment to the flailing arms. They were not shouting for boll weevils. They were screeching, "DEE-VILL, DEE-VILL, CHEERS FOR DEE-VILL."

He pulled back and swore at the bare, overhead bulb. They continued to shout. He leaned forward briefly, smiled an acknowledgment, waved them away. They screeched. He walked around the room, heard their screams. He returned to the window.

"YAY DEE-VILL. BABE RUTHY DEE-VILL."

He leaned out and rasped, "Fuck off."

'THREE CHEERS ON DEE-VILL."

"I shall cut out your black hearts," he yelled.

"DEE-VILL, DEE-VILL."

145

"With the strength of Carnera I will conquer."
"PIPARAY, DEE-VILL."
"I will cleanse the world of your wickedness."
"GIMME DEE-VILL."
"Goddam monkeys, gorillas."
"DEE-VILL, DEE-VILL, DEE-VILL."
"It is my mission to civilize you."

As they started again, he ducked inside. He walked to the sagging bed, kicked it. He returned to the window, eased himself out. The screeching began. He pointed to the gate, to the enemy. Silence. A small boy stepped forward. He recognized the bellhop. A high, thin command, the troop about-faced. Another command. Spindly legs whipped up and down, reached out, marched to the gate, marched through it, disappeared. He pulled back in and headed quickly for the bar.

"Whatsa story mornin glory?"

He looked carefully around. Nothing. He looked down. The bony little boy dressed in British khaki, including shorts, leaned on a spindly leg, one hand resting on his hip.

"Go away," Cleveland said.

"Goddam bastid you fulla shit." The boy smiled.

He rotated slowly on the worn velvet of the bar stool. "What did you say?"

The grin exposed gapped, brown teeth. "Bullshit bastid," the boy said cheerfully.

"Don't say things like that. The Black Devil does not like things like that. But I will like you if you go back to your men."

In a neat, rocking motion, the boy shifted to the other leg, which bowed even more. "I don wanna fuckin march. Hey Deevill. You got a fuckin smoke?"

"No."

"You got a fuckin Scotch?"

"What's your name?"

"Lucky Strike."

"What's your real name?"

"Lucky Strike. Hey Deevill I smoke what you got. Fuckin Ol Gold?"

Cleveland reached into his jacket and brought out the pack of Camels. He flipped and a cigarette flew out. The boy caught it. "Got a fuckin light Deevill?"

The gold lighter clicked. The boy sucked in smoke and lighter fluid fumes. "You okay for a fuckin bum." The boy smiled between puffs. "I tell alla fuckin wops you okay." He puffed some more. "Kill the bastid wops," he said happily.

"No Scotch," Cleveland said.

The sagging shoulders shrugged. He stood there smoking in a hungry rhythm. He interrupted the rhythm to hold the Camel daintily away from him. With a huge smile he said, "Walda-Ab fuckin dead."

"What was that?"

"I don kid you pal. Walda-Ab pushin up fuckin daisies."

"How the hell do you know?"

The boy puffed. "Sure I know. He go up an fight fuckin wops with my fuckin ol man. They catch a bomb. They dead as fuckin doornails. Honest I swear."

Cleveland finished his Scotch. "I don't believe you," he said, although he did.

Paper-thin hands clashed together. "Fuckin Musslini bomb. I catch Musslini I cut his balls off an eat his meat." The boy puffed ecstatically. He said, "You got some fuckin money, Dee-vill?"

"Where do you live?"

"Behind a fuckin hospital."

"Which hospital?"

"Wop hospital."

"That's Mussolini's hospital. He built it."

"Sure. Wop hospital."

"Does your mother live there?"

"Sure."

"Who else lives there?"

"You got some money for my fuckin mother?"

"I don't know."

"Fuckin mother got nothin to eat."

"What about Mussolini's meat?"

"I eat his meat. Gimme money for fuckin mother."

He swiveled off the stool. "Let's see where you live. We'll talk about money later."

The boy cocked his head to the side and puffed. "Okay. Hey Deevill you eat B'doglio's meat?"

It was a wooden railroad flat. Front room, kitchen, parlor, bedroom, another bedroom, a window overlooking a weedy garden and a low-slung hyena who stared back at him. The boy's mother, the wife of Walda-Ab's dead cousin, sat in a stained *shamma,* looking out beyond the hyena. He touched the boy's shoulder. "Tell her I'm sorry about what happened."

The boy nodded and spoke in the jagged waters of Amharic. As he spoke she turned once and stared briefly, then turned back. The boy finished. Cleveland said, "Maybe I'll come back another time." The boy spoke again. This time she responded, without turning. The boy hunched his shoulders and Cleveland heard the cartilage click. "She say she goddam happy you come around an my ol man happy too up in heaven you come around you fuckin wanna she say you got money or a smoke she take it because ol man say you great big shot I swear."

He patted the smiling head and looked at the smooth brown of her face, skin stretching tautly over high cheekbones. Her hair was black and puffed up thickly. It smelled of rancid butter.

"What's your mother's name?"

"Terunesh. I tell you what it mean you gotta smoke."

"Tell me first."

"You honest Deevill. Fuckin name mean poor."

The boy picked off a flying cigarette. The lighter clicked, he inhaled, sighed.

"Why did they name her poor?"

"I tell you dat. She a good baby when she come outa fuckin mother so they name her poor."

"You mean pure?"

"Yeah poor."

He looked at the unblinking profile. "Does she sit here all day?"

"Yeah she sit, sometime she don sit."

"Anyone else? Brothers? Sisters?"

"Players Please. Don tink on him he love all fuckin limeys."

"Your brother?"

"Yeah. Suck aroun fuckin limey 'gation. Cheap bastids I tell him alla time Yankees beat em up Baby Ruth ah the dumb fuckin kid." He crunched the half-smoked Camel under a bare foot. "Hey Deevill you got a smoke?"

"You've had enough."

"Goddam bastid anyting you say."

Suddenly, fluidly, the mother rose. A quick, jagged sentence, then tall and erect, she walked out of the room. The essence of hair and butter remained.

"Where is she going?"

"You got some fuckin money?"

"Where is she going, sonny boy?"

"Fuckin marketplace. She like it. Dead ol man never let her go, now she go, she sell some fuckin tings."

"What kind of things?"

Grin. "Lotta shit in house. Ol man he know it he beat her up but he up in heaven poor bastid. He don beat her up never enough everbody tell him beat her up dumb bastid now he sorry dead fuckin doornail."

Cleveland shook his head slowly.

"Hey Deevill you give me a lighter I tell you someting good."

"No."

"I tell you anyways you a good fuckin Yankee not bullshit limey hey Deevill fuckin mother say a ting bout you."

"And what was that?"

"Why a sonny boy bring fuckin nigger in her house?"

2

The next day he walked to Ras Makonnen Street as the city filled with tall men from the hills who carried their spears and kept swearing loyalty to the Emperor. He walked through them while they chatted of Adowa and the death of the Left-handed one. In the marketplace of the street, other tall men were doing business with wood, dung cakes, hides, honey, wax. Also doing business were the people of Addis with their gold earspoons, leather amulets, iron bangles, neatly worked iron spearheads. Women that Walda-Ab had identified as slaves sat and wound around their hand a cotton thread that came out of a floss-ball held between their toes.

She wasn't there.

He wandered away to the Armenian stores, then continued to walk through the warrior city. In the middle of the afternoon, he found himself across the street from the railroad flat. He crossed over and knocked. A little boy, cut squarely, sharply, squinted up at him. He smiled down. "Players Please?"

"Yeah."

"Is your brother here?"

"No."

"Is your mother here?"

The boy squinted up. A flow of words cut through the flat. The boy frowned and pointed. Thank you, Cleveland said, and walked through each partition-room, the little boy frowning behind.

She was sitting in the same place, looking out the window at the weeds and the scavenger. He cleared his throat and held out his hand holding three thalers: Maria Theresa of Austria, 1780, thick and bosomy. He heard the boy say in a heavy whisper, "Hey I take your money." A graceful arm reached, picked off the thalers, dropped them into the *shamma*. A door opened, slammed.

"Hiya Deevill how's your tricks?"

He looked down at the grinning big brother. "Hello, Lucky, did you have a good day?"

"Fuckin day. Germalist guys fuckin cheapskate." He held out a grimy hand. "I make goddam three talers. You got fuckin money for your *paisan*?"

He drew out another thaler and flipped it. Lucky caught it in his mouth, spit, snatched it in mid-air, pocketed, saluted. Cleveland nodded, cut his eyes to Terunesh. She was staring at the hyena as he prowled unhappily through the weeds.

She was there the following day, in the marketplace. Squatting, chatting, arguing. A long, white thread ran from her fingers to the floss-ball between her toes as she sat talking and arguing with the slave women. Some of the men with spears stopped and talked to her. She shook her head, they walked on, grinning. He stood behind a stall all afternoon. When she finally rose with the stretching grace and barked good-bye to her friends, he walked quickly away in another direction.

He moved in. Lucky Strike grinned, Players Please frowned, she gazed out the window. At first he wore his white suit, but after three days, he put on the clothes of her husband, heavy western clothes. When he did that she got up and glided away into the kitchen. In the stiff, black suit, he sat down in her chair. The hyena pulled back.

The jagged voice called.

He got up and walked into the kitchen. A steaming dish sat on the table, beside it a teaspoon. He sat down and picked up the spoon which said on the handle in raised letters, "Chicago World's Fair, A Century of Progress." He dipped in. Meat and pepper stew. Burning hot. He reached for the glass of *tedj* and gulped. He tried a smile. "Aren't you eating?"

She stared at him.

"Okay." He carefully dipped into the stew and forced it down. Then finished his *tedj*. She rose, glided to the table, collected his bowl, spoon and glass and washed them in a basin of cold water. As she worked he could smell the butter in her hair. He looked at her outline inside the *shamma*. When she finished and straightened up, he looked quickly away. She glided out of the room. She was standing now by the window, her slender profile sharp against the afternoon sun. He inhaled deeply, felt slightly ill.

"Deevill," she said in a jagged voice.

He touched the gauzed shoulder. She turned swiftly.

When she had carefully wrapped up in the *shamma*, he sat against a dark green pillow and said, "Where are you going?"

Barely moving her shoulders, she glided away. He swung out of the bed and, still naked, ran to the door and blocked it.

"I asked where you were going?"

She flicked her shoulders, reached for the doorknob. He twisted her hand away. "I don't want you to go there," he said. She looked at him blankly, reached again for the door. Very firmly he removed the tautly curved hand from the knob. She reached up and tugged at his shoulders. He pushed her away. She stumbled, awkwardly caught herself and, crouching down, stared at him. "I don't want you sitting with the slaves," he said. Suddenly she began to moan, softly at first, then loud, hard, jaggedly. He stood to one side. She was up and sweeping past.

Each day she left earlier and came back later. Each time she returned he said, "You've been there again?" She never answered, but prepared his food, set out his *tedj* and sat watching in the corner. After he had finished, he would stand behind her as she washed his dishes. He would stroke her back. She would turn, they would come together.

She puffed at the cigarette and he reached over and touched the stiff, kinky hair. "You must not go there," he said. She looked at him and shrugged. He slapped her hard. She blinked, suddenly clawed at him, ripped his cheek with a dirty fingernail. They struggled until they both lay back, exhausted. Then she got up, dressed and walked to the door.

3

The small rains came. She remained in the marketplace well into the evening, returning when the legations were bright and the searchlight looking for enemy planes flickered. She was wet, mud-stained, silent. He ate a little of what she placed before him, drank *tedj*. After she cleaned up she sat at the window, then undressed and went to bed. When he got in bed beside her, she pushed him away. He said, "Go fuck yourself," walked to the window, drank *tedj* and stared out at the eucalyptus hills.

CONQUEST

IN DESSIE, SEVERAL KILOMETERS NORTH OF ADDIS, MARSHAL PIE-
tro Badoglio climbed out of his bomber and into his Studebaker.
His army of 12,000 climbed into Fiats, Alfa Romeos, Fords, Che-
vrolets, Bedfords, Studebakers. A squadron of light tanks, peaked
with goggled faces, stood at attention. Eleven batteries of long-
muzzled guns guarded the tanks. Two hundred horses clattered
in their trucks; at the gates of the capital, Marshal Badoglio and
his staff would leave their motor cars and properly enter their
new city.

He nodded once. His driver mashed with a booted foot. The
engine flared. Hundreds of engines flared. He pointed. The
American tires on his car spun and dug in and caught, pulling
behind him his iron-willed army.

In the capital, in Menelik's palace, Ras Tafari sat with the
empress and the Imperial Council.

"I will fight here as long as I can."

"With what?"

"Myself if necessary."

"You speak like a European."

"I'm the Emperor."

"Then go to Geneva."

"For betrayal?"

"You've already been betrayed."

"Why then?"

153

"To show them how much better we are."

"I'll show that by fighting on the Nile."

"With what?"

"I'll poison the Nile, ruin Egypt, make England beg. I'll move the capital to Harar."

"Graziani will take Harar."

"Then I'll die like Theodore."

"They'll only call you crazy."

"Is there nothing left?"

"Go to Geneva. Shame them."

"Menelik would fight."

"Perhaps. But he's gone."

"What would Solomon do?"

"Shame them in Geneva."

"I must have my dignity."

"GOD IS YOUR DIGNITY. OUR GOD IS THE ROCK OF OUR REFUGE. AND HE SHALL BRING UPON THEM THEIR OWN INIQUITY, AND SHALL CUT THEM OFF IN THEIR OWN WICKEDNESS."

"I go to Geneva."

Taezaz gazed down at the man in the bed, leaned over, touched him once, twice, then rubbed his fingers against his suit. The man in the bed did not move. Taezaz looked at the woman in the chair and asked a question. She shrugged like a pillar of water, raised her cupped hand to her mouth. He turned and with long strides walked out.

2

On the day that Tafari left for Djibouti, thence Geneva, the chief of police of Addis got out of his bed, dressed in his best and cleanest uniform, got into his car and had his chauffeur drive him slowly along Ras Makonnen Street. He sat in the back of his car and told everyone through his bullhorn to remain in his house or he would be very angry and punish any who disobeyed with very severe measures. He then sat back and ordered his chauffeur to drive to the foreign legations where he got out and shook hands all around, chatted with old friends and drank many cups of tea and coffee and ate some interesting sandwiches, and assured his hosts that the situation in the city was one of calmness and order. While he finished a roast beef sandwich, shots rang out. The chief of police, a very brave man, and one with excellent training, jumped into his car and ordered his waiting chauffeur to rush him back to headquarters . . .

The foreign legations slammed and bolted doors; all sat down and drank their tea and coffee and ate their sandwiches.

If an Italian pursuit plane, with nothing to pursue, had dropped down low over the city, it would have seen this:

The citizens of Addis, streaming out of back streets, alleys, *tukuls,* clotting and forming a solid, yet internally fluid mass, this mass like an electrically charged octopus rolling in great gulping spasms to the stores of the foreign section. It would have seen the fluid mass ingest the first shop it came to, roll over it, leave it with no roof and scattered insides. The safe, curious plane would have seen the fingers on the tentacles of the fluid mass detach themselves from the flailing whips and wrap up in exquisitely cut western clothing, then go darting off in a dozen, crazy directions. The uncaring heart-mass would then have been observed to roll toward the other stores, crushing them, eating their contents. The plane would have seen, at the center of the mass, its frenetic, ecstatic eye, a woman in a stained white *shamma.*

If the plane, smiling with satisfaction at such barbarity, would then have banked away to the outskirts of the city, it would have seen the *shiftas*—the bandits—and the soldiers of disbanded regiments stream out of the hills, flow together, forming their own boiling nucleus, and this mass in its own turn rush toward the ball of fire that was now the foreign shops. The plane, nodding, would have seen the police, led by its brave chief, step forward in front of this new mass, hold it off for the briefest moment, then step by step bravely retreat before it. The plane's wireless, if it understood Amharic, would have heard:

"THE PALACES ARE OPEN."
"THE EMPEROR HAS FLED."
"TAKE WHAT IS OURS."

The clean, bright airplane, daintily sniffing in the thin air, would have seen the bandits and the soldiers brush the police aside, would have seen this second spastic mass lurch toward the palaces, would have observed with scientific detachment how it gave birth by splitting apart, then split again, the smaller new masses now rushing up to and through the gates of each palace. Of course, the original fluid mass was already inside Menelik's palace, ripping, tearing, flinging, dancing—the children of the great king—who in this ecstatic moment were somehow with him in the sky and defending him from the world, yet still condemning him for abandoning them, for shaming them, for leaving them to the European savage. This was the mass led by the woman in the stained *shamma,* the wildest dancer of all.

As the plane diligently made notes for its masters, it could have seen the bandits and the abandoned soldiers hurl themselves against the walls of the lovely rooms, clawing at them and actually running up their vertical length until gravity caught them and hurled them back on their comrades, but not before a tapestry had been ripped away and covered the writhing, flailing forms, and the plane—horrified—would have seen now these terrible disembodied forms prancing, careening, crashing like drunken ghouls into tables, windows, great gleaming urns and then into each other so that the palaces, pierced with Roentgen-Ray vision, were thickly clotted, boiling masses of all colors, and the disgusted plane rose a little higher, lifting its skirts as it climbed.

If the plane had hovered there, it would have been rewarded by the sight of a dozen streams pouring out of each palace, mingling and re-forming as a wild, rainbowed amoeba that with a controlling intelligence, even as it bounced this way and that, still moved out through the gates and flailed its way to the caves (the plane smiling) where the weapons were stored. One glance at the onrushing terror and the watchmen (naturally) fled. And moments later, with rifles of every calibre and length waving, shooting in every direction, the boiling mass would have been seen to send out excrescences and these horrible end pieces to break off and rush off to the next inevitable place. The observer on high, clear of all the filth, would have seen these things rush to the wine shops and with a knowing curl of its spotless lip would have seen casks split open, bottlenecks shattered, and grinning, skeletal heads bathing in the spurting liquid or craning back and gulping, even choking. Then (of course) the police, ignoring their brave chief, and having already been tempted by the tapestries, would have torn off their layer of civilization and fought their way through the drunken flotsam to the casks and, as the plane indulged in splendid reflections on the royal *carabinieri*, fought for their proper share of the spoils.

Now a swoop back to the streets and a splendid view of what would soon be called the Battle of Addis Ababa. But the battle, with drunken illogic, would have nothing to do with fighting the enemy, except that the enemy was now (and truly?) revealed to be itself: Ethiopian Christian against Ethiopian Moslem, Amharas against Gallas. Soldiers against citizens. Bandits against bandits. Until all, or almost all, realized there was even a better and supposedly weaker enemy, and the wildmen (and women) of Addis rushed off to the foreign legations, and the plane would have a moment's trepidation—but only a moment—as it would have seen the graceful and civilized people of the legations, with their faithful servants from the hills of India, easily hold off the ignorant hordes.

Satisfied, the fine and splendidly meshed proportions of western knowledge would now rise higher still and gather in the complete and final tableau: the smoking, exhausted city. Sacked, gutted, defiled by its own people. The plane would now feel something and look up. Rain, a final judgment from above. Beating down, streaming past, sweeping onto the flames and smoke and the shells that had been houses, the blackened hulks of cars and trucks that, as emissaries of civilization, had been turned completely upside down, some with wheels still helplessly spinning. Telegraph wires, the fragile links to the (real) world, hung in crazily tangled nets, or were they webs? For here and there a small, dark figure tried to climb one, actually made some progress, then tumbled with a grin of surprise into the mud. And finally, the plane would note that the bandits and the soldiers and the remaining portions of the writhing masses had suddenly disappeared into caves and alleys and still intact *tukuls*; of course: Badoglio was approaching; if they knew nothing else, the wild people of Addis somehow knew *that*.

The plane would have seen all it needed to see. Clapping its wings in satisfaction, it would sheer off, gather speed and swoop down on the train that struggled like an exhausted black ant through the mountains toward Djibouti. It would drop very close to the thing, examine it, line it up in its gunsights, then with great magnanimity smile wryly, soar up to the clouds, bank and speed away to report back to the marshal in his Studebaker.

In the house behind Ras Makonnen Street, the huge naked man slept on, his snores rising to the hot, paint-flaked ceiling. The woman in the stained *shamma* sat beside the window, from time to time taking a sip of wine from an exquisite, tissue-thin goblet. The garden she stared at sent up climbing vines of smoke into the great pall that hung over the city. A leper prowled in the garbage.

3

Marshal Badoglio looked at the rain-drenched, burnt-out city. He noted with approval that the smoke was curling as in salute thinly up to the banking, rolling planes that played, like small children, with victory. Streaming past and sometimes into his column, slowing it down—but that couldn't be helped—were the refugees, the purest sign, from the beginning of all wars, that it was over. His face wet with rain and tears, Badoglio entered his city.

As he rode he gazed straight ahead, but even so he could pick out in the corner of his conquering eye white flags that hung from every *tukul*. Wet, heavy, they drooped with an appreciation of the moment. Still gazing straight ahead, he nodded graciously as he clattered by a detachment of Ethiopian guards, who presented arms with rifles of every size, a saw-toothed genuflection, sincerely appreciated. Here and there a dark fist was hoisted; the defeated grew instantly shrewd—he had no illusions about that—but some of those fists would prove helpful and indeed loyal when they saw every day what he could do with them. Some of his men threw back grinning salutes. He permitted that, even as he permitted them to wear geraniums in their helmets, for it was part of their outward and generous nature and a good general knew when to ease up. However, he would have wished, as his column rolled past the British Legation, that they did not stick out their tongues.

He rode on. Through the city of the King of Kings, the invincible Lion of Judah. Past the gutted stores, the charred remains of cars, trucks, ambulances, the obediently drooping flags. Straight through, from one end of the city to the other. (A true march, not a D'Annunzio joke of journalists and poets and paper soldiers.) He turned finally into a boulevard lined with Menelik's eucalyptus trees and every bud, every branch breathed apology for Adowa and leaned down for its avenger. Along the chastened byway he picked his way, tall and splendidly erect, until he reached the steps of the Italian Legation.

He dismounts easily. He strides up the steps, turns and stands at attention through the afternoon as his machines roar and rumble through the city, soar above the city. Then in the lovely glow of the Ethiopian evening he briefly turns his head. The tricolor of Savoy is raised above the legation and the cries of joy that follow it up the mast must be heard even in the Venezia. Sunburned knuckles pass across his eyes. A deep breath in the heart-pounding air. He has shown them all: The Scoundrel of Libya, Haig, Pétain, Hindenburg, Foch. Cheers, plunging fists in the air. The waters of heaven. He has shown them: the dwarf with the iron jaw, his king. He has created an imperial hero and an Emperor. He has washed away Caporetto. They owe him more than can ever possibly be granted. But he is a soldier, and a modest soldier. He has only done a soldier's duty, although quite brilliantly. He turns, embraces Magliocco, his victor of the sky.

"We've done it!" he cries.

Magliocco, like most airmen, has nothing to say in a moment

of history. He can only weep. Badoglio looks at his tricolor: Kitchener of Khartoum, Roberts of Kandahar . . .

The Duke of Addis Ababa.

That will do nicely.

.

A LETTER TO THE *TIMES*

Sir:

And so we see that it is over. With great, unexpected suddenness, the impossible has been achieved. The famous military experts who sit before their parchment maps have been thoroughly confounded, and the ancient, impregnable fortress has fallen before their astonished eyes, eyes heavy with the scales of unusable and outdated strategies.

The first measure of the dance thus is ended; the disbelieving world has witnessed a spectacular achievement, and if our indolent governmental custodians are not to go down in the second measure, it behooves them to look at the Abyssinian adventure with a new, clear vision, or they and we will surely be swept into the dustbin of history along with the Spartas, the Persias and Chinas that in their turn never took note of the plunge forward, the stroke decisive.

To begin at the beginning, in itself no mean feat, we must inspect closely and induct from the tactics of the victor. These maneuvers in their scope and precision have exceeded by far anything that has gone before on the dark continent, in particular the endeavours of Robert Napier against the savage Theodore in 1868 which on the surface of the case would appear to have a certain similarity. It has even been suggested that the Italians studied this campaign and copied it in every engineering and military detail. This

161

is complete rubbish. Napier inserted a column; Theodore killed himself; Napier withdrew his column. Simplicity itself. No, we must look elsewhere for the template of victory, and one has done precisely that.

One must immodestly admit that one has long been a keen student of historical parallels. In this case one has found the specific and compelling blueprint for the immense achievement. It is nothing less than Garibaldi's marvelous campaign of 1860–61. One need only consult G. Trevelyan's masterful study of that venture to ascertain the striking similarities: in each case a monarch named Victor Emmanuel was enhanced in person and domain, in each case the colour of the conqueror's shirt was a significant determinant, in each case a leader who was blessed with the anvil G tipped the scales towards victory.

One is well aware that the world in its ignorance assigns the triumph to Badoglio, the tired man of an old war. One is in a position to state otherwise. The heir to Garibaldi is Rodolfo Graziani, who by placing intractable pressure on Selassie's southern flank, by sacrificing his own chance at the immediate accolade, has enabled the tired old man to dance into Addis. One is known for many things, many less than flattering, but one has never been accused of lacking a sense of honour and fair play. That sense must salute Graziani.

And it must salute another.

One's views on the colour question are widely known and have received no inconsiderable attention in the pages of this very journal, yet honour and fair play must be tracked to their innermost lair. Anything less would be the mark of the cad. One states categorically that, graced though he was with the mantle of the unifier, Graziani could not have achieved his ends without the help and powerful support of a quite remarkable individual—none less than the true heir of the House of Solomon, Ras Gallifa, a gallant and faithful son to a wronged, maligned father. A man who in his brief moment on the proscenium arch of the world flashed 'gainst the skies of Mars with a luminous intensity, performed his task with grandiose success, then disappeared from our ken. Speaking as one who was fortunate enough to be privy to the compelling motivations of the Ras, one can only say he did what he had to do.

Can we do any less?

Can we let him go without a farewell salute?

The answer to that fairly posed question is, nay, *must* be: NO. Therefore, one proposes the following: that we honour this man in precisely the way that Rhodesia honours the pragmatist-dreamer who flashed across African skies in the last century. In so doing, one is well aware of the claim of the *chemises rouges*: that the new colony be christened *Garibaldia*. One nods with understanding, but one reluctantly responds, not in this case, history has honoured him enough. One responds in the same vein to the champions of Graziani: Be patient, he will have many a whack at a *Graziani* ere his career is ended.

The prince is quite a different matter. Unless we lift the cudgels in his behalf in this moment extreme, he will sink down forever in the muds of lost cognition. The conquered territory is our final opportunity and we must seize it for him. Let us then do honour to the future in all its bursting glory and at the same time fling a farewell spear at the contiguous past. Let us go forward in the way we have been instructed by a man who has indeed triumphed over his race, his colour, his very heritage.

"All hail Gallifaland!

Very truly yours,
Henry Armitage, K.B.E.

HEROES

MAXIMILIAN JOSEPHSON, KNOWN TO THE WORLD AT LARGE AND TO
the southeastern tip of New York State in particular as The Ace,
leaned back and rested on one knee-high, shining, elegant boot
at the bar of the Hotel Imperial, surveying with gleaming and
porcelained smile the surrounding scriveners, the Swedish advi-
sors sans portfolio, the British Red Cross chaps, the ex-legion-
naires, the White Russian prostitutes who sipped with self-
conscious aloofness—all here gathered to mourn, celebrate or
profit from the fall of a city. As he surveyed and gleamed, his
massive head towering above his subjects, he drank from time
to time from a heavy, half-filled glass of twelve-year-old Chivas
Regal which Mendrakos had hurried up from his private stock
in the storeroom. He managed, as he surveyed and gleamed and
drank, to nod every so often at a familiar eye, but didn't move
from his locked-in position, nor did he move or alter an action
when a bowlegged little boy in short khaki pants, his own smile
a miniature flash of Josephson's, looked up and said, "You got
someting for your fuckin Ace pal?"

Since there was no response, but also no rebuff, the boy
reached up and yanked at an elegant sleeve. "I take anyting I
don tell no lies," he said eagerly, expectantly. The enormous man
this time tilted his head down, considered, set his drink on the
bar, swiftly ripped a gold button from a uniform sleeve and
tossed it at the boy, who snared it precisely with a snapping
hand, studied, rubbed, shoved it into a side pocket, smiled up
again, eagerly, expectantly.

165

"He's out for bigger game, Max," said a man in a baggy black suit who had nodded with hard precision at each move and counter move of great man and disciple. The tall man detached his smile slowly from the little boy as if he were leaning forward and picking it out of the air; he set it down for the man in the baggy suit. Leaning deeper into the booted leg, barely touching the smile, he said, "Selassie or Badoglio?" The boy's head happily followed his words.

"Badoglio," said the man in the baggy suit. "I cover a war, not hasty retreats. That is not a judgment, only a statement." The little head swinging back, the happy face waiting.

"Oh, listen to that," said The Ace, sighting along the smile. The little boy nodded. "The parasite bird picks the teeth of the alligator, hops into the air as the hunter bangs away, clucks a busy tongue, but does not judge. Did you hear?"

"Yeah," said the boy ecstatically. "He a fuckin bum."

"Whore," smiled The Ace.

"Dumb fuckin haw."

"Armistice," said the man in the baggy suit, lifting a fat hand. "You know how we detest the truth."

The Ace saluted with his drink, which he then proceeded to sip with his smile intact, while the little boy leaned hard on a bowed leg and also smiled.

Shaggy head swiveling, the man in the baggy suit said, "Why don't you adopt the little beggar? You'd get scads of publicity." He scanned the headline: "Well-known Adventurer Rescues Bit of Human Flotsam."

The Ace, patting the adoring shoulder, said, "Your aptness of expression is exceeded only by your peristaltic vision." The boy swelled up to the great hand. "Thank you, but no," said The Ace. "He has obviously found his niche, as you have yours. Wrenching him away from it would be too cruel, even for your readers." He patted and the smile below his hand stretched.

The baggy man bowed. "Max, you are an oasis, you really are. Precisely what the doctor ordered after the march of the iron will."

"We endeavor to please," murmured the watching smile.

"And more often than not succeed. You really do. Tell me, how goes it for you in Gallifaland?"

A smooth meshing of gears, a shifting to the other elegant boot followed swiftly by a shift from one thin, bowed leg to an even thinner, more swooping one. "Sufficient unto the day," said The Ace. "We continue to dabble. To peruse and examine. However, we do seem to be in better shape than most of the competition. And you, Warner?"

Eager, challenging eyes bounced to the man in the baggy suit.

"I've been doing quite well, actually. Midst much gnashing of teeth among the Americans. Very emotional lot. The English chaps, with the exception of Steer, are merely quietly envious. Seems that Badoglio has found me utterly *simpatico*. Must be something in my basic nature." An acknowledging bob of the head. "He has dropped numerous hints about a book on his *fantastico* career; he would do the introduction, he assures me. I am keeping him at a seductive arm's length. And there is Ciano, who, in between sittings on Tafari's throne, guarantees a series of perfectly frank interviews."

"And?"

"We are dancing. I tell him I am waiting for his next great success. I'm really angling for the big fish in Rome."

"Nothing like a war for you people," smiled The Ace.

"Absolutely nothing. As you well know."

"Of course. I confess I am working on my own memoir of the occasion." The little boy's head was darting back and forth with expert timing, preceding each line by a precise beat. He swung now to the baggy man who thereupon opened his mouth obligingly and said, "I would expect nothing less. If ever you need a ghost . . ."

The expectant face: "An amanuensis perhaps, hardly a ghost." A nod, sharp, hard.

"I thoroughly apologize. How gross of me. By the way, is it true that you wear two bulletproofed vests?"

"A base canard." The little boy's waiting face beamed. "Circulated by jealous rivals. The truth of the matter is that we do not even wear an undershirt, a ploy borrowed from Mr. Gable of the kinema." Back swung the happy head, challenging, knowing, confident.

"Utterly relieved, utterly." A baggy leg padded a step closer. "Apropos your rivals," Warner Brady said, his voice soft but insistent in the surrounding noise, "I happen to know that Badoglio covets James Dandy as a first-class prize of war. Unless Graziani, a devout believer in revenge, obtains him first. Do you know anything, Max?"

The Ace was properly offended, to the little boy's delight. "I? I go out of my way to maintain an ignorant, if respectful distance between our heroic personae. I have heard it said, though, that he wears *three* impregnable vests." *There,* glowed the boy's face.

"The Fascists are serious, Max."

"Yes?"

"So am I."

"Oh, come now."

"I am, Max. Believe what you like."

"Whores have no hearts," smiled The Ace. None atall, agreed the happy face. "Do you have his exclusive life story?" Yeah, do you?

"Never mind. No. I have my reasons. Whores and lovely scoundrels at least understand each other. Can you pull some of your infamous wires?"

"Heavens, no." Yeah, no, tell him. "We reserve those for your humble servant. In any case, the Black Devil will handle his affairs with his customary skill, I assure you." He sipped, savored, swallowed.

An insistent bony hand tugged at the elegant sleeve. The great smooth head slowly tilted down.

"You wanna Black Deevill?" beamed the little boy.

"Not really," observed The Ace.

"Yes," said Brady, his hand twisting a pointy chin. "What do you know?"

The boy removed the offending hand, cheerfully looked up at The Ace. "Everyting. He fuckin my ol lady."

"Oh my, bad form," murmured The Ace.

"Where?" said Brady. "Where does your mother live?"

A glance at Brady, now back to The Ace, now to Brady. "In my house."

"Where is that, you little brute?"

"My, my," clucked The Ace.

The boy said, "You got money?"

"Good lad," nodded The Ace.

Brady pulled out a thaler and placed it in a dirty palm.

"Two," said the boy.

"Capital," exclaimed The Ace.

Brady slapped another thaler into his hand. "Well?"

"For two t'alers I tell you. For t'ree I take you."

The tall man in the gold epaulettes and the elegant, shining boots and the plump man in the thick, baggy suit looked down at the naked man in the bed, who was breathing heavily through a half-opened mouth. The little boy pointed with pride at his prize exhibit. The Ace patted the splendid lad.

"He has fornicated himself into a state of grace," he said.

"Nonsense," said Brady.

"A coma?"

"Cut it out, Max." He reached down and shook the heavy shoulders. Flickering eyelids, but no movement. Brady looked imploringly at The Ace, who shrugged and looked at the woman who sat at the window, ignoring all.

"Most appropriate," said The Ace. "This is a phenomenon well known among the professors of social and sexual science. It happened to us in East St. Louis in 1917. We flew there to observe at firsthand the riot and its ramifications and found ourself whore de combat for six days. Couldn't move a muscle. Totally and wholly juiceless."

"Stop it, will you? We have to get him out of here."

"Where? Surely not to the Imperial. Ciano et al. would pounce."

"Out of the *country*, for God's sake. Max, for once in your life, will you do something for someone else?"

"I?"

"Yes, dammit."

"Whatever on earth for?"

"Because I ask you. Because he *has* to get out."

"That is not a terribly forceful reason."

"The hell with your damn trivializing. Do you still have a plane?"

"You do offend. We always have a plane."

Brady's pinhole camera that served as a mouth clicked off pictures. "Max, I have Badoglio's ear. I promise you: I will tell him that you shot down Vittorio Mussolini at Mai Chew. He never believed an Ethiopian could do it anyway, I am serious, Max."

"Now, that is too much. You know very well we were not at Mai Chew. Awful place."

"No, Max," Brady said, "I don't know."

"Oh dear, am I being ebony-mailed?"

"I don't give a damn what you call it. I'll go straight to Badoglio, I promise you."

"Which brings us full circle. What in heaven's name has the fallen Devil to do with you?"

"It's a personal matter; even *we* have personal matters. Look, Max, if you do this, you'll be a hero, at least in Toronto."

"Oh, the man is amusing. What of Bridgeport?"

"What a bastard you are, Max. All right, I think I could pull it off in New York. I can't promise, but I think so."

"We are listening."

"I give you my word I'll share the story with Knickerbocker and Matthews."

"Well now."

"Max, the bond of color."

"Heavens, not that."

"All right. Nobility, compassion, footsteps in the night, man to man, modesty, splendour, Ace to the rescue."

Folded arms, narrowed eyes. "Will you telegraph it to Winchell?"

"Word of honour."

"Yes or no?"

"Yes."

The manicured hand descended, tightly clamped the little

head. "Get me some cold water, a pailful of cold water and no nonsense about money, chop chop, quick, fast, hop it."

"Sure ting," beamed the head in the vise. "I be your fuckin Babe Ruthy good time cholly."

They hustled out of the house, The Ace on one side, Brady on the other, led by the boy, stepping out in great, curving strides. Smiling left and right to the small, gathering crowd. The man between The Ace and Brady walked draggingly for several steps, then sagged. His eyes were still closed as he shook his head.

"Don't be a pain in the ass, old man," said The Ace. He reached down for a better grip. Now Brady did, too, panting. The boy turned around and waved.

"Have . . . talk . . ." said the deadweight.

"Not now," said Brady. "Please, later." His mouth clicked off pictures of the curious passersby who now stopped to stare. "That's a good lad, just a wee bit further."

"No."

Brady looked imploringly at The Ace who said pleasantly, "Now, stop the shit, old friend, and move along."

The deadweight shook its head. "Must talk . . . she . . ."

"She does not talk, old chap," said The Ace.

"I . . . me . . ."

"You? Talk?"

"Yes . . . She . . ."

"Please speak correctly. Do you wish to speak to *her*?"

"Yes . . ."

"Oh Christ," said Brady.

"The lady," said The Ace, "has shown no desire to converse with you."

"Must . . ."

"I can't hold him," Brady said in despair.

"Well, let him sit in the mud." He let go and the huge man crashed down into a shallow puddle. He rolled over and The Ace yanked him to a sitting position. "There you are," smiled The Ace. "Now, about the lady. Surely she cannot understand you. In any case, I promise you another when we get out of this sinkhole."

The stubborn head swung slowly from side to side.

"Persistent chap," said The Ace.

"Do something, Max."

"I'm racking my brain, old chap."

The little boy glowed up to him: "You wanna fuckin ol lady?"

The Ace sighed at him. "Very well. But please hurry. Warner, you are bad news."

The boy disappeared into the house as Brady smiled at the curious faces around them. "Man very sick," he said, pointing. The faces smiled back. The man on the ground stared at the puddle of water. A hem of a *shamma,* dirty, ragged, grazed the puddle. Slowly, the man looked up. She glanced at him, then off into the trees. The Ace said, "Well, spit it out, old man, she waits with baited breath."

"No market," muttered the man.

"You do not wish her to play Wall Street, old chap?"

"Cannot . . ."

"Well not right now, my dear fellow."

"Slave musn't . . ."

"The slave market, Max," Brady said.

"Ah."

The boy said, "She like a fuckin market he say no she say go cut off your meat hey you wanna fuckin ol lady?"

"You, sir, are a little rat."

The boy smiled happily. "Black Deevill fuckin bum you beat him up he ain got some guts."

"I would not go *that* far, little hustler. The man has a few credentials."

"Damn right," said Brady.

"No . . . market," said the man, swinging his head.

"Tenacious fellow," said The Ace. "My dear woman, do you think you can tear yourself away from the marketplace?"

Terunesh turned and spoke hoarsely to the boy. He grinned. "Hey big shot Ace she say you a fuckin bum she don like no niggers don you talk to her she get fuckin friends stick a fuckin bullet in your mout dago friends you *capish*?"

"I dare say I do."

"Max," said Brady, "let's get a move on."

"And leave mother and child?"

"No . . . spinning . . . slave . . . no . . ."

"I hear you, old man. But she seems to be rather headstrong."

"Deevill fuckin bum you a fuckin man."

"Why thank you, my boy."

The woman ripped off several more sentences. The Ace raised his hand. "No. Spare me, I am deaf and dumb."

"Hey I give you fuckin ol lady."

"Thank you but no thank you. Well, Warner, this little man has a brilliant future, what's your view?"

"Max, please, I *beg* you . . ."

"Right. Here we go. Enough. We must be quit of this sadly erotic household. Contact."

He rubbed his soft hands together, squatted, grasped the heavily breathing man under his armpits, rose quickly and slung him over his shoulder. He stood erect for a moment and tossed a flash-smile at the surrounding faces that shrank back. Then he stepped forward.

"This is known as the fireman's carry, Warner. Please describe it with accuracy."

A FEATHERY INTERLUDE

LADIES AND GENTLEMEN, AND EVERYBODY ELSE WHO WANTS TO KNOW *what's happening in current events, step right up and cop a long, hard gander at the wide-awake fellow who is tall, dark and handsome and master of the good ship* Solomon II, *this fellow being a stunt man, a strut man, a wing man, a tail man and also a charter member of the caterpillar club, at this moment flying his very own Gypsy Moth, boned, honed and grooved to his own specifications and even carrying behind him his very own passenger just like he was Chamberlain and this fellow was Charley Levine, except this one does not look too good whereas Charley could look like a million when he wanted to, but whoever said anybody ever looked good alongside the rootin, tootin flyin fool of an Ace? And you don't hafta answer that question mainly because you can't.*

Now these two specimens are where they are after bidding bye bye blackbird to a pithy and plump phrasemaker of a newspaper man in the dawn's early bright and with much vim, vigor and vitality on the part of the man with the joystick, also a fair amount of high ethyl petrol, they have climbed up over the terrifically high mean elevation that represents the Shoa portion of Ethiopia and are in the process of winging their headline-catching way west and in due time as they chase the sun they pull into themselves, plus their aircraft, the sensational Soudan where no buffalo roam, but dervishes, Mahdis, jihads and Khalifas sure did back behind the veil of the year 1900, sometimes called the

175

turn of the century because it gave the whole world some turn, but that is another story and you might want to look it up in Van Loon. For the time being, we got to be concerned with the two flyguys winging across the White Nile which roars up to meet sister Blue at a famous old town called Khartoum, or the elephant's trunk, but that is also another story which you could pursue, along with exotic old Omdurman, by perusing the journal of another Charley, this one tagged Gordon, or the log book of Horatio Herb Kitchener of your country needs you fame, but none of which our heroes have time for, to say nothing of a hot-shot passion, for they are now cutting south and winging over two more historical blokes named Jack Speke and Dickie Burton, who, if you are hep to exploring jive you have met before; and sure enough there they are squaring off down there in another round of their endless imbroglio, which you could look into by consulting the folks at the Royal Geographic Society in London, but for the nonce the flying fools have time only for a hurry-up nod as with an extra shot of ethyl Sol II *roars its wind-biting way over the lip of the desert and plunges into the jungle skies of the Congo, still another one for the history books, in particular the brown-silver-spurting-lurking-spitting-meandering ribbon of the same name, also known as Boomlay Boomlay Boomlay Boom, a most appropriate location for our passenger to scan (except he's not in such great shape for scanning) for as everybody in or out of his right mind knows a Kongo man can fly, especially back to or over his own country and this chappie is no exception to the rule, is he? and you* especially *don't hafta answer that question.*

But one thing you hafta admit and that is this Charley Colored Levine sure knows how to look green around the gills and with his head rolling around like a tipsy pinball he sure ain't been doing but very little going downtown lately, in other words he is a mess, as down below the shadow of their Moth flees across the forest faster than any twittering colobus monkey, faster than any scarified whistling chameleon, faster even than the amazed little Pygmy who races it loping stride for stride and cries out in the roaring silence:

"Oh hurtling star on your way
*   to paradise*
do you have a heart within
*   your brightness?*
And does your heart, if you have one,
*   call out*
for the mother who awaits you?
*   Quiet*
in the brightness of waiting
*   mothers*
and frowning, sad, disapproving
*   fathers?"*

His twirling head sure rises and falls and rises again when he hears that one and it swells up near to bursting, it fills with the sounds of the jungle, it seeks out Marty and Osa Johnson but they are at the Loew's Victoria playing Congorilla, not to mention Clyde Beatty snaking his whip, parrying with his magic chair, so his telltale hands they beat out a Savoy-stomping drum-roll on the sides of the flying machine and if you didn't know better you'd swear the 369th Infantry was marching straight through the Congo Free State alongside Jim Europe's syncopated jazz band. A striped Gallant Fox clatters by down there, and you hafta wonder if he knows that Jim Dandy is around, but our pilot is too busy to think about the sport of kings, and now he heels over and they go down, down, down, in fact dive, dive, dive, right across the edge of the jungle, above a clearing, still down, skimming now, to a sliver of a runway alongside a one-zebra town called Stanleyville, in honor of the great stonebreaker, also called Bula Matari, and so the Solomon II rides to a shuddering, grinning stop.

He waves, looks around at his dozer, grasps gunn'ls, swings upward, scissors, clears cockpit, plants boot, steps down, leans against aircraft, lights cigarette with cupped match, surveys scene, nods at three chaps in short pants and adoring eyes, "Guard this machine with your lives and that man with your conscience," strides away to corrugated tin structure. Enters same, looks, drops into battered leather chair, crosses elegant boots, flicks spot off pointed toe, relaxes with his Old Gold, chats, explains, cajoles, congratulates, interjects, rises, crunches butt beneath elegant heel, strides out, across strip, followed by dozen cans of petrol on worshipful heads. Points at tank, supervises, pats thin, happy backs, waves a clearing hand, climbs, turns, salutes, turns, grasps, scissors in, flashes, bellows "Contact!" Flashes once more, nods at mellow roar, rolls forward, turns, rolls back, steps on the petrol, joyfully sticks, lifts up above reaching forest, waves farewell to cheering throng, spirals up, heads west. While his lolling cargo lolls on.

Little does the latter know, or care more or less, that he started out in this very forest—this Ituri—eras ago. Fact is, he is coughing up now, a thin, greenish drool that drips down on the Ituri forest, also the sides of Solomon II, *which the owner is not so crazy about, but whoever said you could compare a Devil with an Ace? and you can answer that question, whether you're so or not inclined.*

Speaking of inclines, the tough old Ace with a rock for a breadbasket now shoots up, up, up, finally to stall and hang, then with a fancy smirk dives, spins, brushes leafy arms, pulls out, glances at his white-eyed partner, gleams, then low and smooth and calm traces out Henry Stanley's old course of discovery and adventure as it snakes, crashes, dickers, bludgeons its (heroic) way through its darkness of horror. A bend here, a loop there, a hump north, a curving back, on and on toward the west and the spilling mouth. To presume on the good, sick doctor. Filling up with accolades, headlines, plus a few raspberries, then back to the pulling homeland to search out Emin Pasha, the wandering Jew, now west to east, to meet himself coming and going. Poor, hooked Henry.

UP HERE, HANK, PUSH THOSE FEVERISH EYES UP HERE!

This is the way to go, this is tomorrow, Hank, with this baby you can take all of the Boomlay Boom and hand it over to foxy old Leopold, so forget Emin Pasha, he is soft as a grape anyway, this up here is the real McCoy, screwing the soft Shebasky, producing a race of airmen who can easily put little Belgium over the top.

What's that, Hank?

AFRICA AIN'T BIG ENOUGH FOR THE BOTH OF US?

*So be it, go chase your looney bird, no hard feelings, but we
are rushing toward tomorrow, low over your stinking, winking
river, low over the cathedral forest, where we will make a little
magic. See that Bantu six-footer, Hank? See him freeze, caught
in our sensational moment? Now look. He bounds away, za-
roooom, a regular Jesse Owens, yelling to his ancestors, and what
is he saying, we will tell you what he is saying:*

> *"What is this that blots out the sun?*
> *Is it the angel of death*
>   *come*
> *to end the world?*
> *Or is it come to save us*
> *from all our sins?*
> *I don't care. I only know we*
> *will never forget the time you*
>   *hurtled through*
>   *our lives.*
> *We will tell of you*
>   *forever."*

*Us, we, ourselves, tomorrow. He snaps off a salute, pats the
lean flanks of his machine, pours it on, races his shadow to a
bend in the river, wins. He sees now the twin cities on each side
of the river, hears the evil old King who owns one of those
cities scream up to the penetrated sky: "WE CAN USE YOU,
MONSIEUR!" He winks at his joystick, we shall see what we
shall see; he banks, glides, sails over applauding branches, slides
neatly into the receiving chute, plunks down in Leopoldville.*

LEO

THE LOBBY OF THE HOTEL ALBERT. BLACK BOYS IN PALE BLUE
uniforms. Gliding, staring. Black noses snubbed against the great,
sparkling window. A circle of pen-poised men with red faces,
necks spilling over spotless collars. The target of the circle: an
elegant man in tailored uniform, legs comfortably crossed.
Johnny Walker Red. Beside him a large man, slouching, head
down, eyes barely open. Lights, action.

"You may ask me anything, Messieurs. If it does not violate a
confidence or a state secret, I shall do my best to respond with
sincerity and candor."

Pens swoop. Scratch. The surrounding noise level lowers; the
pale blue, black boys glide and serve and stare. The pens lift.

"Monsieur Josephson, can you tell us precisely why you have
come to the Belgian Congo?"

"Yes, I can tell you." The elegant man sips the Scotch, rolls
the glass briefly across his forehead. "We happen to be a rather
good friend of your King." A gracious pause for the pens. "He
has given us *carte noir,* as it were, to visit if we were in the
vicinity, in much the same way that his grandfather spread the
welcome mat for another American over a half century ago, as
I'm sure you will recall." An elegant sip, a weary but gracious
sigh. "We happen to live alongside a famous river in America
ourselves. We hereby cordially invite your monarch to drop in
sometime."

The pens descend, busily. Outside, on the wide boulevards

great white convertibles swish by. In neat tearooms Belgian wives, their hips overflowing thick, padded chairs, nibble at croissants, sip cafés filtres. Stanleypool, majestic, bottomless, layered with cans and sacks, broods on its fabulous history. The pens look up.

"But if I may say so, Monsieur, that was a business matter with Mr. Stanley."

"Well"—a camera wink—"you may draw your own conclusions. As the well-known Emin Pasha would say, 'business is business.'"

Ah. The slashing of T's, the stabbing of I's. The whistle of a tiny steamer. Two paddle wheels churning. Screaming parrots chiding the ship as it heads upriver.

"The gentleman beside you. What might his role be in your affairs?"

"I can only say that a friend of ours is, per se, a friend of the king's."

The pens, thick, solid, black, each rubber bladder thoroughly filled. Heineken, Amstel breaths cooling the hot words.

"Could you comment on why he is so silent?"

"Yes, I can. He was in the thick of the second battle of Tembien. We needn't tell you veterans of the great war of the effect on the mind of mortar, shell and machine-gun fire." He closes his eyes for the briefest instant. The elegant epaulettes tremble. He opens his eyes, glances at his companion, composes his features. From the "Belge," the native quarter, sounds of drums, phonograph records of American jazz, arguing voices. "We will speak for him if you don't mind. Needless to say, neither he nor we flew out of the country with personal rewards or viatica." He smiles and delicately pats a drooping shoulder. Murmurs in the fluorescent twilight, pens, craning necks. A bright, flushed face.

"Monsieur, did the Italians use mustard gas at Tembien as has been rumored?"

"Ah, as has been rumored." A faraway tug at the corners of the mouth. The words, calm, composed: "Let us merely say that we used our gas masks." A smile. "And it was not to frighten naughty children."

Indignation swirls across good Brussels bond. On the banks of

the Congo, bustling black porters. Men of every color selling
Belgian money to the visitors from Brazzaville. Other men, black
and white, stand and stare into the river.

"Monsieur Josephson, did the Ethiopians mutilate their
prisoners?"

Splendid stalks of papyrus sail down the river, wait for an
answer.

"We will be quite frank." The Ace spreads his wings, refolds
them, talons squeezing the glass of Scotch. "I have seen a castra-
tion knife in the kit of some of my colleagues who were fighting
for their homeland. However, we did not personally see its utili-
zation. Now"—a qualifying slash of a smile—"that does not mean
it was not used. You, of course, understand that I was occupied—
preoccupied—with the war in the air."

A young, eagerly flushed face. "Did you have success, sir? It
is rumored—"

"Again rumors; ah well, *c'est la guerre et aussi la conte de ma
vie.*" Thick nods, the papyrus smiling, the steamer approving,
the parrots understanding. "In point of fact, we accounted for
five enemy aircraft. No more, no less. I suppose that makes us
the first colored Ace of Aces, an achievement I do not point to
with egocentric pride, but merely point to."

The faces pressed against the window are blank. The boys in
their pale blue uniforms walk softly. Pens swoop, swirl. Droplets
of perspiration. Bellies, chests heaving. Heads up.

"Is it true, Monsieur, that Badoglio has set a price on your
head?"

A simple, modest shrug. "I'm afraid it is. On the other hand,
we would have been amply rewarded if we had trained his people in thin-atmosphere dogfighting. Naturally, we refused."

A boy in a pale blue uniform taps with his fingernail against
the window; the faces draw back. The boy saunters to the desk;
the faces return.

"What are your plans now, Monsieur?"

"As a professional courtesy we plan to meet with your governor general and apprise him of the military situation in the
Horn."

Beyond the faces, beyond Stanleypool, across the Congo, Brazzaville gazes enviously at the splendors of Leo.

"Is there yet a military situation, Monsieur?"

The weary head looks briefly to the east. "Would we tell your governor general any less than we would tell our President?"

Tinkling glasses, soft laughter from the bar. The boys in pale blue speaking quietly of arguing, resisting girls of the "Belge." Understanding smiles. The journalists grapple with the world situation.

"What would be the desired outcome of such a discussion, Monsieur?"

"As we all know," the patient man says, his face a study in forbearance, "Belgium is a land of freedom and democracy. Did you not stand up to the Hun in the great war? We can only say, gentlemen, that we are quite certain Belgium will make the correct response. Not, mind you, an eleemosynary response, but one that springs from the recognition that Ethiopia, in the larger sense, fights for Belgium."

Dining rooms, restaurants, cafes begin to fill.

"Do you speak then of a military gesture, Monsieur?"

"Oh, my goodness, we never speak for kings; we have our own troubles. However, we certainly offer our services in the same spirit that Mr. Stanley offered his to the king's grandfather. And to a far less mercenary degree, although, naturally, we do have our worldly needs. The monarch in question, who incidentally bore the same name as your incumbent ruler, was wise enough to accept Mr. Stanley's proposition, so to speak. We can all profit from a study of the past, *n'est-ce pas*?" The elegant man nods with finality, unfolds and stands, towering above the busy pens. He waits until the pens look up. Then he says, "I believe that this colony, King Leopold's dream, was once known as the Free State. Need we say more, gentlemen? And now I fear we must say *au revoir*, although not, I trust, farewell. My friend's lungs that were touched by some rumored yperite are laboring in your democratic air and he must rest. May I say that I wish all of you the greatest success in your extremely difficult endeavors. Finally, may I personally convey the best wishes of our President to your own sovereign and thank him for the courtesies he has extended to us. *Bonne nuit* and *bonne chance*."

At two o'clock in the morning a man in a white linen suit and heavy black shoes rides the *ascenseur* to the third floor of the hotel. His fingers tap against the mahogany paneling as he rises. He gets out, strides down the corridor, knocks quietly but for a long time. The door finally opens. Whispers, nods. He enters. Thirty minutes later he emerges and rides down in the *ascenseur*, fingers tapping against the mahogany. At four o'clock in the morning a lovely Gypsy Moth aeroplane springs into the Congo air, circles the governor general's mansion once, twice, three times, climbs steeply with a crackling roar, then speeds west and north for the Gulf of Guinea.

The lobby of the Hotel Albert. The black cashier in the pale blue uniform dozes against his cage. The black bell captain in the pale blue uniform cradles his head on his arms at his desk. A journalist, his chin disappearing into the folds of his neck, sleeps with his notebook on his lap. Metal urns filled with sand. Smothered cigarettes. A Brussels paper. Half empty bottle of Heineken. Half empty bottle of Johnny Walker Red.

Part Four

LAND OF LIBERTY

THEY FLEW ALONGSIDE THE GOLD COAST AND THEN THE IVORY Coast, the *Solomon II* dipping down to match land to chart, flirting with the waves, skipping back up to three hundred. When the pilot was ready, he feather-touched the joystick, curved his airplane inland and gently angled down onto a muddy airstrip that ran straight as a spear alongside a low spray of buildings.

He taxied to a soft stop and smiled from the cockpit at the three men in khaki shirts with "Frontier Force" banded on their arms, who trotted alongside the *Solomon* and finally stood at attention. The Ace swung one polished boot over the side, then the other, stood down on the wing.

"May we be of assistance, sir?" one of the men said.

"Is this Monrovia?"

"Yes sir."

"In Liberia?"

"Yes sir."

"Thank God. Gentlemen, I am Brigadier General Maximilian Josephson of the U.S. Army Air Corps. That is Major James Dandy. Please inform your President that we have arrived. Tell him also that we are thoroughly delighted to be here, and we are prepared to open talks immediately."

The red and white stripes of the flag sparkled brilliantly. The white star of liberty, as smooth and spotless as a shirt out of a Chinese laundry, flashed against the dark continent's field of

189

blue. The Ace seemed to be in deep thought, then suddenly smiled. The man in the swallow-tailed coat and the high white collar acknowledged the smile, but did not quite return it. "Your companion is being ministered to," he said in a deep, official voice. "Your mind may be at ease."

"Thank you, Mr. President. I am completely at ease where my friend is concerned, fully satisfied that he is in the best of hands." The swallow-tailed man acknowledged again. "May I say at the outset," The Ace continued, "that it is an indescribable thrill finally to be here, to breathe the air of freedom, to know at long last that you do in fact exist."

"Was there a doubt?"

"Oh, sir." The Ace leaned back and closed his eyes. He sighed. He opened his eyes. "I have thought these many years that perhaps, after all, you were but a young boy's dream—a Treasure Island, a Graustark, a Ruritania."

A solemn twinkle. "Mayhap they too exist."

"Well put, sir. You are a man after my own heart. In all sincerity I have not said that to many men."

"I am sure you are sincere."

"I say it very sincerely, Mr. President."

"Of course. In any case we *do* exist, though surely in many ways we have been a dream. The twain have lived side by each in our history. But for those requiring corpuscular proof, we are flesh, blood, sinew and unceasing worry."

"In all sincerity I am satisfied again, sir."

"Good. Good. Now to you, General. I confess that it has been *you* whom we feared did not exist. Naturally, we have modern communications here and we have been kept in constant thrall by your miraculous escape and your dedication to a sick friend. Truly, we all had given you up for lost. Even I had some doubts."

"I am a difficult man to lose, sir. When you've pulled through a number of scrapes, and I say this with all sincere modesty, you have a bit of confidence when the next scrape shows up."

"I must tell that to my cabinet."

A modest nod. "Still, I have to admit to a grave miscalculation after our narrow escape."

"Oh yes?"

"To my consternation, yes. After Ethiopia and its rigors, I wanted only to find the friendliest territory I could. In situations of extreme personal urgency, and this was assuredly one, I actually allow my aircraft to guide me. We are very much one of a piece, my *petit* friend and I, much as the Lone Eagle and his faithful *Spirit*. Well, it conveyed me to the Belgian Congo, in the sincere and innocent belief that I would find welcome and comfort there. My little friend, ergo I, was mistaken, much to our mutual consternation. We were asked to depart the premises, a request, I am sure, that emanated from Rome, via Brussels. With disillusion in our souls, we soared up above the erstwhile free state and cursed the brittleness in the backbones of men. Then my aircraft, which I fully intend to rechristen *Monrovia Dream,* spun about and pointed to the northwest. As it did, a great force seized me, an airy vector of such power that I had only to shift to automatic pilot and sit back and enjoy the sights and sounds of your admirable continent. Time and distance accomplished the remainder. And so, here we are. At last. To sum up succinctly, surely the love of liberty brought us here."

For the first time, a smile dabbed at the solid black face. The face, the dignity, the speech, Josephson decided, were in their old American solidity a revisiting of no less then Henry Clay, John Randolph, Tyler, Calhoun, all frozen in time, yet miraculously here. As if in verification, the smiling nineteenth-century statesman intoned, "I am pleased." The Ace inclined his head, the measured basso profundo lapping at his ears: "And I will in every way endeavor to succeed where the Belgian government has failed. I do not pass judgment on my fellow leaders, but to nurse the sick is the very least any of us can do."

"So true, sir."

"Now I have a question to put to you."

"Of course."

"It concerns your friend. My personal physician is quite nonplussed. Though admirably trained at Fisk and Harvard, he can find no bodily illness in your friend. In fact, the body is remarkably sound, even powerful. Yet, ill he is. Could you shed some light on the dilemma?"

"I believe I can, sir. You see, he suffers from a sickness of the blood, not an organic sickness, but the kind that flows from a sad heart. All of this stemming from the failure of the noble nations of the world—that is, the League—to save Ethiopia, the right, the simple thing to do. It is a sickness the strong experience when they see cowardice where they had presumed strength. I have known it myself in tight corners."

"I see." The glasses flashed in the moonlight that flooded the room. "Alas, I believe I might have saved him some of his agony, for this is too often the case. We here have had similar experiences with the strong, great nations. Recently the United Kingdom offered us to Germany if only she would return to the League."

"Monstrous!"

"The usual thing." The heavy shoulders flicked. "Your own country has not been a notable exception, if you will forgive my saying so."

"Ah"—a sigh—"you may always say such things to me if they are true. And in the Ethiopian matter, my government has not covered itself with glory. *That,* for my friend, was the *coup de grace.*"

"All becomes clear." The Henry Clay-ness rose. The presence was thick and square, as tall as The Ace. "Well then, you must be doubly weary." The rumbling voice grew brisk. "You and your companion will remain in the Executive Mansion tonight as guests of this poor nation. For the morrow and beyond, in fact as long as you wish, I have made arrangements which may be to your liking. A longtime friend of mine lives in a pleasant house in a pretty little town close to Monrovia. It is called White Plains, a name which may lessen the burden of being so far from home."

"But sir, in a very real sense I *am* home."

The glasses flashed and the smile was a polite napkin at each corner of the mouth. "We shall see."

"Of course. Please excuse my presumption . . ."

"Tut, you are excused."

"Thank you, sir. Sir, might I be so bold as to change the subject?"

"Of course."

"Might I raise a business matter with you?"

A raised hand.

"Ah, let us not sully this moment with mundane affairs. Let us only be grateful that you and your companion have been spared." An inclined head. Two inclined heads. Now the solemn face of Henry Clay. "To the guest room, then. My adjutant will escort you. In the morning, you will journey to the Plains of Whiteness in my personal car."

"You overwhelm me, Mr. President."

"Merely simple courtesy. Yet, for me, there is one final point before you rest . . ."

"Sir?"

"I would inquire, if I may . . ."

"You may ask me anything and everything."

"Then, I would inquire how it is that you have achieved such a high rank in the armed forces of your great country? I am far from expert in these matters, but to my knowledge, such as it is, no African-American has risen to the rank of general."

"Sir, may I point out that there are two hundred forty-six colonels in the state of Kentucky. They have not been commissioned by the United States Army, yet they are colonels."

"Ah yes, I believe I see what you mean." The eyes behind the thick lenses were large and bright. "As to colonels, sir, were you not one yourself when you left Ethiopia?"

"I was indeed. I promoted myself en route, in the complete certainty that my superiors, had they existed, would have approved such a step, were it in their power to do so."

"Just so. How simple when you explain it." The splendid solidity rose, stood beside the desk; he was planted there like an ebony tree, his hands locked beneath the swallow tails. "General, we must *surely* discuss business. But now, you are weary. The hour is late. Good night to you, then, and welcome to the dream that lives."

They broke their fast with Kellogg's corn flakes, ham and eggs and Liberian coffee. The sick man in bed was served on an ivory tray by a young man and woman padding in and out of his room on Liberian rubber. Down the hill from the Executive Mansion, Monrovia awoke, stretched, stirred. Smoke curled. Ships in the blue harbor moved slowly. Josephson ate silently, masticating with expert delicacy. The President drained his coffee and a young man darted forward and refilled his cup and turned to The Ace.

"Thank you, no; I always cease just short of complete satiation." The young man stepped back into the wall. "It is a cardinal rule," Josephson added.

"I am in mind of worse rules," said the President. A nod, and the magnificent china disappeared noiselessly. "Would you care for a cigar, General? Dutch? Havana?"

"I seldom partake of tobacco, but if I did," said The Ace, "I would prefer a Liberian cigarette."

"As would I. Alas, at present I cannot help you there."

Josephson looked out at early-morning Monrovia and sighed. Then he turned back and said, "If I may presume, sir, Liberia really ought to stamp its presence on the world market. Unlike present company, the world does not nourish itself with the stuff of dreams."

"A pity for the world, General."

"No doubt, none at all. Still, the world is out there. It does surround you."

Henry Clay nodded, mildly observed, "We do a bit with rubber."

"Do you, sir?"

"A bit."

"Rubber . . ."

"Yes, General."

"Is it *your* rubber, sir?"

"It *does* grow here."

"Is it *yours*, sir?"

"Well, it does not belong to the League. Not yet."

"Does it belong to Mr. Firestone?"

"Well, well."

"I am merely asking, Mr. President."

"What do you think, General?"

"I have heard, sir, that in large part, it does appear in that gentleman's inventory charts."

"Let us assume that there is some veracity to that rumor."

"Thank you, sir."

"You are welcome. Assuming that, General, what then?"

"Bully for Mr. Firestone."

"Bully, General."

"Sir?"

"General?"

"Do you know Mr. Goodyear?"

"I have never had the pleasure, General."

"Mr. Goodrich?"

"Nor him."

"Mr. Kelly? Mr. Springfield?"

"Alas, no."

"Pity."

"Pity."

"Splendid gentlemen."

"I am sure. One does one's best in meeting new people. We are a small nation."

"But you are a big man."

"Thank you, General."

"Mr. President?"

"General?"

"It would seem, and I am surmising here, a rather dull existence for Mr. Firestone in Liberia."

"Do you really think so?"

"I fear that might really be the case."

"We have a cinema, although I have never been."

"Of course not. Nor would Mr. Firestone. He is, and again I am presuming, a decent chap?"

"Most decent."

"You would like to see him happy?"

"I would like to see all decent chaps happy."

"Sir, he is a businessman."

"I can attest to that."

"If I may, sir, persons of that persuasion have a certain type of mentality."

"I have observed that on occasion."

"Thank you, sir. If I may press on, that kind of person, with that type of mentality, absorbs his pleasure, his excitement, his *happiness*, in his work."

"I think I can understand that."

"It is so good to talk to you, Mr. President. Well then, his work is his qui-viveness, as it were."

"Yes, General?"

"Sir, this work, I fear, is dull."

"Dull?"

"Dull."

"Ah."

"Sir, to return to Mr. Firestone's inventory charts, might I further assume that a condition of monopoly exists here?"

"Let us, for the sake of discussion, grant your assumption."

"A monopoly, sir, though profitable, is a dull thing."

"You think so?"

"I am convinced of that, Mr. President. I have seen many a decent monopolist in my country become bored to tears."

"Mr. Firestone is certainly decent. And I thought, when we met, quite happy. But one never knows."

"Exactly, sir."

"Would you have some inkling of how I might help him?"

"I have."

"Please, General."

"Sir, have you ever heard of the Ace-Liberio Interlocking Gutta Percha Association, Incorporated?"

"I cannot say that I have."

"Might I introduce you to this group, sir?"

"I welcome the opportunity to meet any or all groups."

"I had a feeling you would say that, sir."

"We are a democracy, General, and that is a democratic policy. Do I perceive that you have some connection with this group?"

"As usual, you are perceptive and correct. I am, or will be, the chairman of this combine, said combine to include the gentlemen previously mentioned, whom you do not as yet know, plus U. S. Rubber and General Tire."

"Pray continue."

"In this capacity as chairman and founder of Ace-Liberio, I would be the recipient of the first ten percent of all net profits.

Liberia and Gutta Percha to be equal recipients of the remaining ninety percent. Unless I have been misinformed, this would generously exceed your arrangement with Mr. Firestone."

"Are you speaking of competition, General?"

"How perceptive you are, sir. Competition, free market, call it what you will. The point is that my group—our group—would at long last impart some happiness into the dull existence of Mr. Firestone."

"Well, at last. Mr. Firestone and his happiness."

"At last, sir."

"I would not see any man unhappy."

"I was absolutely certain of that."

"What else are you certain of, General?"

"I can only say that when decent but bored monopolists become happy, their high spirits know no bounds. In his new and bubbly state of mind he could well offer you a more interesting working arrangement."

"Thereby enlarging *my* happiness."

"We are nothing if we cannot help those we admire."

"I must tell that to my cabinet. Of course, you do know the gentlemen to whom you referred?"

"They will be known."

"Foolish question. I withdraw it. Let me ask another, which will probably also turn out foolish; yet, I would ask it."

"Anything, sir, anything, foolish or no."

"Gutta Percha, General. Is not that Malaysian rubber?"

"An excellent question, sir, one that does you credit, and tells me that you know your rubber. You see, sir, this will only make the game more enjoyable for Mr. Firestone. Throw him off the scent. By the time he has gotten back from the Malay Peninsula and returned to the track, he will be so ecstatic that we could call the group Little Boy Blue and it would not matter."

"You certainly know the pleasures of the world of commerce."

"I know people, sir, and these are only people. Taking their bit of fun where they find it."

"Quite, quite. I wonder, General . . ."

"Sir?"

"Are you absolutely committed to the title of this combine?"

"I am committed to listening to you, sir."

"You are kind, General. What would you think of a slight rearrangement so that Gutta Percha would be preceded by *Liberio*-Ace?"

"I would think it utterly discussable, Mr. President."

Birds twittered, voices chattered, the sun burned. The square, black man rose. A huge, thick hand reached across the table and a beautifully manicured one grasped it. Three quick, strong pumps. The flag sparkled.

SUBURB

THEY DROVE PAST A PYGMY HIPPO WHICH STOOD AT THE SIDE OF the road and stared, then waggled into the forest past a black mamba, curled and limp and everlastingly still, past tiny plots of corn, larger plots of sugar cane and rubber and palm. The road of powdered laterite rushed by and they skittered over potholes and rotting timber. Cleveland's head bounced off his chest, it flopped from side to side as if his neck were made of rubber. The Ace twisted this way and that, gazing at the flying-by forest, the sugar cane, the rubber trees.

The president's adjutant sat tall, stiff, correct and very much aware of his official responsibility. Bouncing, swaying, correct, they flew toward White Plains.

A tapper materialized, but he ignored them. His life, his future, his entirety focused on his tree and his latex and his daily quota. They squealed around a hairpin curve, twisted hard away from another mamba, this one alive, leaving it swaying and dazed as the Hudson darted down the red straightaway. More turns, protesting Firestones, more straightaways. Then a final, showy burst, a screech of brakes and the car crunching to a rocking halt, flinging up clouds of clayey dust. The adjutant coughed politely.

"This is your destination, gentlemen."

A huge, two-storied house with bug-eyed, green shutters loomed above them in the clearing. The porch, sagging prominently with age, was fronted by four columns that supported a cupola that stared down the road. All of it, except the shutters, shone with a gray glitter in the morning sun.

199

"Aluminium?" asked The Ace with technically squinting eyes.

"The finest zinc obtainable, sir, covering the finest Liberian woods."

"Zinc. Of course. Most impressive."

The adjutant stepped stiffly out of the car and opened the back door, stood to one side. The Ace climbed out, reached in and said, "Last stop, old boy." He grasped Cleveland's arm and slowly drew him out. Cleveland stood quietly beside the car, one hand on the door, one hand on The Ace's arm. He looked down at the running board. The adjutant walked to the steps of the zinc-covered house where a man in morning coat and top hat stood beside a woman who was covered from neck to ankle with a black dress. The adjutant and the man clasped hands, then, as they drew their palms away, snapped their middle fingers. The adjutant then turned to the woman and bowed with his head. She said, with a crinkly smile, "You are a rogue, only deigning to visit us on state occasions."

"My days are one long round of responsibilities."

"Still, you are a rogue."

He bowed again with his head. "May I present General Maximilian Josephson and Major James Dandy. General, Major, I am pleased to present to you Dr. Abraham Simon and Mrs. Abigail Simon. He stepped aside stiffly. The Ace shook hands with the Simons, American style. Dr. Simon hesitated, then patted Cleveland tenderly on the shoulder. Mrs. Simon nodded encouragingly. Cleveland lifted his head, dropped it quickly and stared at the bed of white quartz beneath his feet. The Ace smiled and said, "He'll be fine."

"With guidance from above," said Mrs. Simon, "there is absolutely no doubt. General, you are most welcome, as is your poor friend." She turned. "Ruth, Joshua!" A small, thin black girl in an orange print dress and a sliver of a young black man stepped out of the dark of the doorway between the columns and walked down the steps to within several paces of the group.

Mrs. Simon said, "These two rascals are our foster niece and nephew from up-country. They will take proper care of you." Her voice deepened. "Now, you two convey our guests to their chambers. Then return for their belongings. Look smart and do not dally, for I will know it." She smiled at The Ace. "General, you and your companion must rest after your journey. While you do so, this villain will join us for a beverage." A bow. "General," she continued, "if this pair do not perform their duties well, please inform me. Abraham?"

The man in the morning coat snapped to and said with a high, clear voice, "If you pay heed to the little things, the big things will take care of themselves." The young man was a black carving, the small girl hung her head. Dr. Simon cleared his throat. "On behalf of the citizens of White Plains and environs, we salute you, we greet you, and we bestow on you our admiration. Sirs, we doff our hats to you." He doffed his hat.

DANDY DRIFTING

THE ROYAL COBRA SLITHERED UP THE STEPS FROM THE MAIN FLOOR and made his way into the first guest room, leaned against the wall behind the mahogany chiffonier and breathed hard for he had just been into it with the mongoose, and he looked as he leaned into the circular eyes of the man half-sitting up in the bed. The man looked back, yet he did not look back; he seemed rather to be looking at the wall even though his eyes were on the cobra. The cobra, too tired to worry about that peculiarity, rested, pulled his eyes away from the man and looked at other things in the room. The only things of interest after a while were the other two men. Since he spent a good amount of time in the house, he recognized the man standing beside the bed. He was Dr. Abraham Simon, who wasn't a bad fellow, in fact tended to live and let live, and when he came across the cobra clucked at him in a friendly way. The other man, standing a few feet away from the bed and Dr. Simon, was completely different from anyone he had seen in White Plains. He was very tall and he was dressed in clearly splendid clothes, for they took one's eye completely away from Dr. Simon. He also smelled different from anyone in White Plains, man or woman. Perched on a branch of a palm tree close to the open window was the colobus monkey. The two men were looking at the half-sitting, half-lying man.

Simon: He does seem somewhat aware of his surroundings.

Splendid man: Without question. He is a very clever fellow. Too much in himself, though.

Simon: Africa does that on occasion.

Splendid man: I have heard only to the white man.

Simon: A canard. A misperception. It can capture any man with a mind. (Steps closer.) Tis odd.

Splendid man: Oh, he is very odd.

Simon: That's as may be. The oddity I was observing is that he is the expectorating image of a fellow I knew as a young bucko in the Congo.

Splendid man: The Congo?

Simon: (smiling cagily, wistfully) Oh my, yes. Not all of us hail from your sainted nation. My better half and I both hail from the Congo. I must also plead guilty to being a bit of a hades raiser when the cotton atop this pudding head was black as coal. (Sets glasses far down on nose.) Oh my, yes.

Splendid man: Yes, what?

Simon: It is he.

Splendid man: He who?

Simon: Bless my soul.

Splendid man: WHO?

Simon: Mirambo. Bless my soul.

Splendid man: Mirambo?

Simon: (peering) To a Tee. The nose, the chin, even the tight-fitting ears. Even so.

Splendid man: And who is Mirambo?

Simon: Oh, you wouldn't ask that back in the Congo. Oh my, no.

Splendid man: (Sighing.) I am asking it now, Doctor.

Simon: Suppose I told you that he was feared, loved and hated for hundreds of miles around? Suppose I told you he was a great black prince of a fellow? Suppose I told you he was a devil, too; what would you say to all that, eh?

Splendid man: I'd say he was quite the lad.

Simon: Suppose I told you he was up to those tight ears in the slave trade, what then?

Splendid man: I would have to believe you, wouldn't I?

Simon: Oh, you wouldn't have to. But if you had any sense, you would.

Splendid man: I have complete faith in your veracity, Doctor.

Simon: And well you might, for wasn't I there? Didn't I see the ruffian swagger through the land? See him with Tippu Tip, the Arab slaver, who was thick as thieves with Henry Stanley?

Splendid man: A slaver?

Simon: Who sir, Mr. Stanley?

Splendid man: Mirambo.

Simon: Of course. Worked cheek by jowl with Tip. Had a ticking eye, did Tip; tick, tick, tick, that's why they called him Tippu Tip; but don't mention it in his presence, dear me, no.

Splendid man: I won't, sir.

Simon: Split you in half like a goat for supper. Tick, tick, tick. Oh my, no. Lovely teeth, though. Smooth as glass, white as a full moon.

Splendid man: And Mirambo was his partner . . .

Simon: Yes, oh yes. Hated most Arabs, but got on famously with Tip. Very big chap, Mirambo. Twenty-five wives, made them all happy. The Napoleon of Africa. (Stares at man in bed.)

Splendid man: He could fight then?

Simon: Eh?

Splendid man: Mirambo, sir. He was a fighter?

Simon: (Looking out the window.) Oh, you could say that. But don't abide by me. Talk to his Ruga-Ruga. Big chaps. With red cloaks and a feather headdress. Talk to them, if you're not too scared. Ran the show from Victoria to Tanganyika. Go on, talk to them. If you stop running, they'll tell you about Mirambo, the fighter. Got on famously with Tip. The one Arab he could stomach. Twixt the twain, they ran all the white and black ivory you could want. (Peers down.) And there he is, big as life.

Splendid man: Well, my friend has been called many things in his time—

Simon: Who, pray, has called him the Napoleon of Africa?

Splendid man: No one but you, sir.

Simon: Very well, then. (Reaches down, gently touches ear of man in bed.) Always wondered how it was they lay so flat. Thought of glue, but no glue there. (Turns, walks slowly out. Splendid man winks at man in bed; turns, follows. Only sound in room is man breathing. Joshua and Ruth walk into room.)

Joshua: The slaver speaks of slaving. Be careful, girl, or Prince

Napoleon will sell you down the river. (Ruth holds hand to mouth, steps behind Joshua, who shakes head.)

Joshua: Come on, you can look in from time to time, but I've got work to do, and the overseers will be checking up. (He turns, exits. She hesitates, hurries after. Room, aside from breathing man, is quiet. He stares at, through wall.)

"So," said the colobus monkey, hopping onto the window ledge, "there lies the famous, the infamous Mirambo."

"No, no," said the royal cobra, sticking his head out from behind the chiffonier and flaring his sheath, "he merely *resembles* Mirambo."

"I prefer to consider that he is."

"That," said the cobra, gliding up to the bed and looking deep into the man's round eyes, "is impossible."

"Well," replied the monkey, with a flip of petulance, "it is impossible that we are talking together, yet here we are doing so."

The royal cobra waved its diamond head and glittered its eyes and the monkey knew it was in for an argument. "Oh, no," said the cobra, "that is a very poor analogy. You see, we are engaged in a form of animism, one of the religions of this country, so it is perfectly, even reasonably possible. After the Catholics and Protestants, we rank number three. Consult any student of these things."

"I refuse to get into it with you," said the monkey, hopping around on the ledge. "You are impossible after the mongoose." He scratched his head till it hurt, then he jumped down from the ledge and skipped to the bed. "In any case, Mirambo or not, this fellow here thinks he is quite another person."

"Another person from whom?"

"From the one lying there."

"And who, oh clairvoyant one, might that be?"

"A little boy named Cicero."

"And how would you know that?"

The monkey spun so fast his tail blurred. "Isn't he from the Congo? Am I not from the Congo? Don't I have family there? Don't we keep in touch?"

"Hmmm, I suppose so."

"You suppose so? I refuse to argue."

"Don't be so touchy. Heavens, I was only commenting."

"Well, be careful how you comment. Shall I continue?"

"Heavens, yes. So touchy . . ."

"All right. I happen to know that this great, strapping fellow is little Cicero. See there, he smiles. For Cicero is doing things."

Cicero was indeed doing things. In fact, he was flying. As a Congo child, naturally, he certainly could fly. He was flying across the ocean, a Spirit, a Gypsy Moth, a Winnie Mae. From the plains of South Carolina, he was flying to the country that surrounded London, and since he was good in geography, he knew this had to be England. He landed on top of a great cathedral, sighted, took off. He hit all the tops of all the great cathedrals around London, sighted off the last one, revved up and took off for the big city. He landed on top of a tower that was filled with grinning heads. He smiled back, made himself invisible, as a Congo person could, then ran downstairs past the guards, who were eating beef and guzzling gin. He kept on running through the streets of London town until he came to a great palace. Still filtering air, he hurried up the steps of the great palace, past the stiff, unseeing guards, and down the hall, through an open door that led into a neat little bedchamber. A few ladies were waiting there, but to these he paid no heed. He had eyes only for the Queen, who was sitting above the waiting ladies and staring at a globe that was painted practically all red. She looked very moody. Feeling very sorry for the moody Queen, he walked up the three carpeted steps and tapped her on her royal hoop. She turned slowly. Since she was a queen, she could see the invisible Cicero, and he certainly could see her. He whistled like a polite chameleon, for he was gazing into the royal face of Queen Victoria. She also gazed and as she did said *"Oh,"* for he was a comely little fellow. A strange thing then happened, strange, that is, if you weren't from the Congo. Right after Victoria said *oh* her face began to shift itself around as if it were clay, and Cicero was sick in bed and playing and pushing the clay features this way and that. Then her whole body, hoops and all, became this clay, this rubbery type of clay, and it, too, started to shift and rearrange itself. The clay Victoria was busy all over and then, just as she was going like sixty, she stopped. The staring (but polite) Cicero was not seeing V. R. at all, but was looking straight at Gashouse Lil. ("One of the most famous managers of houses of ill repute in all New York, if not the world," explained the colobus monkey, who also had relatives in Central Park; the royal cobra nodded his impatient head.)

"And wada*you* want?" Gashouse Lil out of Victoria asked, adding, "as if I didn't know."

"A number," said Cicero.

"Ain't you kinda young?"

"Yes, but I still want it."

Lil smiled. "Well, it's never too early to start. Blonde, brunette, redhead, light, dark or in between?"

"Not that kind of number," said Cicero as the monkey and cobra exchanged glances. Lil winked, pulled an opium pipe off the shelf and lit up. She took a few puffs. "Something special, eh?"

Cicero looked with a frown at her relaxing face. "I didn't know you kicked the gong," he said.

"There's a lot you don't know, sonny boy, but I'm willing to learn you." She leaned back, inhaled noisily, pushed the smoke out like she was blowing bubbles. "How about some Indian meat, junior? *East* Indian."

"No, thank you."

"Esquimaux?"

"No," he said. "I don't want any of that. I want a *real* number."

She shrugged her ample shoulders. "Mick?"

"No, no, please." He sighed, for the smoke was getting to him. "A real number. A *perfect* number."

"Listen, buster," she said coldly, "I *never* have nothin to do with children."

He paced about the throne, stopped in front of the inhaler. "I am talking about a winning number," he said, spacing out his words. "An Arabic number."

"Cheese an Crax," she said, "kids are shot to hell today. You don't want my place. Go over to Crazy Moe's."

"*Integers*," he yelled. "One, two, three."

". . . You mean like money?"

"*Yes.*"

"Whyn't you say that?"

"I said it. I said I wanted the perfect number."

Another ample shrug. Then she rapped on a real gong. In strode a man Cicero instantly recognized as Sir Henry Armitage. They regarded each other. (Obviously, he was visible to Lil's friends.) As they did, Sir Henry pulled a hand over his face, like Edgar Kennedy wiping off a smile. When his hand had reached his serious chin, Sir Henry had been wiped clean. Cicero was looking into the wiseguy face of the well-known Abadaba. ("Coney Island's pari-mutuel king," said the monkey. "He fixes all the numbers, and I *do* mean fix." This time, the cobra was an enlightened nod.)

"What's on yer mind?" said Abadaba.

"The kid wants a number, a perfect number," said Gashouse Lil.

"Who don't?" Abadaba said. He made a circuit of the room, meanwhile stealing little glances at Cicero. When he came to a halt in front of the throne, he said to the boy, "You don't look like a bad kid."

"I try to be good."

" 'at's what I like to hear. Listen, kiddo, I wanna get it straight, right off the bat. I ain't givin you no perfect number; you think Abs is cuttin his own throat? Never. Tell you what I'll do, though. I'm startin a new racket, it's like crossword puzzles. It's called the perfect letter, and you're in on the ground floor. How'd you like to run some letters for me?"

"No, thank you."

Abadaba snorted with his eyebrows. "Up thine. Call me when you're ready to deal. Seeya Lil." Out he breezed, whistling "Barney Google." The waiting ladies conversed in soft tones; Lil seemed deep in thought. Finally she said, "Sit tight, poopsie, you're aggressive like I was, you got getupandgo." She rapped twice on the gong with her pipe. In walked two well-dressed gentlemen who were clearly William Gladstone and Benjamin Disraeli. Naturally, they were arguing. However, as soon as they saw Gashouse Lil, they stopped arguing. They about-faced with a neat little two-step. When they had two-stepped back, Gladstone was Mad Dog Coll, Dizzy was Gurrah Shapiro.

"The kid has a question," Lil said. "I want you to help him out. Shoot, junior."

"I am looking for the perfect number," said Cicero bravely.

"See Waxey, said Gurrah."

"Waxey?"

"Yeah, Waxey Gordon. The Khartoum character."

"That nut?" burst out Dog Gladstone. "He don't know his ass from a hole in the ground."

"You do, I suppose?" said Gurrah.

"You know it, babe."

"Sez who?"

"Sez me."

"Oh yeah?"

"Oh yeah."

Lil hit the gong and yelled, "All right, all right." Cicero covered his ears. As if he were blessedly deaf, he saw their mouths flapping, their teeth gnashing, heard nothing. Turning round and round, he closed his eyes and lifted off. When he opened his eyes below the fog, treading air, Gurrah and Dog were still swinging at each other.

"What now?" said the cobra.

"Don't be so nervous," said the monkey. "He's only resting for a while. That was a very taxing interlude. But don't go 'way. This boy is as solid as Finland."

He hung over London for the remainder of the afternoon. Then, he said to himself this was getting him nowhere fast, tapped his solar plexus and zoomed up over the fog and east until he reached the Channel. Without hesitating, he left the coast and powered through the choppy ozone until he reached some more land. He cut south and headed straight for a big city in a brave little country. When he reached Brussels, he buzzed

around until he found the grandest building in town. He landed
on the roof of the palace, stepped carefully across the tar paper
and down the first staircase he came to. When he saw an open
door and a man bending over a desk and writing, he changed
himself into a doughboy, entered and asked where he might find
the king.

"Par là," the old gent said, saluting. He saluted back and
walked down the hall and into a throne room that was crowded
with groveling people. Tightly putteed, he strode through the
grovelers and approached the shrewd-looking fellow on the
throne, who was juggling two balls, one of rubber, one of ivory.
He walked up to King Leopold I and without a moment's hesitation said, "Your Highness, I'd like for you to help me."

The king paused in midair, grabbed the balls and squeezed.
Immediately, his face began to writhe like a dozen lady wrestlers
who had bathed in olive oil. After several minutes of this facial
carrying on, he suddenly came to rest above the neck and Cicero
was gazing into the mug of Charley Lucky, right up to the thin
right eye.

"Whatwuzat?" smiled Lucky Leopold.

"I need your help."

Lucky smiled through the slit of his right eye.

"You came to the right party," he said. "If I can't square it,
who can?"

"It's not that."

"Whatever it is, anything; just spit it out."

"All right, I want the perfect number."

"I can get you some action at Gashouse Lil's."

"I've been there; I don't want her action."

"A ritzy kid, huh? How about Jennie the Factory?"

"Aw, not that. I mean a *real* perfect number."

"Cokie Flo got some very wild stuff."

"No . . ."

"You're a funny little guy, you know?"

"I don't agree. I'm just looking for—"

"I know, I heard you. You wanna book for me? Polly A needs
a booker. You'll get 'em fresh off the train; it's the chance of
a lifetime."

"No"—sigh—"thanks."

"How about some shylockin? I'm openin up in Queens. Lots of fresh air."

"No, I'm—"

"Please, not again." His eye was very thin, his legs short. "You're really hooked on numbers, hah?"

"Yes."

"Okay, I'll give you a lead. For numbers, you gotta see the Dutchman. He goes to his church, I go to mine."

"Where's his church?"

"What? Oh, a wise little ass. But I like your style, so I'll tell you; the Dutchman'll shit a brick."

"Yessir?"

"He's in the goddam Congo, and if I know Dutch, which I do—it's the secret of my success—he's sugarin every goddam chief in the territory. Scram now, I'm expectin a very important call from Sicily."

So he scrammed. High above the clouds of Belgium, while King Lucky cozied up to the mouthpiece of a telephone, he took a powder, swallowed hard, and flew out over the North Sea. As powerfully as Johnny Weismuller, he beat a tattoo through the resisting air and frothed across the Atlantic. As dawn broke, he saw below the darkly mysterious continent. He dropped down several layers and examined the tight-packed forest, heard the birds and animals and the clank of a hundred machetes. He dove through the trees, braked and landed gently on the spongy earth alongside a man in a pith helmet and mustache who was leading an enormously long column of men (and machetes) alongside a surging river and bawling out orders like he was selling tobacco.

"*Bula Matari,* sir?" Cicero said loudly.

The man stopped yelling, cursed because he could not see well in the darkness, turned, looked about him.

"Down here," said Cicero.

Henry Morton Stanley, for that is who he clearly was, looked down and saw a small boy in a loincloth. "Odd, most odd," he said, and pushed back his pith helmet. At once, the pith helmet, the neat khaki clothing faded away as if they have been made of cheesecloth and it was a windy day. Along with the clothing went the face, the form, the persona of Mr. Stanley. In their place was no hat, a thirty-five dollar gray pinstripe from Crawford and a surly, nondescript fellow.

"What did you call me?" he said.

"*Bula Matari.* Stone Breaker."

"You better not mean ballbreaker, kid."

"Oh no."

"Okay then. Talk American."

"Mr. Schultz?"

"Say that again?"

"Mr. Dutch Schultz?"

The surly, nondescript man looked around, then wagged his head intensely. "Ain't nobody here with that handle," he rasped.

"But I thought—"

"Don't. Yull get all tired out. The name is Flegenheimer. Arthur Flegenheimer, not Dutch blank."

"But I thought—"

"You got wax in yer ears, kid? Thinkin is a man's game. How are you in twenty questions?"

"Fair."

"Okay, I'll give ya question number one oney: Do you believe 'Flegenheimer' is too big for a newspaper headline?"

"Not for the *Sun* or *Telegram.* Maybe for the *News* or *Mirror,* but they could always shorten it to 'Flag.' "

"Hey, yer awright, kid. Arthur Flag . . ."

"Or even Art Flag."

"Yeah, yeah, Art Flag, sureashell beats 'at other name you better not mention."

"Thank you, Dutch, er, Art."

"Okay. Okay. Art Henry Stanley Flag. Don't you fergit it. Let's hear it."

"Art Henry Stanley Flag. And the hell with the headline writers."

"Okay then. But I ain't got no money."

"I don't want money, Mr. Flag."

"I don't need no runner, controller or wheelman. Anything else, go see Lucky."

"He told me to talk to you."

"Sure." He swatted at a tsetse fly. "When it's a tough one, send em to Art Flag. Okay, what's your grift?"

"I'd like to obtain the perfect number."

"Oh shit, see Abadaba."

"I did. He didn't tell me a thing worth knowing."

"Oh Jesus," Art Flag said, "me, always me. I been a good son and a good provider, but I always get the business. They wanna find a nutty doctor who don't wanna be found, send for Art Flag. You wanna locate a crazy Jew who loves it back in the bush, get Art F. and sit back an fiddle your diddle. You know what I am, kid?"

"The numbers king?"

"Lower yer voice, kid, an knock off that goddam language. What I am is a patsy; that's what I am."

"Yes sir."

"Me an Waxey, doin all their goddam dirty work, and where do we get it?"

"Where, sir?"

"In the end, that's where."

"I'm sorry, Mr. Flag."

"Yeah, I bet. All right, what's yer beef?"

"The perfect number, Mr. Flag."

"Oh yeah. Jesus, you an two million others. Hey, Tip."

A swarthy gentleman dressed in a white burnoose and carrying the flag of Zanzibar in his left hand trotted up to them. Both eyes were blinking like the bed of the Pennsylvania Railroad was in them. It was Tippu Tip. But after a hundred fast blinks, resplendent in a Palm Beach suit, it was really Sol Winograd.

"Yes, Arthur?" Sol said.

"This kid wants the perfect number."

Tip Winograd blinked like an Eastman Kodak shutter that had gone into business for itself. "That's rich," he said.

"Don't wise off," said Arthur. "He ain't a bad kid. Can you help him out?"

The eyelids fanned. "Hey, Mirambo!" Sol Tip bellowed.

A giant of a man, carved out of black stone walked over. If Cicero didn't know better, he would have sworn it was Hollis Cleveland.

"Cut out the raidin for a little," Tip said, "and see if you can help this kid. Arthur give me the green light."

"Does he want to be bought or sold?" The voice was softly powerful.

"Neither," Cicero interjected. "I would like . . . Well I want . . . I'm looking for the perfect number."

The gigantic black man folded bulging arms and poured waves of laughter, deep, rich and powerful laughter, onto the small head that was cocked to one side. "And . . ." gasped the giant, "what . . . do you . . . want . . . with . . . that . . . ?" and this time he doubled over and laughed all over the spongy ground.

Cicero said quietly: "I'd give the perfect number to my ahnt so she could get better."

John Henry Mirambo Cleveland stopped the laughter as if he had sliced it off with his great machete. So did Sol Tip and Art Henry Stanley Flag. There followed a deep African silence, which is deeper than any other silence. Then the enormous black man said in a voice that was almost a whisper, "I'm sorry, son. I'd like to help you, but it's a little out of my line. Have you tried Cokie Flo?"

Something clicked in Cicero's head. "You mean in Addis in Ethiopia?"

"Yes."

"I've tried her. She can't help me."

The black giant turned to Art Flag.

"How about that crazy Jew you're looking for?"

"Bugs? He don't know the day of the week."

"I'm sorry, son. I don't think I can do anything for you. If you'd like to be sold to a decent American, I could arrange it."

"No, thank you; I'll just keep on looking."

The great shoulders, as wide as the Hotel Theresa's main entrance, hitched up, then drooped; Mirambo Cleveland walked away, studying the ground. Cicero looked up at Sol Tip, who was going with his eyes, and at Art Flag. The two of them reached down and grasped Cicero under the elbows. He stiffened, felt himself being whirled through the air, then felt himself being gently set down on a camp stool beside the pounding river. There he sat while the tremendous column of men filed past, delicately hefting their huge bundles on top of their heads. Arthur shouting, cracking a long bullwhip. Sol blinking as men kept running up and slapping money into his outstretched hand.

Thus it went for the remainder of the dark afternoon: the men struggling, Arthur shouting, Sol blinking. Until another scrim of darkness told him that night was falling, and the men had all filed past, and Arthur and Sol had caught a dayliner to sail upriver and regain command of the column; and he was alone, but not quite alone. Wiping his eyes, Cicero noticed that, sitting near him beside the track, with a lion, elephant and leopard cavorting in a little circle about him, was an old gentleman with a leonine head, elephantine skin and a sprinkling of sunspots on his face. The old gentleman, who seemed a bit careworn and creased, albeit optimistic, was writing in a lined notebook. From time to time he would pause, look up at the treetops and cross himself, then return to his work. Cicero at once recognized that face, form and careworn but optimistic saintliness; but even in the moment of recognition, there was a flashing superimposition of another man upon the first, then a melding of the two, and finally a splendid and logical integration. He stepped right up.

"Longy Zwillman, I presume?"

The new, yet old, man looked up from his notebook.

"Yeah? So?" he said.

"I guess I have found you," Cicero said politely.

"You want a medal?"

"No, sir."

"Dutch found me, too."

"I know."

"I never ast to be found. Don't do me no favors."

Cicero waited while the man wrote a bit more and crossed himself several times. Then he said, "You've been busy converting the heathens, haven't you?"

The animals continued to cavort. The old man sighed and rested his pen on his page.

"You think it's easy?" he said.

"I know it isn't," Cicero answered quietly.

"Betcherboots. I'm spending a fortune in sugar. You wanna know the real problem?"

"I suppose."

"Don't do me no favors."

"What is the real problem?" Cicero said quickly.

"People don't know what's good for them."

Taking a deep breath, Cicero said, "*I* know."

"Sure, kids today know everything. You got a Fatima?"

"I don't smoke."

"Sure, you know everything, and you can't even handle a butt."

"Still," Cicero said, his eyes stinging, "I know what's good for me."

"Oh Christ. Awright, what?"

"I know I desperately need the perfect number."

The animals hesitated. Longy nodded and they started again. He said, "Hey, you wisin off? At your age, I was awready hittin the shape-up. You know what a shape-up is?"

"Yes."

"Sir."

"Yes, sir."

"Well, do it. An don't wise off to me about no numbers; I got my own troubles. Ast the Dutchman."

Cicero opened his mouth to reply, but as he did, the old-new man got up suddenly, folded his camp stool, thrust his notebook into his gabardine tunic and, with his three playful companions, turned and plunged into the jungle. Cicero waited and, sure enough, the voice, nervous, patient, coaxing, demanding, calm, frenetic, wafted back to him: "Listen, chief," the voice said, "play along with me, and you get a hundred percent protection." Then, all was quiet, except for the humming, buzzing, screeching sounds of the forest.

Cicero sat down on the damp ground. It wasn't good for his kidneys, but he was tired and needed to sit down. He was also disgusted. Go back to the Dutchman, go back to Lucky; that's all they could come up with. Didn't anybody operate independently in this darn continent? Nerts. He leaned against a huge, gnarled, thousand-year-old tree. The tree leaned over him and grinned crookedly. So did its friends. Soon everything around him was leaning, grinning and laughing, including the thick undergrowth, ants, anteaters, wet earth, taproots. Nerts! He sat and absorbed for awhile, then filled his lungs with the dank, heavy air and shot straight up like a goosed autogiro. Branches, leaves, astonished flying squirrels flashed past. And now he was free and clear, high above the jungle, high above the Congo River; even so, he soared higher. Until he could see the entire length of Flegenheimer's column, could even see beyond it to its target: crazy, mixed-up, laying-low, Bugs Emin Pasha Siegel. And that wasn't all. From atop his *amba* of air, he could make out Cokie Flo in Addis, in her house, at her window, motioning. He shook his head and swept the area spread out beneath him. He saw Tip Winograd and Mirambo Cleveland counting the *honga*, divvying up the take. He shook them off, zoomed in on Lepke Lugard humping away and cursing the black woman under him. Nerts to Lepke. Head swiveling, he saw Waxey Gordon's knucklehead bouncing down the steps in Khartoum. Everywhere, everybody, motioning, sugaring, counting, divvying, humping, bouncing. He was fed up to here. He tanked up on the fetid air and yelled down:

"Hey, you mugs, you gorillas!"

They all stopped whatever they were doing, looked up, way up.

"I am not fooling around anymore!" he yelled. "I want that perfect number and I want it now!"

The faces stared, glanced at each other, stared back.

"Oh yeah?" they said.

"Yes!"

There was a moment of tremendous hesitation; then, all together, like a hundred angry Inkspots, they roared, "Well, ain't that swell. Okay kid, but we got some news from home."

"Oh yes? Well, spit it out, you mugs!"

"Sure. We ain't got the perfect number, see? Never had it. But we got somethin else, somethin *better*."

". . . Yes?"

"Yeah."

". . . What?"

"The perfect goddam phrase."

"The what?"

"*Phrase*. Ain't you been to school?"

"Yes, I've been to school."

"Well, we got it. The perfect phrase."

Suddenly he was tired, oh so tired. He had a headache, his ears rang, his eyes were burning. He spit on his hands and wiped his eyes.

"Very well," he sighed down. "I will settle for that."

"Don't do us no favors!"

"All right, yes!" he cried. "Half a loaf is better than none. Well, what is it? Defecate or get off the pot!" Oh, but he was tired, so tired . . .

There ensued a great, tumbling-over-itself silence, the silence he always heard when he looked out over the East River at Ward's Island. Now, from his vantage point high in the Congo air, he stared down with his saliva-slaked eyes. From far up he could easily see every mouth wide open, right to the gold molar fillings, and as he looked, all the mouths blended into one mouth until he was truly examining the world's biggest mouth. He nodded grimly, threw a lightning glance to the west, across the Atlantic. Sure enough, Lucky's snarly yap in Brussels had joined the party. Another glance: so had Gashouse Lil's in London. He pulled in the thin, fetid air; Oh God, if only he had a ton of Sen Sen to sprinkle down on the amazing mouth. For here it came: the words, stinking, rolling, cracking, thundering up at him, as if they had blasted out of Theodore's giant cannon, as if they had been tattooed on Joe Louis Barrow's reaching cement gloves:

"H-E-L-L-O-O-O S-U-C-K-E-R-R-R-R-R!"

The royal cobra ducked and slid behind the chiffonier. The colobus monkey reared back, hopped, sailed out onto the palm branch beside the window. The man in the bed was twisting, kicking, jerking, swinging his arms as if a thousand mosquitoes were swarming about his head. The cobra and the monkey pulled into themselves, peered out and listened. The breath of the man came in short, hard bursts, and it seemed that his nose could not hold such breathing, but somehow it did, as a charging bull elephant's trunk did. The cobra flattened himself to the floor, the monkey half turned, ready to leap away. But the man did not come at them; he was too occupied with his bed enemies;

his kicks, twitches, jerks, air-punches, flying water seemed to fill the room, pushing against the walls, the floor, the ceiling; even the outside zinc coating seemed to bend away under his striking power. Then two others were in the room, standing bravely in the path of the bull elephant: Joshua at his head, holding down the great slab arms, Ruth throwing herself onto the kicking legs, being tossed aside like a wood chip, returning and hanging on until they were down, making only birdlike nervous movements. Both, all the while, speaking softly, purringly to the man. Until slowly, painfully it seemed, but obediently, he was settling back and becoming still all over, except for the nervous legs and his fingers which stretched out and closed. Until, with a great sigh, legs and fingers, too, were still. The staring eyes then fixed on Joshua and their round black centers grew smaller.

"Hello," the man said quietly.

"Welcome," Joshua said.

The man's eyes observed Ruth holding his ankles. "Am I in the Congo?" he said.

"No," said Joshua. "Liberia."

"The land of the free?"

"The home of the brave." Joshua nodded.

"Oh."

The man breathed very quietly. Joshua said, "Could you manage something to eat?"

"Thank you, yes. I'm hungry."

"Good. When the Lord's away, the serfs will play. Ruth?" The girl slowly lifted one hand, then the other, then looked up at Joshua. He said, "Go and fetch some of that magic brew of yours." She nodded gravely, checked once more on the quiet ankles, then tiptoed out. Joshua stepped back and looked down at the now quiet man. "She'll bring you up some Campbell's chicken soup; it's Legree's favorite." He smiled. The man smiled back.

The royal cobra settled down for a nap. The colobus monkey noisily scolded a friend who had wandered too close to his branch.

WALTER WINCHELL IN NEW YORK

... AND NOW A TIP FOR THE BIG-BOARD WATCHERS, STRAIGHT OUT of the horse's mouth ... rather the Ace's mouth ... cozily ensconced in Liberia in the middle of all those dripping rubber trees ... keep an eye, keep all *four* eyes, on *Firestone* ...

PAWNS

HE BEGAN TO DO HIS ROADWORK, JUST AS IF THIS WERE POMPTON Lakes and Jack Blackburn was beside him on a Columbia, pointing, pouting, cajoling, coaxing, coaching, bawling. Straight down the red laterite road he jogged, shoulders folding and meeting, winging back, abdomen pulling and rolling, stone fists clipping the redolent ozone with six-inch jabs, chin-snapping hooks. The bamboo palms and the fan palms and the coconut palms leaned over the road and asked for it, then in panic tried to draw back—too late; they took his best, toughest, Sunday punches and their green snouts weaved back and forth with delicate dizziness. Feeling even stronger, he took on the teak, ebony, mahogany: Carnera-tall, stiff, easy. Naturally they took their bone-hard lumps. He smiled up at the grinning orange ball, turned and barreled down the road: Jesse Owens vs. Eulace Peacock. Step for step. Now he broke into a quiet trot, a fast walk, a side-step, cross-step, then a Bojangles back-pedal, fast and light-tappy, whirl about, another Owens-sprint, breaking the tape a winner as the track and field nuts screamed their approval. Then a swim in the cool, shadowed stream that ran through the corn plot behind the house.

A week after his first restoring workout, he became so full of himself that he cut off the red road on a late afternoon, ducked under the palm trees and ran with head turtled through the forest. The vines clutched and whipped but he enjoyed that challenge and ducked lower, slitted his eyes, drove ahead through semidarkness. Up ahead the darkness closed to a black wall; he charged and broke through. Staggering, he recovered and dug the sweat from widening eyes. Joshua and five other men sat cross-legged, staring up. Joshua was pointing a rifle at him, the dirty white stock jammed against a tattered shirt.

"Good afternoon," Cleveland said. "Terrific day."

"How did you find us?" Joshua said softly.

He flexed the muscle wings beneath each armpit. "I didn't *find* you." He looked at the slightly bent rifle sight. "I just happened to run this way. He tried a smile and it didn't feel too successful. He noticed then a thick, black cicatrice on each forehead.

Joshua said, still softly, "Why weren't you doing your silly running on the road?"

"I told you ... It just happened ... I *was* running on the road ... I just veered off ... I felt like it ... what do you mean, silly?"

"Why did you veer off?"

"Go fuck yourself."

He turned and took a step. Three of the men were suddenly blocking him. He turned back. The ancient rifle was down, Joshua was smiling. Cleveland walked to him, stopped, looked at the men.

"Joshua, what's going on?"

"Joshua? I beg your pardon. The name is L'Ouverture. Preceded by Toussaint. And this stalwart fellow is Henri Christophe. On my right you see Jack Savage. Before you, Tom Wild, Jumping Jack and Black-Man-Trouble. Gentlemen, this is the man I have told you of. The famous American hero. You must treat him with the respect due all American heroes." No one smiled. Joshua-Toussaint bowed with his neck. "Tarry a while, Major, or is it General? I am always bewildered by high-ranking officers. Join us, won't you, in our little conference circle and I will tell you some fancy things."

They sat in the clearing and the men looked to Joshua-Toussaint who said this: "The white men came to Kru Town and they adopted us and named us Joshua and David and Aaron. We prefer other names. True, they also are theirs, but we prefer them."

"The white men?" said Cleveland.

"Why, yes."

"Abraham Simon, the ebony tree, a white man?"

"Certainly."

He looked at the six foreheads. Touched his own. "And that?"

"Our mark of freedom. Scraped away by the overseer. But we paint it back on when it pleases us, as it does now."

"The white overseer?"

"You are getting smarter. Oh, we wash it off when we return to the plantation. We are very proper." Teeth flashed.

"And of course your President is a white man?"

"Of course. We do believe heroes may possess a brain. One fine point, however. He is not our President. We did not elect him." He smiled at Jumping Jack, who nodded. "Jumping Jack, tell our American hero what the President's Declaration of Independence says."

Jumping Jack bounced up, closed his eyes. "It begins," he said, "thusly: 'We, the people of Liberia, were originally the inhabitants of North America.'" He opened his eyes and sat down, leaned forward. Joshua-Toussaint pointed to each man. "Are they from China?"

"It really says that?"

"Yes, my hero."

"You're slaves then."

A murmur.

"Not quite. One must be careful with words. Pawns."

"As in chess?"

"Oh, I think not."

"As in pawning your watch?"

"I am not familiar with that business."

"Where I live, to borrow money, you hand over your watch." Another murmur.

Joshua-Toussaint said, "And when you pay back the money, then you are given your watch?"

"Yes."

"Then, there is a closeness to your pawning. However, these watches never seem to be given back."

A snort of laughter.

"You're not adopted then?"

A snort, almost a cheer.

"Now, lads. In a way, he is right. Adopted forever and ever. Forever. Forever." Silence, inward eyes, forest sounds, the sound of a smoothly racing motor, squealing tires. The exhaust of the car pricking at his nose.

"What will you do?" Cleveland said.

"Resist adoption."

"With that?" Gingerly he touched the bent sight.

"Why not?" The sight was stroked by L'Ouverture fingers. "Major General, I have to ask a favor of you. Truly speaking, I must *command* this favor. You will not tell of the naughty children meeting here and talking together. You will not do so, will you?"

"No. I promise. I would like to know . . ."

"What would a hero like to know?"

"If I may help . . ."

"But are you not a white hero?"

"Sometimes. Not always. In any case, not today, not now."

Joshua-Toussaint studied his rifle.

"Perhaps. But do not expect us to transform you into a black hero. We have no time for nonsense. And we have been helped before. We are familiar with help." He leaned forward and touched Cleveland on the forehead. "Go back to your running now. Stretch out your legs and whip up your heroic heart. Enjoy your body, feel good. Return to the pretty house and have a pleasant beverage, partake of friendly conversation. Enjoy yourself in your land."

Supper. Polite conversation. Good drinks. Thick, expensive cigars. Polite conversation. A liqueur. Friendly, aromatic, polite, enjoyable evening. Soft good nights. Polished mahogany stairs. His room, whirring, comfortable.

He sat on the bed and waited, heard steps on the polished

stairs, well-fitted doors meshing. He got up, slipped out, walked down the Persianed hall, knocked.

"Who?"

"Dandy."

"Enter."

He opened, stepped in, closed snugly. The Ace was sitting on a cane chair, one foot soaking in a bucket of water. "When your feet are sad, you are sad all over," he said.

"That's what my ahnt always says."

"Deep thinker, your ahnt."

"Tough day?" said Cleveland.

"It is up there with the toughest. Idiots abound."

"I agree completely."

Josephson eyed him as he pulled up another cane chair, sat down, leaned.

"I have to talk to you."

The big soaking toe looked up.

"Talk."

"You're well-connected in Monrovia."

"I will not argue the point."

Cleveland inhaled the gentian violet.

"Do you know where to get any guns?"

"Which guns?"

"Any guns."

The soaking toe wriggled.

"We always know where guns are. We have a saying: Find out where the guns are, and there you will find itchy fingers."

"I'm serious, Max."

"*Moi aussi.*"

Cleveland said, "I would like to know where the guns are; I can supply the itchy fingers."

The Ace stared at the wriggling toe; its nail was black, green, blue. "It's pretty," he smiled down. "Fungus is so pretty."

"These fingers," Cleveland said, "belong to some people who would like to use their fingers."

"This," said the Ace, "is not the ideal place to combat fungus. Fungus loves it here. Sings, dances, cavorts, shrieks with delight."

"People who have received a royal screwing."

"Would you care to rhumba with a fungus?"

"Pawns."

"I'll wager my fungus can do the conga."

"Joshua is a pawn. So is Ruth."

"One, two, three, kick."

In one sweeping motion Cleveland stood and his chair was rolling back to the wall. The Ace said, "No, no, you must kick sidewise."

"Can it, Max. Listen to me—"

The Ace looked down, sighed.

"I have been listening. Guns, fingers, arms, slaves, pawns, Joshua, Ruth. Keep your stupid nose out of it."

Cleveland retrieved the chair, planted it, sat.

"You know?"

"Know. Understand. Everything."

He sat back; the cane creaked. "Your stately friend in the Executive Mansion is on top looking down."

"I believe," observed the Ace, "that my toe has an upset stomach. I think I will give it a Seidlitz powder."

Cleveland stood and walked to the window, looked down the road. It was blood red in the White Plains night. He turned.

"There'd be money in it for you."

"Perhaps a Tum. A Tum for its tummy. Please take your money and do the usual with it."

"There will also be headlines."

The sick toe wriggled.

"*I* handle headlines around here."

"I'll write to Brady, tell him you're Zapata and Juarez."

"Peasants?"

"Geronimo. Sitting Bull."

"Losers?"

"Name your ticket."

"I would like to be Fred Astaire. But I have a fungus."

"You're a genuine prick, Max."

"Yes, I suppose, but you are a dumb sonofabitch." He stood and tenderly patted the toe with the edge of a soft towel. He painted with an inky liquid. "Got this from a medicine man. I believe it is Coca-Cola, but perhaps it isn't. Or if it is, it just might work."

"Max—"

The Ace pirouetted on one foot like a graceful stork. "You and your pawns. Infants. Mongoloid infants. Wandering about in the jungle like Tantor, Edgar Rice's elephant, not nearly as bright, at least he made some money for Edgar. Now listen well, little one. Leave this to the grown-ups. We make no promises, but we will see what we will see. We have a great deal on our mind. And on our toe. Please go away and play at heroism, the poor toe cannot take any more."

Walter Winchell in New York: The latest from Africa is a *hot* flash! In a certain liberated nation, the sound of revolutionary drums disturbs the tropical night and it ain't Gene Kroopa. Fact is that Trader Horn has pulled in his horns for the nonce, so have all the wildabeasties in and around a metropolis named for Uncle Samuel's fifth Prez . . . Now here's the tangled thing: tiz bandied about that the leader of said uprising is none other than a certain diabolical chap who was formerly plying his trade in Addis Ababababy. While, now pay *attencion,* the "enemy" is this fellow's erstwhile rescuer, protector and all-around buddy. The question making the rounds in the sepia continent goes zumzing like zo: What ever happened to gratitude und appreesheashun?

Darla Dixon's Hollywood: If Louis B. Mayer and his Prince of Creativity, Irving Thalberg, have their way, MGM's top script-ers will soon be presenting them with treatments of a hard-driving, real-life drama being played out in Dr. Livingstone coun-try. The only tsetse fly in the ointment is the obvious fact that the conflict is being directed by a pair of colored Americans. But this could be BIG, so Louis and Irving are currently leaning toward a Foreign Legion slant starring William Powell and young Ty Power, whom they would dearly love to beg, borrow or steal from 20th Century to fight on opposite sides of the Nile. Plus which it is heavily rumored that Janet Gaynor and Norma Shearer are *both* campaigning hard for the role of the luscious Zulu maiden . . .

2

Cleveland pointed his '03 Enfield, U. S. Army, out of the bug-eyed attic window, balanced the curve of the red road on top of his sight, slowly tightened his finger and got ready for the next appearance of the Frontier Force. A white flag peeked around the corner. Followed by a gleaming brown boot that felt, planted, pulled in its mate. Both boots followed by an elegantly wrapped torso, commanded by an elegantly balanced head. Cleveland yelled down to the Martini-Henry pointing out of the kitchen window: "Hold it; that's Josephson." He twisted to the cupola and again to the roof: "Don't shoot. Signal Christophe and Savage. They want to talk. Tell them to hold their fire!" He waited for the drums. "Yes, tell them to pass it on!" He heard drums in the distance, receiving, sending. He pulled in the gun, turned, walked downstairs, out onto the porch, cradling his rifle. He looked down the road. Josephson was walking slowly, planting each pointed toe like a ballet dancer walking on for his bow. The white flag was tied to a long, straight walking stick and held at shoulder arms. He reached the verandah steps, stopped, removed the flag from the stick, leaned over and swiped at his boots. Straightened up, tied the flag around his neck, then climbed the stairs slowly. Ahead of him stretched Cleveland's hand.

"So good to see you again. Splendid show. Futile, but splendid. Do you have anything to slake a parched throat?"

They sat in the kitchen: Cleveland, Joshua-Toussaint, Josephson. And in the breakfast nook, neatly, comfortably trussed-up, mouths taped, the Simons. Beside them, Ruth (Lady Dessalines), tall, proud, flushed, fierce, slightly apologetic. The Ace drank some Lipton's tea, smiled around the room, nodded at the mute Simons. "Are they in good shape?"

"Are you all right?" Cleveland said.

They cut their eyes to Ruth-Dessalines and nodded happily.

"Never doubted for a minute," Josephson said. "Not a minute. I trust you implicitly, James."

Joshua-Toussaint said, "We are not giving in."

Josephson smiled at Cleveland. "Melodramatic lad you have there."

"Yes," Cleveland said. "What do they want?"

Josephson sipped his iced tea. "James, my boy, I am authorized, empowered and instructed to tell you that you have made your point, peculiar as it may be."

Mrs. Simon sighed in her chest.

Joshua-Toussaint said, "Go on."

A bland glance, and Josephson said to Cleveland, "Please assemble Coxie's Army and accompany me to Monrovia. All will be settled there in a proper setting. We will talk like gentlemen."

"Talk to *me*," Joshua-Toussaint said.

No glance this time. "Cannot abide repeating myself, James. It is redundant, superfluous, verbose and tautological."

"I don't like your white friend," Joshua-Toussaint said.

Josephson and Cleveland exchanged smiles. The Ace said, "The young are the young—East Saint Louis, Paris, Liberia." He stood, carefully sipped his tea, set the cup on the inlaid table. "You may translate for me, James. I will depart the premises. I will apply pedal locomotion along Lincoln Highway till I reach my lorry. I will tarry there. All hostages will be delivered to the three lorries parked close by in the next hour. They will be unbound, untaped, unhurt. Ninety minutes from now, I will leave, with or without. Inform your young friend that I will be happy to intercede with Dale Carnegie on his behalf. Pleasure."

He ballet-stepped across the floor. Down the steps, one pointed boot, then the other, landing squarely on the sick toe. Planting each foot precisely, the toe curled daintily, The Ace marched down the road.

"Untie them," Cleveland said.

"Just a minute, don't be so trusting—"

"Untie them, dammit. Get up on the roof and tell the others what he wants. I'll meet you in his truck; don't screw it up."

He found himself planting each foot in the red dust. He heard the drums.

The New Lincoln was on Broad Street. It was an office building that had overnight become a hotel. (The office workers were given a sudden two-week vacation.) It looked very much like a hotel he had stayed in on 126th Street in 1931, but the Sheridan was in better shape than the New Lincoln, although they were clearly out of the same cookie cutter: four-story square, red brick building, filigreed down the Broad Street side with fire escapes, sutured on the other sides with the jagged-white cracks of the settling process. Eight Krus and Cleveland were put up on the second floor in large pink wainscoted rooms. All of the new guest rooms contained half-sized, zinc-coated bathtubs. Cleveland's room featured a table-model Atwater Kent, Joshua-Toussaint's an Emerson. Cleveland's worked; he pulled in Paul Whiteman, and Isham Jones from the Firestone station in Monrovia and clipped news reports from Freetown in Sierra Leone.

They were fed in the Nancy Hanks Dining Room beneath a portrait of a patriarchal Lincoln, at a separate table covered with white linen that had embroidered in its center the seal and motto of Liberia. Every evening after dinner they were asked by a black-suited, tortoise-shelled manager if everything was satisfactory; he made careful notes on a teak clipboard of all that was not; after three days, Joshua-Toussaint had a new radio, a Majestic.

For five days they lived, ate, looked, listened, wondered. On the sixth day, at eight in the evening, after dinner, they were escorted into the Gettysburg Room by the manager and introduced to the secretary of the interior, a heavy, black Ickes in a white Palm Beach suit, who pumped each hand with official firmness, waved everyone to waiting chairs, cleared his throat and welcomed them in the name of the President, informed them that this was at best an imperfect world and asked them what their grievances were. The Krus and Cleveland looked to Joshua-Toussaint who stood, reached inside his shirt and drew out a large, thick sheet of paper that was folded in thirds. He unfolded.

"The Kru people," he read in a low, flat voice, "are an ancient, proud and independent race who have never been enslaved, although we have been duped, tricked, twisted, cheated and pawned." He looked at the secretary, who looked back officially; he clasped his hands and placed them over his watch fob; he waited. Joshua-Toussaint returned to the paper. "We have always been like the wind; we have gone anywhere, sailed anywhere, and always our freedom was planted on our foreheads . . ."

Each cicatrice was shiny and thick.

". . . our confederacy was founded five hundred years ago by the great Abron when your Washingtons, Lincolns, and Monroes were still in the sky . . ." The secretary nodded politely.

"We have always resisted the slavers. We did not care where they came from; we resisted. The English, the Dutch, the Americans. However, you Americans never cease when it comes to slaving." The secretary stirred. "Let history show that one hundred fifteen years ago you came and spoke smoothly and with your coaxing ways to King Jack Ben, who, being a kind and trusting man, allowed you to enter *our* land. But not being content to remain in what is now this city, you spread out like the leaves of a giant palm tree . . ." The secretary's right index finger moved. "Then more of you came from your colonizing society. You formed *your* government, wrote *your* Declaration of Indepredance, *your* Constitution . . ."

The secretary smiled politely.

"Still, we did not give in; we did not lie down for you or your masters in Washington. We stood and fought in 1838, in '52, in '75. In this century, in 1910, we rose up again; you cried out for Washington. The Americans came on a warship and they saved you. In 1915, the world was at war. But you and your Washington bosses fought only us . . ."

The secretary carefully crossed his legs.

"Four years ago we fought again for our lives, our fortunes, our sacred honor. You sent a colonel of the frontier force to investigate. His investigation left behind more than a hundred of us who would never rise up again."

Joshua-Toussaint lowered the paper, stared at the secretary, who stared back.

"We turned from arms," Joshua-Toussaint said, "to your democracy." He was not reading now. "We voted for the People's Party, which understood us, unlike your Whigs which are called True. *True*. For this, we have been punished, hounded, maligned. We cannot speak or write against your President. If any should tell of our misery, he is guilty of a thing called sedition. *Even your masters across the sea killed such a law over a hundred years ago . . .*" The overhead fan, heavily oiled for the occasion, whirred smoothly. The black Ickes upcurved his mouth, drew his clasped fingers apart, riffled them gently against the fob. He and Joshua-Toussaint looked at each other like two schoolboys in a staring duel. The secretary sighed, coughed politely, covered the cough, murmured "I beg your pardon." He cleared his throat, said "Well then, well then. A very sound presentation. No split infinitives, not one dangling participle. Logical structure, proper topic sentences. Very sound. The Booker T. Washington Institute, was it not? Cannot have been too bad, must have had a proper academic teacher. Well then. Let us reflect. Naturally, I must file an official report. But we will meet again, never fear. Patience. And fortitude. Rome was not built in the proverbial day. Nor Monrovia. Mr. Jones-Smythe, pray bring in the violinists."

3

A knock, he sat up in his Kru shirt and pants, swung to the floor, padded to the door, opened it. The Ace, in gray mufti, bowed. Behind him, in the shadows, three men.

"Good morning," said The Ace. "did we wake you?"

"Yes."

"Good, the early bird, rise and shine, time and tide, ask me no questions, may we advance?"

He stood to one side. "Advance."

The Ace walked in followed by The President, the secretary of the interior and a mustached ramrod, the size of the Lion of Judah. He was dressed in a double-breasted gray suit and wore spats. The Ace said, "Of course you know our hosts. May I present Lord Michael Beechwood, gentleman, scholar and famed Scotch drinker."

"Max, you rogue," Lord Beechwood said.

"No false modesty, milord. This is the famously infamous James Dandy."

Cleveland shook a very firm hand.

"Lord Beechwood," the Ace said, "is from the League."

"National or American?"

"Jolly good," Beechwood said, smiling with his entire face. "We *are* a bit like cricket, aren't we?"

"I warned you," the Ace said after the President and the secretary glanced at the ceiling. "Now, James, old man, do behave. Tell Sir Michael everything and anything. Be candid, impetuous, angry, indignant, mortified. Be yourself."

"So early?"

Lord Beechwood murmured carefully, "The human animal is most usefully spontaneous in the morning. I learned that valuable lesson at Versailles. We did nothing but dawdle and nap in the afternoon."

"Sit down."

The Ace, the President, the secretary were about to sit; Beechwood held up a tiny hand. "The brain works better on its feet." Everyone remained standing; the Ace sighed. "Milord," he said, "and mine hosts, Major Dandy does not dissemble. He acts from a sincere heart. Gentlemen, if Florence Nightingale had dallied with the great Zulu chief Cetewayo—if, mind you—the result would be the scowling but admirable fellow standing here before you."

"A fatuous woman, Max," said Beechwood.

"I said *if*, milord."

"The Zulus were so volatile," said the President.

"*Chacun à son goût*," said the Ace.

"Get off the pot," said Cleveland.

"Of course, of course." The Ace beamed all around. "Well, then, I can tell you this, gentleman. Major Dandy can be most efficacious in helping you, in helping the League, in helping the world, as it were."

Beechwood nodded a tightly combed head. "Very well, let us get to the heart of the target. Major, just what do you think of this business? The government is quite beastly, I hear, but I do mean to approach this with fairness."

"Thank you," said the President as the secretary thinned his eyes.

"You really want my opinion?"

"On behalf of the League I respond with a categorical yes."

"Okay." Cleveland cut to the Ace who was leaning on his sick toe. "The place is a badly run sewer. Not that I have anything against sewers per se. There have been some highly effective sewers, like the East India Company." Beechwood beamed. "My advice therefore," said Cleveland, "is to bring in real American know-how, not a rubber company or a bank, but a team of our efficiency experts. They would study the mess and put it on a paying basis faster than you can say Machine Gun Kelly."

Beechwood fished out a small notebook from his inside breast pocket and jotted that down. "Kelly with an e?"

"No e."

"Do go on."

"After all, *we* screwed it up."

"Hmmmm, I rather like that. America created this mess, now have America straighten it out. Jolly good."

"On the other hand," said the secretary, "I must—"

"Let him finish," said the President. The secretary smiled and frowned at the same time and Cleveland said, "I'll give you specifics, Okay?"

"Please do," said Beechwood; the President smiled.

"There are several people who can do the job. Mr. Charles Luciano, a proven businessman, could step right in at the top." Beechwood took notes. "Mr. Vito Genovese would be excellent in the exchequer—"

"Are these individuals Italian-Americans?"

"Yes. They represent a firm called the *Unione Siciliano*."

"Interesting."

"Mr. Dixie Davis could handle the judicial system. Mr. Abner Zwillman could take care of maritime matters, which greatly involve the Krus. He would shape them up in no time at all."

Beechwood looked up from his notebook. "Quite an array of talent. Indeed. The *Unione Siciliano*, eh? It occurs to me that we might even approach Mussolini via that avenue, perhaps even coax him back into the fold. *Quel coup pour La League*."

The secretary said, "Mussolini is a hideous dwarf with no legs and a prognathous jaw."

"Careful," said the President.

"Yes indeed," said Beechwood. "But James Wolfe was a poor, sickly thing and Nelson in no wise resembled Bunny Austin."

"Nelson," said the Ace, "did not play tennis."

"How do you know that, Max?"

"I much prefer Ellsworth Vines," said the President.

"Come now," said Beechwood.

"Does Mussolini play tennis?" said Cleveland.

"I doubt it," said the Ace.

"Ah but Ciano does," said Beechwood.

"Really?" said the President.

"Charles Luciano plays golf," said Cleveland.

Beechwood made a note of that and they spent a very pleasant morning discussing golf and tennis and Bobby Jones, Ellsworth Vines and Bunny Austin . . .

DIPLOMACY

THEY GATHERED THREE NIGHTS LATER, THE KRUS AND CLEVE-land at their own Liberian table with the seal of the nation gleaming from the center of the tablecloth. The Black Ickes sat at another Liberian table with the blank-faced President. Beside their seal was a teakwood carving of the *Monitor* with an elongated teakwood man standing on deck, arms uplifted in freedom and victory. At the raised dais sat Lord Beechwood and Maximilian Josephson, chatting. The Ace wore one star on the collar of his freshly laundered and starched shirt. Waiters in white uniforms walked on rubber-cushioned feet about the room, holding high trays of Haig and Haig, Canadian Club, Four Roses and Green River.

Dinner, featuring tins of salmon, tuna fish, bully beef, fresh-killed goat, yams and apple pie was served, followed by coffee, Drambuie and cigars. After which Lord Beechwood tapped his beautifully cut Waterford glass. Cigar smoke rose and twirled through the hush. Lord Beechwood coughed several times and all heads lifted and turned toward him. He stood up stiffly in his desert boots.

"The time has come, my friends," he said, "to gallop straight out to the veldt, as Cecil Rhodes would so aptly put it . . ." He swiveled around the room; the Ace solemnly nodded. "I have been hard at it, let me assure you," Lord Beechwood said as The President nodded, "and I can tell you this, in so far as priv-a-cy will allow . . ." Secretary Black-Ickes slightly frowned. "I

239

have been in touch with Geneva and after conversing far into the nights, both Swiss and African, I have arrived at certain conclusions, both grave and portentous in gauging a future whose lineaments we are only now beginning to discern . . ." He smiled and lifted his tumbler of Drambuie and sipped. "The fact is," he continued, "nyether the Kru race, and I do believe them to be a race in the Darwinian sense, nyether the Kru race nor the sovereign nation of Liberia, for whom I hold a deep, nationalistic affection, nyether of these can go it alone." He sighed and smiled. The President also smiled. The thin voice was high but calm. "Therefore, my good friends, I shall recommend to Geneva that the Kru coast will henceforth become a League mandate. To that end I have instructed my people to contact Mr. Charles Luciano of New York City, America, so that he may come over at his earliest convenience and begin the process of governmental reorganization in order for this great nation's affairs to be at long last effectively managed without the rulers losing their chartered rights and the ruled their rights of birth and place." He bobbed his head at the President and Joshua-Toussaint, and said in the high, calm voice, a bit nasal now, "And the old-boy Americans, as it were, and this new mandate shall go forward into the light of a fine, trusting and trustful day." He lifted his tumbler. "A toast, my friends, to a slicing of the Gordian knot, as it were."

A drumbeat of rain filled the hush.

"NEVER," yelled Joshua-Toussaint.

"Quite impossible," loudly murmured the President.

Cleveland jumped up, so did Joshua-Toussaint, followed by Krus who had suddenly materialized. With Cleveland leading the way, all of them strode to the center of the room that was spotlighted by a gleaming chandelier holding a hundred bulbs. With a quicksilvery nod by Cleveland, a shiny Martini-Henri protruded from the shoulder of Joshua-Toussaint. Lord Beechwood stared blankly, his small eyes beginning to wet with incipient tears; he wiped each eye carefully with a yellow handkerchief that matched his tie. Liberians at a corner table looked to the President who flicked a shoulder. Five Enfields emerged and pointed at the Krus.

"THAT WILL BE QUITE ENOUGH."

All heads, including those of the waiters pressed against the walls, swung away from the rifles. At the dais, Maximilian Joseph-son rose very slowly, as if he were unlocking each joint in his body. His eyes swept the room. "Gentlemen," said The Ace into the rain-clattering hush, "I have up to now been a very patient spectator and a listener." His voice was very deep and his words measured. "I now become a participant."

Lord Beechwood discovered that he was still holding his tumbler of Drambuie. He looked at it rather angrily and plunked it down, spilling some on the white damask tablecloth; a waiter whispered, "Oh my." Beechwood frowned, then turning, said, his high, thin voice now stern, "I say, Max, you have no official status in this affair, please remember that."

Smiling easily, The Ace said, "With all due respect, I *have*." He reached into a side pocket of his uniform jacket and drew forth a sheet of yellow paper. He waved it once. "I have this morning, gentlemen, received a telegram from Washington. Let me say that Postal Telegraph service in this city is first rate." He smiled at the President who touched his forehead in salute. "This missive," continued The Ace, "categorically bestows on me official status. Let no man doubt my sincerity." His now-solemn gaze carefully swept the room.

"Ah then," said Lord Beechwood.

"Thank you." The Ace held up the yellow paper and read, spacing each word: "Am tonight dispatching cruiser *Farragut*. Stop. Liberia must and will remain sovereign nation. Stop. The United States government guarantees that sovereignty. Stop. However, this government also recognizes the plight of native peoples with justifiable grievances. Stop." Even more slowly now. "Kru people entitled to proportional representation in the Congress of Liberia. Stop. Cordell Hull, Secretary of State, for Franklin Delano Roosevelt, President." He looked up. *"STOP."*

The rain now pounded like drumbeat-fire.

Lord Beechwood said, "But see here—"

"One moment, sir," said the President, rising.

"Eh?"

"Lord Beechwood, we thank you."

"But I say—"

"We thank you for your herculean efforts in undertaking this complex and not inconsiderable mission. Of course you shall remain overnight as my guest in the Executive Mansion. You must not refuse me."

"Heavens, no."

"On the morrow," intoned the President, "I shall arrange transport on a government vessel so that you may proceed to your great naval station of Gibraltar. There you of course will wish to freshen up and transfer to one of your own ships which will carry you to a train that will in turn hurry you to Geneva, where you will, I am sure, present your official report."

"Indeed, I shall . . ."

The President smiled and half-turned. "Mr. Toussaint L'Ouverture, if you and Major Dandy would care to join me in twenty minutes in the executive office we can begin the pro-cess of mutual accommodation." A half-turn back. "And now, on behalf of my countrymen all, I thank you again, milord, and the nations that sent you, and the League that serves those nations so well." He spun smartly and walked out through a curtained side exit, followed by his thoughtful Ickes.

All the guns were lowered with a sigh.

Cleveland and the Krus looked at each other and Cleveland shrugged and with Joshua-Toussaint L'Ouverture followed the President and his secretary. The Ace shook Lord Beechwood's hand, and, chatting, they walked out through another door. Liberians donned new raincoats and hurried after them. The Krus lingered, and some of them talked to cousins and nephews who were cleaning up.

COMMERCE

THE ACE WAS FRESHLY BARBERED, LOTIONED, LAUNDERED AND pressed as he leaned back on the leather cushions of the four-door green Packard and looked out at the city of Monrovia passing in review. This was indeed a place of potential, of possibilities: an Automat could find a pleasing location on Ashmun Street. There was an appropriate space for a King Kullen or an A&P on Randall Street. And, of course, as Broad Street glided past, Gimbels. One might, if one were so inclined, drop a line to Adam re the merchandising potential of this metropolis. He would even waive the finder's fee; Adam was such a decent fellow. He slid his wrist through the leather loop behind the window that was marked in front by a cut-glass vase of newly cut roses, African roses. He sighed.

Now he looked at the rigid spine of his chauffeur. Good lad, Samuel. Alert shoulders and neck. Square cap on an observant head. Unequivocal hand signals. Might even have it in him to be an assistant section manager in the menswear department in Gimbels of Broad Street. Another sigh.

They passed through the gate of the Executive Mansion and he waggled a finger at the guard, who saluted. Samuel shifted smoothly into a lower gear and they rolled slowly to the circular driveway fronting the White House. With a foot of feather, Samuel braked, and then sat quietly. The Ace said, "Well done, Sam."

"Thank you, sir."

243

"Do you have a wife, Sam?"

"Oh yes, sir."

"Children?"

"Oh yes, sir."

"Lucky lad."

"I think so, sir."

"Are you a Kru?"

"Oh no, sir. Mandingo."

"Ah, I see. Sorry about that."

"Quite all right, sir. We don't mind the Krus."

"Do you get on with them?"

"We don't mind them, sir."

"Of course. Do not wait for me, Samuel. I will send for you. No, do not get out."

"As you wish, sir."

The Ace opened the well-fitted door, slid out, closed it gently. He glanced at the stiff Samuel staring through his gleaming windshield, turned, mounted the long sweep of steps. He returned the salute of seven guards, stopped, knocked with ungloved knuckles.

"Come in, Max," called the familiar voice.

He entered, walked to the desk and shook hands, snapping middle fingers, with the President, who was standing and wearing his heavy black suit, but also a soft, benign smile.

"Sit down, Max."

He sat. The President sat.

"Cigar?"

"No, thank you. My habit of late is to have one after breakfast and one after dinner. None in between."

"A Schimmelpennick, Max. Beechwood gave me a box before he left."

A smiling no.

The benign head wagged. "Would that I could instill that sense of discipline in these quarters."

He inclined graciously. "I do believe it will come in time."

"Do you really?"

"Yes, I do."

"In time . . . Max, I wish to express my gratitude for what you did last evening. This nation is beholden to you."

A freshly manicured wave. "I merely did what had to be done."

"No, Max, I beg to differ. More, much more. No one but you could have done it and with such splendor."

"Well sir . . ." A glance at the late-morning city that was bustling toward the fire of noon. "I'm afraid I'll have to agree with you."

The President slapped the desk. Then sat far back in his swivel chair beneath the flag. The square face was set in a smile. "That is why it grieves me so to say what I must say."

The Ace sat back, folded his hands on his khaki, crossed legs. "You have made inquiries," he said. "I assure you, sir, I can readily obtain that telegram, or its twin brother, from Washington."

"Tut, Max, I am certain you can. Tis something else."

"Oh, sir?"

"Max. Max." The President was suddenly standing and looking out at his city. Slowly he rotated, so slowly that it seemed his suit was weighing him down. His gaze was elsewhere. Then he said, "How goes it with Gutta Percha?"

"Apace, sir. Not rapidly, that would be unwise. Apace."

A flash of glasses in the sunlight that was dappling the room.

"Have you talked with Mr. Goodyear, Max? Mr. Goodrich? Mr. Kelly? Mr. Springfield?"

"I have put out feelers, sir. That is not to imply that anything has been firmed up. I would not mislead you on that score. Time, sir."

"Yes." The President sat down heavily. "Of course you have been in touch with Mr. Winchell?"

He smiled at his well-buffed nails. "I was once a leg man for Walter. In the dear, dim days almost beyond recall. I toss him an item from time to time."

"I see, a leg man. An apt expression. Max, how much is Firestone paying you?"

The Ace reached for a Schimmelpennick, sniffed at it, nodded and tucked it into his handkerchief pocket, behind the carefully stuffed handkerchief. "I will definitely smoke this tonight," he said. His face matched the beneficence of the man's behind the desk. "Not officially Firestone, sir. Merely a chap in their office."

"Well placed?"

"Always, sir."

"How much, Max?"

"Really not very much. Nothing that approaches what we are worth."

"I am absolutely certain of that." The President webbed his square fingers over his vest; "I should like to ask, why take *any*-thing and jeopardize Gutta Percha?"

"But sir . . ." He wished devoutly for some malevolence in that face. . . . "Sir, Gutta Percha *will* be born. I would never jeopardize *that*. You have my solemn assurance. And, eventually, as we discussed at the outset, Firestone must know about Gutta Percha, thereby coming round to your terms." He smiled through his Yardley. "I am merely playing with those who are eager to be played with. You must know by now, sir, that we never do the expected."

"Well do we know."

"Then, do not be concerned. It will all come right in the end; each knot will be securely tied, never fear."

"Max, Max. They know our every move."

"Oh no, not every. Never that . . ."

An interminably benign sigh. "Max," said the President, "do not quibble. It is so much more. So much—"

"I am not quibbling, sir—"

The hard, traffic cop's hand . . .

"For one thing, Max, it is not right . . ."

The Ace opened his mouth. The cop's benign hand closed it.

"For another, we cannot afford such a game. Our predecessor had to resign because the finger pointed too hard at him. We are on the international stage, Max, and the whole world is watching, avid to pounce. The electric lights of the righteous shine into each Liberian loophole. The Kru business would be as nothing compared to a *scandale de commerce*. And here in the Executive Mansion."

He felt the pain in his solar plexus, the bull's-eye pain, like the pain he had over Lake Erie, motor smoking, and the sudden realization that he had not packed a chute. He said, "But sir, they *all* do it," and instantly he wanted to reel the words back; The Ace never used excuses, especially legitimate ones. As if he had read his mind, the President nodded and said, "neither Liberia nor we can afford such luxuries."

His head dropped.

Gently: "We must be above reproach, Max."

He looked out at a building that would never be called the Hotel Josephson. Looked back into calm eyes. "Of course you must, sir."

Another interminable sigh. The face kinder than ever. "You must go, Max," it said softly.

"Absolutely."

"Quickly."

"Without doubt."

The morning sun flared. Suddenly the rain came, hard, tough, inexorable. The President stood, squared himself, walked around the desk and held out his hand. The Ace got up stiffly. He grasped the tough hand and they shook, snapping middle fingers hard; thank heaven it was not a gentle handshake. The President said, "We have arranged for you to receive the Chevalier of the Order of the Star of Africa."

"Might I have the Grand Band?"

"Max!"

"The Star of Africa is perfect, sir."

"We want your solemn promise that you will divorce yourself from the rubber business. Completely."

"Oh, you have it, sir. Sir . . ."

"Yes, Max?"

"Will you . . . carry on with Gutta Percha?"

"We will try. I honestly do not know if we can succeed without you."

The breastbone pain again.

". . . But we will try. You have pointed us in a good direction. We thank you for that."

"Ah, sir, you are most welcome. Might I ask a favor?"

"Careful, Max . . ."

"Oh, nothing complicated, I promise you. Only this: in case there are any monies due me from Gutta Percha, would you see that Samuel, my driver, receives them? Not all at once, please, spread it out, it will be better for him."

"You are an interesting piece of work, Max."

"I have been told that, Sir . . . just in case there are any monies . . ."

"We will see to it, Max."

"Now *I* am beholden."

The kind, bemused head shook slowly. "Max, again, the nation and we proffer thanks . . ." At last, *finalmente,* the paternal face clouded. The President took off his glasses, breathed, carefully rubbed them clean with his three-pointed pocket handkerchief, put them back on. "We are so sorry, Max . . ."

"No. Do not be sorry, sir." The most brilliant smile he owned lit up the room. "I deserve the sack. Plain and simple. I was stupid. I deserve nothing less." He turned brisk. "Would you arrange to have Samuel bring my car round?"

The desk received a slap. It hulked there in teaked splendor as its master looked it over, then raised his head and studied the flag, the seal, the national motto. The big head sighed, said, "Yes, Max." The Ace turned, walked precisely out of the room, leaving behind a cloud of Yardley aftershave. The President remained standing, hands tightly webbed behind his back; he gazed out the window at Monrovia surrendering to the pounding rain.

EXEUNT

CLEVELAND LOOKED AT THE *SOLOMON II* STRAINING AT ITS CHOCKS. He said, "I thought you were going to change it to *Monrovia Dream*."

"So I was." The Ace drained his whiskey and soda, threw the glass far out into the gentle surf. Squinting into the setting sun, he shrugged, "Never quite got around to it. Too much the man of affairs. I am considering *A la Recherche de Latex Perdu*."

"What about, 'Nailed with my hand in the cookie jar?' "

"Oh no, that would never do for our little companion." He tenderly touched a wing. "His is a soul of romance. He would falter beneath such a weight."

"Have it your way."

"More or less always do."

Cleveland held out a hand, The Ace took it, they shook Liberian style.

"Where to, Max?"

"Oh, I believe I shall frisk about a bit over open water, then try the coast."

"Kru coast?"

"I would think."

"Kru Town?"

"Bunny Town, old chap. Had a long talk with Sir Michael before he departed. As you know he is in love with tennis and has a particular fondness for Bunny Austin. No, don't frown, tis true. He has promised to send private monies to us providing we change the name of the capital, as noted, and also the country—"

"To Fruit-Cake Land?"

"Heavens, no. To Austinia."

"Oh shit."

"Oh yes, tis true. Fact is, these passions arc not too rare. Knew a chap in Patagonia who was thoroughly gone on bridge. Would write ten page letters, single spaced, to Ely Culbertson. Shivered when he heard, 'No trump.' "

"Oh shit."

"Word of honor."

"Beechwood's a fucking ass."

"But of course."

"And a respected leader of the civilized world."

"But of course."

"He runs the world while we scratch at the door."

"We? I, never. Do not even knock. Enter face akimbo. Once came up on the dumbwaiter. She was enchanted."

"Oh shit."

"Oh but she was."

Cleveland looked at the glistening ocean, shook his head, turned back. "I thought the President wanted you out of Liberia."

"He does. But now the natives of Austonia have fame and some say in government. Not much, but enough so that he would never exclude me from my people."

"Your people?"

"Indeed. Seems your friend L'Ouverture is not as dense as originally perceived. Came to me with shining eyes and said it was their considered wish that I join them. How could I refuse?"

"By saying no."

"I do not see how I could, really. They want me as their Paramount Chief. Quite touching. How could I disappoint?"

Cleveland grabbed the whiskey bottle and heaved it into the forest beside the runway and stared out at the Atlantic.

With a blue kerchief The Ace dabbed at the Canadian Club stains on the wing, leaned against the *Solomon II*, folded his khaki arms. "They have suggested that I be called Abron, after their great chief of five hundred years ago. I told them we must first see how things progress."

"Shit."

The Ace smiled and then his face was solemn. "My, my. *You* hoped to be anointed."

"Like hell . . ."

"Ah. James, look here, I simply will not do business with the green-eyed monster. I shall abdicate at once. In your favor."

"Forget it. I don't give a shit who they bow down to."

"You don't?"

"They can have Beechwood."

"They don't want Beechwood, they want me."

"Congratulations."

"Thank you, James."

"Whathehell can you do for them?"

"Now that is a foolish question. Really. As a matter of fact, I have already cast an appraising eye on the diamond situation in Sierra Leone."

Cleveland sighed. "Smuggling?"

"Now, James. Mr. Rhodes and Mr. Barnato would prefer 'quiet negotiations,' as do we. See here, old chap, it is not too late; do you wish to be Abron? Or better yet, King James?"

"They didn't ask me."

"Quite right." The Ace straightened up. With a small smile, he said, "Well then, will you try to be a good fellow?"

"Go fuck yourself."

"Splendid. Now, do not drop your head, James. Never drop your head. That's the ticket. Perhaps one day . . ."

"Yop. Perhaps."

The Ace turned very quickly for a big man, hopped onto the impatient wing, vaulted into the cockpit. He eased down, pulled the goggles over his eyes.

"Contact!" he bellowed.

The two frontier force men screamed, "Contact!" reached up for the propeller and yanked. It caught, the motor coughed. They jumped aside, doubled over and slapped away the chocks, then ran to the edge of the improvised runway. The *Solomon II* quivered, rolled forward on the red laterite. Daintily it picked up speed, gathered and skipped into the air. It smoothly arrowed out over the ice-blue, rocking Atlantic. The Frontier force men whirled their caps high over their heads and yelled, "Lucky Lindy! Lucky Lindy!"

Cleveland slowly dropped his arm. The Ace had never looked back.

Part Five

BLACKIE

SOL WINOGRAD HAD OFTEN BEEN TOLD THAT HE WAS A DEAD ringer for Al Jolson. He liked that. Sometimes he would call his wife Dixie, even though her name was Bernice, and he would ask her for a Dixie melody, which always made her sky her eyes. No matter, that was Sol in his Jolson mood. He could whistle like Jolson, even with his fingers. But best of all was his "Mammy." That was his big one. Right in the middle of a business meeting, he would screw up his face and yell "Mammy!" and keep right on going. Sometimes he did it during a working lunch, especially dairy, which he was on because of his ulcer. No matter when he did it, his colleagues would merely pause, then carry on with the deal or the sour cream and there would be no noticeable change in the results. Sometimes it even helped, although he'd never tell them, for after the "Mammy" he could get a damn good idea. Every now and then, a newcomer would poke his neighbor in the side and say "What's this 'Mammy'?" He would be told—later—that that was Sol, forget it and, above all, don't stare or laugh. One new boy who did both wound up back in Canarsie.

There were other "Mammys"! He loved to give out with a big one when he jumped into the surf at Atlantic City, hands high, legs pinwheeling. It was the first word he belted out when he was whisked to the top of the Chrysler Building in '30 and saw his beloved city spread out beneath him.

When Sol's boy, Scott, named for the great author of *Ivanhoe,*

255

was thirteen, Sol heard Jolson on the radio sing "Mammy" all the way through, verse and chorus. He went right out and bought the sheet music and gave it to Scott with directions to learn that song and to learn it on both knees, not just one. Scott was a good boy, always did as his father said. Thereafter, during his years at Collegiate School, he performed "Mammy" at all of Sol's parties, and throughout his first year at Yale, when he was home, he was invariably the finale at all the social affairs in the Winograd household. And often in a face blackened with shoe polish. It was during this period that he picked up the nickname, Blackie, and it stuck until the last month of his sophomore year. In that month, after a flock of beers off-campus, he sat down and typed out a letter to Sol which consisted of one sentence repeated two hundred times: "I WILL NEVER NEVER NEVER AGAIN SING 'MAMMY'!" Sol was very hurt, of course, and said to Dixie-Bernice and to his mother—*his Mammy*— that's college for you, you would think it was hurting him to give me a little pleasure, but on all of Scott's vacations, he no longer pushed the song; in fact, there was a little bonus here for it was a decision, and if this kid could make a decision, even a *never* decision—even against his own father—it was still a decision, and this Sol could buy.

But then, dammit, he began to make other decisions: In his junior year at New Haven he joined a group that called itself the Eli Ras Tafarians. On top of that, three months later he told his father he had to go to Ethiopia. Sol swallowed, said shit-Mammy to himself, said to Scott, "Who gave the order— Pershing?"

"It's an internal order. It came from within."

"I know what internal means. I'll let you visit the *shvartz* Ethiopian Synogogue on a Hundred Twenty-fifth Street. I bet you never knew they had Jews in Africa."

"I knew."

"Go over to a Hundred Twenty-fifth Street. I'll set you up to meet the *reb*."

"Not good enough."

"I'll send them a check. How much?"

"Not good enough."

"I'll send a check to Ethiopian War Relief."

"Not good enough."

"Whathehell is a kid from Yale gonna do in Ethiopia?"

"Drive in the Eli Ambulance Corps."

"Where are you gonna get an ambulance?"

"I thought you might buy one."

"Why the hell would I do a thing like that?"

"Because the capitalistic, cartel world, of which you are an integral part, has brought the war on and refuses to stop it. It wouldn't be much of a gesture, but it's better than nothing."

So Sol, internally denouncing out-of-town colleges, mouthing innumerable "Mammys"! seeing he couldn't beat him—for how you gonna beat a no-decision kid when he starts making decisions?—joined him. That is, he went out and bought a first class ambulance and sent it and Scott to Africa, first class. For quite a while he got sudden and sharp attacks of the blues, and even Jolson didn't help too much, but he plunged into work and began to pull out of it, to be the old, snappy Sol. He even took the kid's baby picture out of the drawer and put it back on his desk. And every now and then, when one of the boys from Mulberry Street would crack wise about the barefoot niggers and how Mussolini was going to kick their ass up to Siberia, he noted quietly that he happened to know somebody who put his money where his mouth was. A brief exchange of looks and straight back to business . . .

Scott drove the Boola Boola through the tail end of '35 and into '36; there was an item about him and his "sensitive, tough-guy buddies" in *Time* and one in *Liberty,* that mentioned his New York home and parentage, both of which Sol folded and kept in his wallet. He got one letter from Scott telling him to vote for Norman Thomas; that he didn't keep in his wallet.

They liked Scott in Addis, especially the British ambulance drivers. He often drove with John Melly, began to think of him as some kind of saint-savior who would one day lead Britain and perhaps even the world back to sanity. He was close by when they got Melly, helped to pull his riddled body back to safety—too late. He slid into a tailspin then, wouldn't go near an ambulance for quite a while, walked the streets as an inviting target, worried both his buddies and his mates. He returned to daylight for the sake of the Emperor, and with the news of the approach of Badoglio got back behind the wheel as Tafari's train to Djibouti rolled off. He drove through the sack of Addis. He stayed with the corps through the weeks of Badoglio, through the coming of Graziani. *That* was too much. He turned the Boola Boola over to the Swiss consul, told the other Elis he could not live with civilized barbarity and left on the stroke of midnight to join the guerillas of Ras Desta in the mountains surrounding the capital.

He stayed with Desta one month, saw what he and the other patriots were up against in Graziani, realized that without the outside help that only a Melly could have catalyzed, the counter-invasion, and liberation would take fifty years. Unable to face his bravely doomed new comrades, once more on a dim midnight, he slipped away and simply began to walk. He kept on walking and when he looked up he was in the Soudan. He felt life returning, the frustration ebbing away, and when he stumbled across a British film company making a docile competitor for Weissmuller's *Tarzan,* he found himself talking endlessly—if modestly—about his war experiences. He was asked at once if he wouldn't care to sign on as a kind of advisor, driver, all-around good chap and also to do the part of a deaf-mute British soldier who would guide Tarzan through Fuzzy Wuzzy country; seems that the original fellow had gone a bit bonkers in Africa. Although he didn't care for the imperialist slant of the picture, he thought he might be able to tone it down, so he said yes. He stayed with the company through a tinny version of Kitchener's victory—made certain there were some specific shots of bare hands versus steel—then traveled south with them as Tarzan searched for the legendary son of Dr. Livingstone, who would restore the British soldier's hearing and speech. He managed to stick it out to Lake Victoria and through a rather clinging affair with a Manchester Jane who lived in deathly fear of cannibalism of her private parts. At Victoria—the very name nagged him badly—he realized he could take no more of the company's attitude toward its porters, toward its make-yourself-at-home carelessness in the villages they stopped at, and finally with Jane's quite irrational obsession. He left after denouncing the astonished assembly as it munched tinned crackers and grape jelly, advising Jane in a parting shot to consult Dr. Ernest Jones on her return to England.

Again he walked:

Several miles down the lake he fell in with a French novelist whose safari had started out in Mombasa on the east coast, and who was determined to do a book on Henry Stanley that would for all time depict him as the greatest explorer in history, far outreaching Columbus or even Amundsen, Scott's personal favorite. The theme was so outrageous that Scott thought there might be something to it, so he joined the Frenchman, who, aside from the Stanley business, was quite *sympathique,* and they sailed up the Congo in a replica of the greatest explorer's steamboat, broke down nineteen times, relived the fevers and travail of Bula Matari's party, began, around the edges, to bicker over Henri's identification with Henry, and when they reached Brazzaville, came to a complete and noisy parting of the ways, not so much over Stanley, although by then that had become quite enough, but over Leon Blum, who, to Scott, was the political Amundsen of the day. The climax of the odd journey was a fistfight in the *Lapin Jaune,* which ended with Scott's hiking boot from Abercrombie and Fitch atop Henri's paper chest, and the words, *"Vive Le Front Populaire!"* resounding through the city.

From Brazzaville he shipped out on a Swedish freighter that sailed up the Gulf of Guinea, doing business at Fernando Po, which was colonialism at its most disgusting (Spanish), at Lagos in Nigeria, which was almost, but not quite, as bad (British), and at Grand Lahou in the Ivory Coast, which in a sad way was the worst of all because somehow Blum was connected to, if not with, it.

He jumped ship in Grand Lahou, determined to find something that would justify French imperialism as a superior type, implanting the spirit of 1789 in West Africa, thereby getting M. Blum off the hook. He was unsuccessful. But after five miserable weeks a rusted, splintered derelict calling itself the *Pretty Venus* limped into port. He was told by the African stevedores that this was one of the last of the Black Star liners owned by a M.

Marcus Garvey (looking around as they told him) and long since sold to pay off his debts, which he could be sure were unfairly accumulated. Scott forgot the double cross of the French Revolution, realized that here was an ideal still doing a job—pitifully, sadly—but still doing a job; Garvey had *indeed* come back to Africa; *something* in this godforsaken world *had* worked. *Doubly* worked, for it flew a *Liberian* flag. And even though it was a Portuguese ship in everything but registry, and Portugal had an abominable colonial record, he eagerly signed on.

For two poisonous days he dragged through his duties and, when he had time off, grabbed the rail and strained forward for the one beacon of consistent light that pierced the white man's burden. On the third day he saw it.

Monrovia.

He fainted from dehydration mixed with ecstasy.

He came to in a darkly paneled waterfront bar called The Fifth Avenue. He was nourished back to this now-not-so-rotten world (the *Venus*'s skipper long since elated to be rid of him) with tins of Libby's tuna fish, White Rose peas and innumerable slices of Taystee bread, all judiciously washed down by American applejack. All administered by Mr. Millard Van Buren, who owned both bar and rooms above, whose grandfather had come over from Savannah and who was perfectly delighted that he could entertain a countryman. He was a magnificent listener and Scott could now really talk after the bursting of the imperial dam; he told Millard everything he could think of, dredge up, recall about a place that Millard called the good old USA. Millard listened with a look of total rapture on his richly seamed face. And when Scott finally ran down, he countered with news of Monrovia, which to Millard, of course, *was* Liberia. When he came to the mysterious stranger, who, it was said, lived like a second President on Broad Street, Scott leaned forward, even put down his applejack (which he had came to associate with all things free). For he had long heard of such a man. All along the coast—in Lagos, Grand Lahou, even Nanny Po, where one of the pick-and-shovel, sweat-dripping boys had whispered to him through the back of his hand, "Don't be sad, boss, I come out okay when Crazy Guy come to rescue." Scott leaned in, wiping the applejack from his mustache, to hear more . . .

So there he was, living in a pleasant room above a pleasant bar and grill; he helped out a bit with the books and he continued the long and pleasant and enlightening talks with Millard Van Buren and filled up and out on Libby's, White Rose and Laird's applejack. The shaggy spear of a Vandyke expanded into a raven-black Emile Zola beard. He read the *Liberian Patriot,* the *Liberian Recorder* and the *Weekly Mirror.* He read and reread a back issue of Sylvia Pankhurst's *New Times* and *Ethiopia News.* And one cool, dry night, with the gossip from the bar seeping up through the floor, he looked up from Miss Pankhurst and saw standing in the doorway Hollis Cleveland. Millard was standing behind him, peering around a huge shoulder.

"Hello, Blackie," Cleveland said.

Scott carefully folded the paper, laid it down beside the Coca-Cola glass filled with applejack and said, "Please don't call me that."

Mr. Van Buren said, on tiptoe, "I will see you anon," and quickly walked down the stairs.

Scott shook his head and the new beard waggled. "So it's you," he said.

"It's me, Blackie."

"I really would appreciate your not calling me that, Hollis."

"I'm sorry. It's me, Scott."

"Thanks, Hollis. Holy Xmas, come in."

Cleveland closed the door and walked in and held out his hand. Scott got up and extended a forefinger. Cleveland grasped it with his own and they shook three times. "There," grinned Scott. "There. We have been reunited. Sit down on that Grand Rapids rocker, it's Millard's connection with the good old USA." Cleveland sat, rocked once, creaked loudly, stopped. He grinned back.

"It's been a long time," he said.

Scott pulled his chair closer.

"A long time and a helluva busy one, Hollis."

"Yes, a busy one. How's your father?"

The raven beard shrugged. "I'm not sure, but my guess is that he's fine. He's usually fine, isn't he?"

"Sol," Cleveland nodded, "could always take care of number one."

"That he could."

Cleveland's rocker creaked, but he said nothing. Scott grinned. "Close to the vest. Sol would say that."

"Yes."

"And Hollis got it knocked up."

"Probably."

"You know him better than anyone. Sure he would."

"If you say so."

"Sure I say so. Don't you say so?"

The rocker creaked. "You still love to argue," Cleveland said.

"Guilty as charged. Go to the mat with anyone. Even you. Next to my father you're the best forensic man I know. He always said you were two peas in a goddam pod."

"His exact expression was, 'He's a *mamzer,* like me.' "

Scott's knees took a pounding. He lifted the Coca-Cola glass and drank. "Would you like a drink?"

"No, thanks."

A sip, a grin. "So you got it knocked up?"

"No argument."

"Then that's established."

Cleveland rocked and said, "What are you doing here?"

"That's a funny question."

"What circumstance brings you to this corner of the universe?"

A sip, a half-grin. "I have every right to be here."

"That's a Yalie answer."

The grin expanded again and Scott said, "Guilty again. All right, at the moment I'm not doing anything in an external sense. I started out in Ethiopia, did a few things that my father would question in terms of smarts and I wound up here."

"Sounds like me."

Scott pulled at his beard. "How come you're the Crazy Guy?"

"Oh I do roadwork every day and some shadow boxing."

"Is that all?"

"I fought for a while with the Krus. In Monrovia, that's a little crazy."

". . . Did you fight anywhere else?"

"I was in Ethiopia."

"With Afewerk?"

"I knew him."

Scott drank and pulled his beard. "You're the Black Devil."

"Sol would say, the *Shvartz Mamzer*."

"All right. Do you know that Graziani is still looking for you?"

"You won't snitch, will you?"

Scott cackled. "Scout's honor."

"Why don't we send your old man after Graziani?"

"I like it, I like it. Sol would eat Graziani for breakfast, Ciano for lunch, Badoglio for supper and Mussolini for a late night *nosh*."

"Check and double check."

Scott clapped his hands the way he had at the circus when he was ten. "The three of us could give them fits." He leaned forward. "I've heard some very intriguing things about you."

"Rumor. Inuendo."

"Come on. Hollis, I am going to tell you something."

"So tell."

"You are wasting your time here."

The Crazy Guy on Broad Street nodded. "I was thinking the same thing."

"Perfect! Now tell me if you agree with this: Liberia will make it one way or another. The American economic royalists will see to that."

"Historically correct. Probably still is."

"Okay, close to the vest. May I continue?"

"Be my guest."

"*We need you in Ethiopia.*"

"I've been."

"We *still* need you."

"Who the hell is we?"

"Listen," Scott said, hitching his chair closer, "some of the top leaders took off for the mountains just before Badoglio marched in. Ras Desta, for one. I was with him. But what could we do?"

"Nothing."

"Well, not too much."

"Nothing."

"Okay, Okay. Less than nothing against Graziani."

"I'll buy that."

"All right then. You know what they need?"

"Me?"

Scott got up with an awkward jerky movement, swung his arms overhead; for a moment it seemed that he was about to sink to one knee and break into "Mammy." He circled the rocker and stopped in front of Cleveland. "How about it, Hollis?"

"You're the crazy guy."

"Like hell. I'll write to my father. He'll send enough stuff to wipe out half of Chicago. We'll go back up there."

"Sol, the royal insurgent."

"Why not? He owes Ethiopia."

"Jesus Christ, Blackie."

"See? You're getting hooked. I'll even overlook Blackie."

"You'd better overlook Sol, too."

Scott hesitated, then began to pace back and forth in front of Cleveland, who sat very still. "All right, just you and me. Together we'll nail the fascist pricks. I know we can. The people will stream down from the mountains when they hear the Black Devil is back. Ten seconds to say yes."

"Here's five back. I'm going home."

Scott sat down hard. "Hollis, I'm going to be very frank with you."

"Shoot."

"All right, here goes. Ethiopia, in the deepest meaning of the word, *is* your home."

"Who says?"

"That insistent voice in your guts."

"That voice keeps saying, 'Get your ass back to Lenox Avenue.' "

Scott sat up stiff, tall, with his thin shoulders squared. He drank some applejack and shook his head slowly. Cleveland rocked a few times, then said, "Why don't you come back with me."

The head kept shaking. "You really mean that?"

"Sure I mean it. You're not cut out for this shit. Neither am I."

The head grew still. "Hollis, you are very naive, do you realize how naive you are?"

"Yes. So I'm getting out."

Scott stared and then half-smiled. "I asked and you have responded. I'll go back myself. I'll raise a corps of volunteers and go back."

"Good luck, friend."

"And the hell with you."

"Okay."

"Go back to that world you call home."

"Okay."

"Sure. You and my father think you have the world by the chandeliers. You've got a lot to learn."

"Come on back and educate us."

"Are you serious?"

"A hundred percent."

"Hollis, I have a job to do here. Two jobs. Yours and mine."

Cleveland suddenly stood and the rocker creaked to a gentle stop. He glanced out at the brilliant night. Then he said, "Get paid. Twice. So long, Blackie."

"You prick."

Cleveland turned. "Oh sir," he heard. "*Señor* Diablo? Before you stalk out, I have something for you." Scott got up and walked to his jacket hanging beside the window. He drew a long envelope out of a breast pocket and walked to Cleveland and held it out. "Go on, it won't bite." Gingerly Cleveland picked at the envelope with two fingers, held it away from him. "It's a letter from my father," Scott said.

"How the hell?"

"My father, as you well know, sees all, is aware of all. His world boils down to New York, Chicago and Miami Beach. The rest is someplace else. If two people go someplace else, they are destined to meet."

"That's Sol."

"Precisely."

Cleveland folded the letter and tucked it into his shirt pocket.

He walked to the door and opened it. The downstairs voices blared up. He looked back at Scott. He saw the *New Times and Ethiopia News* held by eight tight fingers. The Florsheim shoes were toed in.

DEAR HOLLIS

How goes it, old pal? Hey, not old in years, not yet anyway, but old in the fact that we go back a long ways together
and made our share of local history, right? Right. And like
a good education—as my father used to say—nobody can
take that away from us. At least, that's what it says here in
small print at the bottom of the page.

Like always when I start out with the big intro, and you
are the first to know it, I got something on this thing called
a mind. We both know, don't we, that when either one gets
a brainstorm there is h to pay between the ears and it
d——n well better come out or we'll get constipation of the
head. Well it refers in large measure to that word which
you see upstairs. ED-YOU-KAY-SHUN. Yes sir, that has got
the old sawdust stirring. To be specific, Hollis, it's how that
word—that item—applies to my kid Scott. You remember
Scott? If you don't, receipt of this letter is bound to jog your
memory, because if you're reading, he sure as h handed it
to you. And by the way, not that I have to butter you up,
but facts are facts, that kid always thought you were the
cat's pajamas, did you know that? His hero should be Albie
Booth and he picks out a *shvartz* hustler. Kids. Well, back
to education. First off, I'm not crying, just explaining. I'm
not the brightest, but I'm not dumb. You pay your money
with a kid and take your chances. There might even be
fathers, and I'm the first to admit it, who would think he

was the Prince of Wales, although frankly I am not too high on the P of Wales. But you get my drift. Gene Debs would love my kid. So would Upton Sinclair. They'd love him. But I'm not Debs and I'm not Sinclair, I'm just not built for that game. Maybe if I'd have been born with the proverbial silver spoon in my mouth, I could well afford to love the whole human race, including all the s.o.b.'s around. I don't know. Maybe I could have shaped up the kid by digging out my old wooden spoon instead of the sterling silver he got. Maybe it's the wacked-up times we live in. Put them together with the silver spoon, mix well with the *great* schools I sent him to, shake up in a dice cup and roll out craps. How the h did I know when Hoover and Mellon couldn't even figure out a way to keep the stocks from crashing? To say nothing of those college professors. When all is said and done, there he is, I didn't turn him out on Mr. Ford's assembly line.

But I am going to say this— Being a patsy for every sit-down striker in the land and knocking the system that put bread in their mouths enabling them to sit down is not what I had in mind when I saw that sensational little tot sitting on the best hobbyhorse in town at the age of two. And please don't get me wrong. I have got my share of beefs and I'm very willing to say all here is not and has not been hunky dory. But it sure is not the last days of Pompay, either.

Another thing— I'm not one of those fathers who want their kid to be this or that. All I ever asked, and you can believe it or not, was that he was tops in whatever he did, outside, of course, of being the top knocker of "Columbia the Gem of the Ocean."

Well, there you are over in Africa, sitting under a palm tree, with coconuts raining down all around you, no doubt surrounded by a bevy of dusky maidens, smiling that smile, and saying what has this got to do with this, that or the other, right?

That is a d——n good question.

And I'm prepared to give you an answer if you will tell

those maidens to go sit in some leafy bows for a while and let the guys talk business.

Namely——

Okay, since you hit the road, took a powder, vacated the premises, I have been doing a lot of thinking and mulling things over. As you can see from all the above. Then one day it hit me like one of those coconuts. What hit me? This: The fact that you and I are stamped out of the same cookie cutter, much more so than Scott and I ever were, or probably ever will be. But that's not all. The plain fact is that nobody else around here has got it upstairs like you have, who I can understand and who can understand me without dotting every eye and crossing every tee. There has been a great gap around here in the area of listening and talking and understanding. So Hollis, we wipe the slate clean AND—

I want you to come back and take a job worthy of your talents and knowhow!

And I am not talking about any runner b.s. You could be tops in that dpt. all the way up to Inwood, so what? Nope, you're ready and able (and willing, I hope) to move up. Nothing less than controller. Right. I will teach you the books and you'll pick it up in no time flat. And get this, you can have river to river, 110th to 145th. That is a good and very profitable piece of land. Believe me.

We will work hand in glove for I need someone I can depend on. You got a free pass up to Castle Hill Avenue any time you want and if the old lady don't like it, she knows what she can do. Frankly, I can handle her. You can live where you want, although there's nothing like minding your own store. But if you're used to the fresh air after Africa you could even move out to Queens.

And, as previously noted—bygones will be bygones!

Well, there it is. I circled all around to get to it, but I had to get a few things off my chest and like I said nobody here talks my language. Think it over. Try it on for size. I'm for it two hundred percent, but you have got to be also. Frankly, I'm thinking of slowing down somewhat and you would have more and more responsibility befitting your brains. There's even things like a season pass to the Polo Grounds and a box at Jamaica and Belmont, so don't say Sol don't know how to sweeten the pot. I'll be waiting for your answer, so don't s——w around too long with those maidens. Besides, Scott would say you are exploiting the natives. See what I mean? To borrow a phrase from Lowell Thomas (I hope),

So Long Until Tomorrow,
Sol W.

Crazy Guy of Broad Street
Toussaint-L'Ouverture

Stood at the foot of the gangway leading to the Danish ship, *Tivoli,* on a sparkling Liberian morning, with the harbor, the city beginning to flare into life. Toussaint-L'Ouverture spoke first.

L'Ouverture: I wish you a pleasant voyage.

Crazy Guy: Oh, I suppose it will be pleasant.

L'Ouverture: I trust you enjoyed your stay here.

Crazy Guy: Not particularly.

L'Ouverture: Well, life is not always pleasant.

Crazy Guy: I trust it will be more pleasant for you and your people now.

L'Ouverture: I do not think more pleasant. A little better, perhaps. You were quite helpful.

Crazy Guy: Thank you. How is Josephson?

L'Ouverture: Do you refer to Abron?

Crazy Guy: Pardon me. How is Abron?

L'Ouverture: He is doing many things, talking to many people.

Crazy Guy: Splendid.

L'Ouverture: Yes, he does seem splendid.

Crazy Guy: Do you like him better now?

L'Ouverture: Like? We *love* Abron. There is not one person who does not love him.

Crazy Guy: What else? And is his life pleasant?

L'Ouverture: We do everything we can to make it so.

Crazy Guy: As does he . . .

L'Ouverture: I am not sure of that. I believe he achieves a pleasant life without working very hard.

Crazy Guy: You may have a point.

L'Ouverture: Well, he finds a way.

Crazy Guy: You said a mouthful . . . Good-bye then.

L'Ouverture: Good-bye.

Crazy Guy: At least we showed the others a thing or two.

L'Ouverture: Oh, that is hard to say. We will see. However, you will be well out of it.

Crazy Guy: Meaning I'm supposed to stay and fight your battles?

L'Ouverture: Oh no, you fight your own battles.

Crazy Guy: Thanks a lot. Never mind, I did very little.

L'Ouverture: No, you did something. But who knows what will happen. Even Abron does not know. The others and we will probably be here forever.

Crazy Guy: So?

L'Ouverture: We will be here. And you will be there.

Crazy Guy: Reading about you as I loll about my plantation.

L'Ouverture: Oh, do you have a plantation? Well then, you will not read about us. Perhaps I will read about you.

The Crazy Guy of Broad Street said something under his breath that had to do with the eye of a pig, hefted his shoulders, tramped heavily up the gangway. He raised his arm once, as though it were very heavy, then walked to the other side of the ship, the side facing the open water.

AN ATLANTIC INTERLUDE

STEP RIGHT DOWN OUT OF YOUR SEDAN CHAIR, LADIES AND GENTLEMEN *and take a real swell look at Noah of the Ark plus Black Devil Bébé Scarlet Gallifa Menelik of Senegal who might not be the great Abron but sure as hell was Mirambo and at one and the same time pip-squeaking little Cicero and ain't that a real kick in the slats to say nothing of a contradiction in terms? But that is not surprising when you think of the continent he is lately rid of and is rid of him, I mean ain't that place some contradiction in terms? You bet your diamond mines, and as he walks the trim Nordic deck on his way to the new world, he is thinking, that is, the chap referred to above is thinking, What Hath God Wrought in John Hawkins' middle passaging conveyance that wasn't no sedan chair but was called with proper awe and reverence The Jesus? And while he is thinking same, he is copping a gander—for who can resist copping something from that kidney pie filled with goodies—at jolly old as well as liberating equality. And as he peeks he says adios to lots of folks: to all them Kru kings. To good old Leo who pushed in a thumb and pulled out a plum. To the nice folks from Surrey in their neat Nairobi houses, and bye bye also to Teddy on safari drawing a bead on them Roosevelt gazelles of his; farewell to the boys who tuck in all them mosquito nets and serve all them Sundowners. Ta ta to Frankincense and Myrrh, goombye to gorillas ticketed for Bwana museums. Ohrevoyer gnu, koodoo, bongo and dik dik. Hey and all them zebras whose hides could be used for baseballs thereby giving us built-in stitching. . . .*

273

Ouch weeder zane Mahdi and Khalifa and Ashantis who win two out of eight from Eton and Rugby which ain't too high in the Scramble League, but how you gonna beat that ol Maxie gun? Aloha silent pix which ain't nixed from Cape to Cairo. Add dee oats phonograph records of Fats and Cab. Bah bah Flit, it's been so nice Reos, Overlands, Caddies, Packards, Chevies, Lincolns, Fords, Fords, Fords, without which no mission could mission.

Yesiree, he is giving it the big good-bye, getting it out of his system, leaving it all back there, cause he got other fish to fry. Such as dressing for dinner and drinking up his cocktail and eating hearty and listening to a neat orchestra. Ohyes. And don't think Cicero ain't staring with big eyes at all that un-middle stuff, specially that suddenly darkened salon and that white screen and them flashing lights and on that screen Simba and Congorilla, and Cicero keeps on staring when the lights come on and the neat orchestra strikes up a lively tune and Mrs. Hilda Swenson asks our friend to please dance the Congorilla for the folks, to which request he politely demurs, stating he does not know that particular step, but does this stop Mrs. S.? It does not; she goes right ahead anyways and does the Congorilla with six other peppy and slightly left-footed folks which earns a great big hand, although frankly Eleanor Powell don't have a thing to worry about, while through it all our friend sucks neatly on his Sundowner.

But after all this and that, don't think he don't go and get somewhat friendly with Mrs. Swenson for whom French Equatorial Africa is one heckuva tonic when civilization just becomes too much; and as they chat about a lotta nice things and sip and gaze, don't think he don't learn her husband is in the zoo business in Stockholm, and believe me when I tell you, as does Hilda, that giraffes are so goldarn annoying for they refuse to stay alive, but all in all it is not a bad way to make a living, is it not so, Mr. Dandy? And pray tell what line are you in?

"Stamps, I am in stamps," *he rejoins with a sip, nodding at a certain Ace, who slaps a genuine leather boot, and please-call-me Hilda is most impressed for in addition to being attractive things, stamps do not smell, especially that magnificent giraffe from Tanganyika, and above all, they cannot die, just increase in price, and her husband should be so lucky, is it not so, Mr. Dandy?*

It sure is so and call-me-Hilda gets real cozy and I do not mean Cole as she confides over a kirchwasser that hubby better go back to school and do his homework because when he says, as he often does, that they are all children and ugly children at that, he doesn't know everything, because, James, just look at you, you may be the exception that proves the rule, but you surely are an exception, although naturally you are a Bantu.

"Why am I a Bantu?" he inquires.

"I tell you," she confides over the kirchwasser. "It is a matter of your tallness. And your bearing. And, you know, something else . . ."

"What?"

"Do you really want to know?"

"Only if you care to tell me, Hilda."

"Then I tell you." Sip. Sip. "It is your cephalic index."

"It is?"

"No question. I noticed it immediately. It is quite good."

"Really?"

"Oh, yes. Pure Bantu."

"I must disappoint you, Hilda."

"Must you?"

"Yes." He gazes toward Kru Town. "I regret to say that I belong to the Eastsaintlouisboogaloo."

But she ain't at all disappointed. She claps them long Nordic palms and says happily, "Then, there you are. Gustav is doubly wrong; there is another decent tribe . . ." And our man inclines graciously.

Well they go back and forth in that vein all the way across the ol middle passage, except they veer up to Copenhagen where our friend is invited to stop off and tarry awhile, even you might say jump up to Stockholm on account of Gustav is muckin about in the London Zoo with some wildebeests and her good German friends would sure fall off their swastikas if they met an African like this one and didn't she have a little bit of the devil in her?

She sure did, he agrees, as anyone can plainly see, thereby gainsaying the old adage that all Nordic women are carved out of ice and did she realize that ice burns? which she sure blushingly did and ah what a shame. Yes what a shame, but business is business as well she knows, which with a Nordic sigh she surely does. But perhaps someday, and she looks dreamily back at the kidney pie: a bit of a meeting in Dakar, a restoration of mind, body and spirit on lovely safari all the way to Timbuktu. To which he responds, yes, who knows? It is a small and coincidental world and he stretches all the way up to his decent cephalic height and bows and she giggles and he goes right on to complete the passage without further ado except that little Cicero keeps on saying JESUS!

Part Six

WILDLIFE

Sol Winograd walked up the steps past Theodore Roosevelt, arched stiff and solemn in the saddle, and hurried into the Museum of Natural History. He didn't look around or hesitate. He followed the crowd, which when in doubt you always do. The crowd didn't let him down. It led him straight down the Roosevelt Memorial foyer and bang into the herd of charging elephants. Sol blinked, but didn't budge an inch. Those were a great bunch of pachyderms; he made a mental note to drop a line to Dr. Akeley's boss, patting the good doc on his brilliant head, who knows, maybe someday he would want a Jumbo tusk in *his* office.

Unflinchingly he walked into the doctor's famous hall. There it was:

AFRICA.

He spent two solid hours there. Slow, deliberate hours. Hands locked behind his back. His appointment book solidly blacked out. And he dug deep, darn deep, for Sol W. could accomplish in two hours what your average explorer needed two months for. So he accomplished: Studied the stand-up, chesty gorillas, baring their ivories, reaching out with their thrillingly close semicircle

279

of hairy arms. Stuck his eyes right up against the outraged orbs
of the springing and calmly furious lion. Grinned at the grinning
monks. Oh shrewd, very shrewd; and sly, oh yes, sly. He moved
this way, stepped that way, danced close, skipped away, did one
terrific job on all that fauna.

And after a while, like all his after-a-whiles, he made a connection. Deep in the heart of Africa. Made a connection. He. Sol.
Made a connection with those big boys, one big boy to another.
When you had a territory, when you *truly* ran it, you understood
each other. Yessir. Otherwise, get your rear end over to Brazil
or India or Norwalk or some other minor league. Yessir. He
breathed deeply of that connecting knowhow, let the thick,
heavy, dank air into his lungs like it was the best of Garcia
Grande. He even moved in a little closer, admired even more
each pointed toe, every bared incisor. Even did what Sol always
did that made him come out on top of every deal: changed
places with the smartest-looking monk. And he grinned out at
Winograd-Jolson. But how would he pose that funny-looking
duck? Head to one side? Slickly winking? Punching ozone? He
giggled inside his stuffed chest. Nah. Not *that* king. And remember, he needed his native habitat. So he reexchanged places,
threw that monk a knowing wink, spun on his leather heels,
walked quickly out past the charging jumbos, kept on walking,
through Teddy's foyer, walked right out of Africa and into the
main hall. Headed for the corner. Slid into a phone booth. For
that is where you would stuff and pose a Sol W. For all eternity,
especially if you wanted to get it right. He picked up the phone
and for his African pals held it in the air for thirty seconds,
hard, tough, powerful. Then he clapped it to his ear and called
Hollis Cleveland.

This time he reached him.
"Don't tell me," he roared.
"What?" said Cleveland.
"You mean I finally got you?"
"You finally got me."
"Well, well, you could knock me over with a feather."
"What's up, Sol?"

"Don't rush me, I just got you. You know where I'm calling from?"

"Where are you calling from, Sol?"

"Africa."

"The Bronx Zoo?"

"What zoo? The Museum of Natural History."

"That's nice, Sol."

"Don't patronize me. You know how I hate it when you patronize me."

"Okay, Sol."

"This is some place, kid, the real McCoy."

"If you say so, Sol."

"You're darn tootin I say so. How are you, kid?"

"Fine."

"I called and called."

"I've been in and out. How are you, Sol?"

"I could be worse."

"That means you're okay."

"Up to a point. Just up to a point. But you are a little peepot and I'm glad you're back; are you glad to be back?"

"It's not so bad, Sol."

"That means you're glad."

"Up to a point, just up to a point."

"You little peepot, what's that supposed to mean?"

"You know how you feel when you come back after a vacation?"

"What vacation? After two days I go nuts."

"Yes, well, it's hard to explain then."

"What hard? I know exactly what you mean. You're turned around, right? When I come back from Chicago, I'm all turned around; it's not so hard to understand."

"That's pretty close, Sol."

"Thank you very much, you little peepot. Did you get my letter?"

"Yes, I got it. By carrier pigeon."

"Some pigeon. A big shot bulldog."

"He looked all right to me, Sol. He's got a beard."

"Cheese and crax, my grandfather!"

"He looked all right."

"Sure, with a lousy Russian beard. He didn't have one of those nutty diseases?"

"Not that I could tell. He looked all right."

"Yeah, all right. Gonad breaker."

"I never mix in family affairs, Sol."

"Thanks again, you little pot. We have to talk, Hollis."

"We're talking."

"Don't *you* bust them. I mean *talk*."

"All right with me, Sol."

"Don't burn up the track, kid."

"Well, you know, Sol . . ."

"Sure, I know Sol, nice guy. Did you *read* my letter?"

"Yes, I read it."

"All right then. We talk. At least I won't have to spell out every other word. Come on up."

"Where?"

"Uptown naturally. I don't change. I'll see you in fifteen."

"Why not sooner?"

"You little peepot. It'll take that long to get there from Africa."

He hung up hard, waved at the charging elephants, hurried outside, skipped down the stairs past Teddy R., flagged a cab going downtown, gave him the address, said, and don't tell me you're going in the wrong direction, braced as they U-turned, said, "You wanna do something constructive for your kids, take them to that place; it is *some* education."

2

Hollis got off the elevator at the ninth floor, walked down the hall to the blue door that said *Class A Investments, Inc.* and walked in. He said to Florence, "He's expecting me." She pointed with her head. He moved to the dark blue inner office door and, as he did, it opened and Sol emerged, peppy, grinning, following two outstretched hands. The hands grabbed, pumped, patted, pummeled a tan gabardine shoulder. "I'm in conference," he said to Florence, who said yes, Mr. W., and then fiddled with some papers. He walked Hollis into the inner sanctum, gee whizzing, holy geeing, myohmying. He made very sure that Hollis was comfortable in a chair that had Hebrew letters on the back and the embossed words, *"Lux et Veritas,"* and he said happily, "Soap and truth, kid; the world could do a lot worse," reached down for the good cigars, clipped, offered, lit, sat, well-welled. Hollis puffed, exhaled, looked at the same old Sol, only not exactly the same: a bit smaller, pressed into himself. His neck, encased in the smoothly rolled Arrow collar, showed a loose ridge of flesh from chin to voice box. The expensive hands were thinner. Cleveland waited; Sol could never stand a silence.

"Well well."

"You're repeating yourself."

"Of course I am. I can't get over it."

"Over what?"

"You know what. You being here."

"I'm here, Sol."

"And I can't get over it. How are the Riffs?"

"Ask Mr. Romberg."

"How's the girlfriend of the whirling dervish?"

"Ask Mr. Kitchener."

Sol slapped the glass-topped desk. The picture of three-year-old Scott on a pony jumped.

"You're something, you little peepot. You act like you just got back from Staten Island."

"It cost a little more."

"Tell me something I don't know. Did you know transportation is a monopoly?"

"Now that you mention it, yes."

"Darn tootin. Between Ford and Vanderbilt and Cunard and Pan American, that's what it is. But, don't worry, it won't cost you a cent. You were on the pad all the way."

"Thanks, but no, Sol."

"No is no. Whatever you say, kid."

"That's what I say. But thanks."

"What thanks? It's the other way around if it's anything. You taught me a darn good lesson and I'm the first to admit it. I learn the hard way, kid. Like you."

The smoke was rich, thick, smooth, blue. Hollis looked through it toward the East River. He could see Ward's Island. He said through the smoke. "Yes, the hard way." Sol flicked some ash on the desk.

"Well?" he said.

"Yes, well."

"What's the verdict, kid?"

"No."

The eager face remained eager. It looked at the cigar and agreed with it.

"I knew you'd say that."

"You know me like a book, Sol."

"Like you were *Ivanhoe*. Which I have read twenty-three times. Got it marked up like a bible. You'll find out more about Jews and goys in there than any school. You wanna learn about people, stick with Sir Walter."

"I prefer Alger."

"You little peepot, you're kiddin me. I'll send you a copy of *Ivanhoe* and *Quentin Durward*."

"Thank you."

"Ah, stop being so goldarn polite. You're a little peepot."

"That I am. What's with all the darns and pees and holysmoke?"

"You noticed. I told Florence you'd notice. I knew it." The desk got slapped again. "I stopped cursing. I took an oath not to say one bad thing till the kid comes through safe and sound. The old lady thinks I must be shackin up, but that's her problem. What the h, he's still my kid, right?"

"Right."

"I told Florence you'd notice."

He got up, perched on the desk, massaged a lisle ankle.

"A lot of water under the bridge, kid, while you've been gone. A lot of excrement bouncing off the fan."

"I'm listening, Sol."

"I knew you would. If only everybody else listened."

"I'm still listening."

"Things are in a state of flux, Hollis. Wide open but also narrowing down. The Dutchman got his while you were effing around in the jungle. Lehman's got a guy named Dewey who's lookin down everybody's throat. Things are goin on a mile a minute. But one thing is clear. Stupid is out. Which is where you come in."

"I'm still listening."

"Forget the letter."

"I already have."

"You little peepot."

"So I forget the letter?"

"Keerect. You got *all* of Harlem."

"All?"

"All."

"Harlem is Sol's."

"I'm moving north. It's yours."

"This is a great cigar."

"Holy shoot, Charley Schwab would make you vice president if he could turn you inside out."

"I don't like steel."

"Don't I know? Look, you'll be on your own. Nobody peekin over your shoulder, not even me. I mean if you need help, I'll be there; but you'll be your own boss. Bygones are bygones. I trust you, Hollis."

"I appreciate that, Sol."

"The proposition or the trust?"

"Both."

"We been through too much, kid. We need each other. Well?"

"I'll have to sleep on it, Sol."

"Sure. A snap decision always snaps back."

"I won't take ten years, Sol."

"Don't I know that? You'll think, then bang. Like me."

The glass top took it again. Sol unfurled and walked over to him.

"Whatever, it's great to have you back, kid. I mean it."

"What can I say, Sol?"

"Nothing. How's your aunt?"

"I think all right."

"Don't think, kid, make sure. You'll feel better. Listen, I sent a telegram to Hull saying he's too darn easy on Mussolini. I signed every name in the office to it, yours truly number one. If they don't like it, they can quit; at least I'll know who the penises are around here. Don't worry, Mussolini'll get his."

"Maybe."

"No maybes, they got Hauptmann, they'll nail Mussolini."

"Don't tell that to Lucky."

"Lucky can go eff himself."

The thin, expensive hand reached, Hollis shook it. "Whenever you're ready, kid."

"Sure. Take care, Sol."

"You too. You're lookin a little drawn, try some yeast cakes, they'll bring you right back. Maybe we'll catch a ball game next week, Hubbell is goin great."

"Sounds good."

He stood, glanced at *Lux et Veritas*, patted it, walked out through the blue door.

Sol said into the phone, "Of course he didn't buy it. I told you he wouldn't." He shut his eyes, screwed them tightly together. "Yeah, but I *know* him." He held the crackling voice away, then pulled the mouthpiece close. "You finished? Look, if you talk crazy, I gotta straighten you out.... Yeah, it's a good deal, yeah, what can I say? They go to college, they know it all, what else can I say, am I Einstein? Will you stop already? Okay. No, I got no time to argue, there's nothin to discuss, stop cryin and carryin on, you're actin like my Aunt Fanny, now listen. He's on his way down ... Right, do what you have to do ... Yeah, I like the little sonofabee, but do what you have to do. That's right. And tell those morons not to eff it up ... Sure I know who I'm talkin to, but who gets all the headaches? ... Will you stop already? ... *Gonads.*"

He slammed the phone down, sighed, twisted his scotch-grain bluchers. Lousy, pointed-toe miseries, Dewey should have such shoes. He chomped on a cold cigar, looked at Baby Scott smiling on his pony.

"I'll send an effing telegram to Roosevelt," he shouted.

GLAMOUR INC.

HE WALKED DOWN TO TWO, CUT LEFT AND CONTINUED WALKING
until he came to a door whose upper half was frosted glass.
Painted in red on the glass was "FOREVER YOUNG—COS-
METICS BY CAROL." He walked in, winked at a secretary,
kept on going with the secretary behind him. The woman at the
desk looked up.

"Christ," she said, "you."

"Hello Babe, I'm back."

"Yes, you certainly are. That's all right, Elsie, I'll see the gentleman." Elsie said, Yes, Miss Wilson, I'm sorry about this, and
swept out. Carol walked to Cleveland. "Should I see the
gentleman?"

"Why not?"

"He never calls first."

"I couldn't call from Africa."

"Why not?"

"That's a very good question. I just didn't think."

"You sonofabitch. Johnny Walker Red or Black?"

"Red is fine."

"I have Black."

"Red is fine."

She whisked away and he looked at the window. Her voice
came through the little room behind her office. "How long you
been back?"

"A week."

"We've got phones in this town."

"I was tied up in a hundred knots."

She clicked back and handed him his drink. "You bastard. Let's sit down." They sat on a green corduroy sofa, she held up her drink. They clinked glasses.

"It's an Orange Blossom," she said. "I hate them but they taste like Florida. Remember Florida?"

"Sure."

"Sure." She sipped some Florida while he sipped Johhny Walker Red. "You see the big butter and egg man?"

"Yes."

"Lots of thunder and lightning while you were screwing around in the jungle."

"Everybody thinks I was screwing around in the jungle."

"What else can you do in Africa?"

"You can go home, can't you? Ask Garvey."

"Come on, baby, you're talking to Carol."

"Okay."

"Here's to Florida," she said. "And Bomba, the Jungle Boy."

"You've got it." He drank and glanced at the window. "Can I use your phone?"

"Can't you just relax?"

"After the phone."

"Go on," she sighed. "May I remain or you calling some Amazon queen?"

"I was in the other jungle. As a matter of fact, Bomba was also located in South America. See—"

"Use the damn phone."

He placed his glass on a rubber lily pad, got up and walked to the phone, lifted, dialed, waited. He smiled at her, she smiled back, he stopped smiling and said, "Inspector O'Shea, please . . . no, no one else will do . . . no, just say a friend is calling. From Cleveland." He smiled at her again, then returned to the phone. "Yes, Terry, it's me . . . That's right, Terry . . . Terry, listen, there are several evil-looking persons skulking about downstairs . . . Yes, skulking . . . yes, in *your* territory . . . oh yes, you know them, I mean I'm positive you know them . . . I would say that's a good guess, Terry, I just talked to him . . . Of course it's no

deal ... Terry, I sort of like the little prick, but do what you
have to do; now listen, one of the skulkers, one of the goons, I
mean, is Willy Southall ... That's right, Willy ... right, Terry,
show him a fist and he blows sky high ... Exactly, Terry, he can't
stand violence, he'll deliver Sol ... Terry, business is business ...
Terry, please, *he* offered me Harlem. Terry, listen: Harlem, the
Bronx and that piece of Yonkers we talked about ... Yes, McNulty's piece ... Well, tell him it's changing hands ... That's *your*
problem, Terry ... Terry, get that inspector on Jerome Avenue
... yes, Macready, that's the one, tell him to see McNulty ...
Of course I'll take care of him. I'll take care of McNulty too if
he behaves himself ... Nothing worthwhile is easy, Terry ...
And please keep Dewey off my back ... How're the kids, Terry?
Spain? Well, that's what makes a horse race ... So long, Terry."

He laid the phone gently in its cradle, walked back, sat down
and picked up his drink.

"That was Terry."

"I had a hunch it was."

"Carol, can I stick around a while?"

"How long?"

He looked at the window. The street noises came up, low,
steady, insistent.

"As long as it takes."

She considered briefly, then got up and walked to the phone.
She ordered two bottle of Piper, '29, ice bucket three-quarters
full, please. She looked at him. "Dinner now?"

"Later."

"I'll call you later," she said into the phone. "If you go off,
make sure Marvin comes on." She cradled the phone, walked
back and picked up her Orange Blossom, but did not sit down.
He smiled up at her. Now he checked his watch and smiled
again. Suddenly he got up, strode to the window, held the curtain
to one side. He flattened himself against the wall on that side
and waved to her not to approach. She shrugged, sat down,
sipped her drink. Then, nodding to himself, he let the curtain
fall into place and walked back and sat down beside her. He
picked up his drink.

"Well?" she said.

"Here's the deal on Africa," he said. "First of all, the jungle is one hell of a location, that's why it's so popular. You have dusky maidens running around all over the place wearing less than Sally Rand, without the fans. Billy Minsky would love them. Then you have these Ubangis with lips like ashtrays. In the middle of all that you've got gorillas suckling white babies. They're always fighting one another over those babies. Then to top it off, you have tons of raw materials. That's why everybody wants a piece of the action. You have gold and diamonds, rubies and slaves, cobras and mongeese. Or is it mongooses? Anyway, even the local tribes want their cut. Now seeing all this, holding up the white man's burden, is this little cat with a big jaw in Rome, Italy. He says, hey, I want *mine* . . ."

The Ace, leaning out of the leather-lined cockpit of The Spirit of East St. Louis, *shouts down through his megaphone,* "Congratulations, James, I always knew you had what it takes, that you would indeed climb to the top of the slippery pole. Now James, as your tutor, I will unblushingly accept any token of your monumental appreciation. Chow, old man."

EPILOGUE

ON A STEAMY SUMMER NIGHT IN 1938, A MAN IN A TAN GABARDINE suit stepped off a bus and walked east from Madison Avenue and 86th Street into Yorkville. Or Germantown, as it was often called. He walked slowly past Park, Lexington and approached Third Avenue. Ahead the elevated loomed. He paused near the Cafe Ludendorff and stood there with his eyes half closed. He folded his arms. He seemed to be listening, but not to the trains rumbling overhead or the street noise. Although, actually, there was very little street noise.

Several people walked by. Two of them brushed lightly against him for he was standing in the middle of the sidewalk. But neither he nor they gave ground. One of those who brushed him turned and briefly stared.

The man ignored that, for he was indeed listening. To a high, thin, quick voice. The voice belonged to a man who was called Taub by his partner, an Angelo Palange. This Taub was talking through the courtesy of Adam Hats, which the man in the gabardine suit appreciated, although tonight he didn't wear a hat. The voice of Taub was filling 86th Street. He was coming out of the Ludendorff, out of stores and open windows.

The man smiled. Adam-hat Taub was some talker. He talked in short, hard nasal bursts and what he was talking about concerned two "very important men." One of them Taub identified as the Brown Bomber. The other important man was called several things: *Un zer* Max, the beetle-browed Hun, the Black Uhlan

293

(although he was very white, especially under the lights that flared about them).

As the gabardined man listened with half-closed eyes, Taub described how the Brown Bomber and the Black Uhlan were coming together some four miles to the north on a small square of firmly padded canvas, surrounded by 80,000 people. Taub said that all these people, plus millions of others, had a significant vested interest in what these men were about to do. The listening man nodded.

The Bomber and the Uhlan now advanced toward each other under the blazing lights on their small, padded square. Taub's voice grew harsher as he described how the Bomber, planting his front foot, struck with his left fist several times, like a machine-gun burst.

Then it was the Uhlan's turn. He looped his fist toward the Bomber's close-cropped head, an act that brought an "ahhh" from the crowd. Taub explained that it was the same looping fist that had apparently destroyed the Bomber at a previous meeting, and the crowd had no doubt remembered.

However, Taub snarled, the looping right hand *missed* its target; the (suspect) chin of the Bomber was safe for the moment. The listening man unfolded his arms, shifted his feet. Even as the Bomber. And then the Bomber flicked out again with his rattlesnake fist. The Uhlan's head bounced, the crowd yelled. Taub's voice punctured the yell: the Uhlan had retaliated with the looping right hand again and this time made contact with the Bomber's chin. The listening man winced, but no real damage, Taub said, and then he got busy with the Bomber's reaction.

He was peppering again, four times in a row; then he drove his right fist into the jaw of the Uhlan.

Taub and the crowd gasped. The Uhlan's head *and* body were bouncing, this time into the ropes that enclosed the small square. Taub regained his voice and became terrifically excited. He screeched that the Bomber was stepping forward with a sliding motion, swinging his right fist. At that very moment, the Uhlan slightly turned. The Bomber's fist caught him just below the rib cage, at the side of the Uhlan's shining body.

Taub rasped that he heard a shrieking cry of pain. The listening man opened his eyes.

The Uhlan, with Taub screeching, was clutching the ropes and the Bomber was stepping away to a corner of the square. Now a third man entered the roar, the screams and Taub's description: This man, Donovan, was dressed in shirt and trousers, and he had a sweat stain in his right armpit. Taub could see the stain because Donovan's arm was lifting, then descending. And he was counting, Taub screamed. But he counted only once. The Uhlan had stepped away from the ropes which was a dangerous place to be. Donovan motioned to the waiting Bomber, and also to the troubled Uhlan. They came together and as they did, the Bomber's fist made clublike contact with the Uhlan's tough, unshaven jaw. The Uhlan suddenly dropped to his knees, and Donovan performed his ritual as the Bomber retreated to the corner. Three times Donovan raised and lowered his arm.

The crowd-noise was wild, strange, consuming. But somehow Taub rose above it with his own roaring-scream: The Uhlan was slowly slowly getting up; the Bomber was smoothly advancing. He chopped at the now inviting jaw with his left fist, then pounded in his right. The Uhlan sank beneath the weight of both and again kneeled on the canvas floor. Taub's voice cracked.

Again Donovan swung the inevitable arm, this time twice. As in a dream, the Uhlan rose and stood waiting. The crowd suddenly hushed. The Bomber materialized, used his left and right fists in what Taub screeched was a combination hook and cross. The Uhlan's head snapped back; he dropped to his ritual position and Donovan began his own ritual. As he did, a white towel fluttered into the square like a wounded bird. Donovan ignored it. His arm rose, fell, rose, fell, continued until it was still for a moment. Then he raised both arms over his head, thrust them apart. Close to his feet lay the gleaming Uhlan.

Taub was beside himself. He kept repeating that only two minutes and four seconds had elapsed, and that this was an *amazing* thing. The thundering crowd shared his amazement. Then suddenly, as if a thousand hands had counted to ten, the voice of Taub, the screaming astonishment of the crowd, were silent in Yorkville.

The man in the gabardine suit looked around. He shrugged and began to walk toward Lexington Avenue, the direction from which he had come. Close to Lexington a very young man came up the steps of the Bavarian Cafe and almost collided with him.

"I beg your pardon," said the gabardined man.

The other man pulled back. The gabardined man scratched his right earlobe. As he did, the young man jerked backward and stumbled down the steps of the cafe. The gabardined man scratched his other earlobe and continued to walk.

He walked past Lexington, Park and Madison. He stopped when he reached Fifth. It was very quiet here, although not the hushed quiet that engulfed the streets to the east. The traffic in both directions was light. The park across the street was dark and calm. A double-decker bus trundled by, brightly lit, with only a sprinkling of riders.

The man stood beneath a street light. Now he heard voices overhead. That is, one voice, multiplied. The voice of Taub's partner, Palange. It spoke of revenge and of a message that had been sent.

The man seemed to think about that. Then, nodding at the voice, he stepped off the curb and walked to the center of the avenue and faced north. He stood on the white line that split each flow of traffic, north, south, uptown, downtown. A car speeding north, or uptown, veered very close to him before the driver blew his horn, and continued on, mouth flapping. The man moved a step away from the white line, still facing north. Another car, doing forty on its dash, squealed to a rocking stop. The driver leaned out, opened and then closed his mouth, pulled in his head and rolled up his window. Another car stopped short behind the first one. A head leaned out again, considered, and retreated as a window rolled up. Horns blared despite the mayor's ordinance.

The man took one more step out into the uptown lane and then glanced behind him. Two more cars. Now he walked slowly to the center of the uptown lane. He waited as the horns grew louder. Suddenly he slanted his upper body far back. He arched his shoulders and head so that he was staring at the gleaming sky. And with his arms swinging, feet pointing down, knees lifting and driving, he stepped high, wide and handsome up Fifth Avenue, leading the yelping, blaring, furious parade.